I0761775

Challenge *down* Under

A Dave and
Katie Adventure

Kit and Drew Coons

Challenge Series Book Two

Challenge *down* Under

A Dave and Katie Adventure

Kit and Drew Coons

Challenge Down Under

ISBN: 978-1-7325783-7-1

Library of Congress Control Number: 2017916734

Edited by Jayna Richardson
Illustrations by Julie Sullivan (MerakiLifeDesigns.com)
Design: Julie Sullivan (MerakiLifeDesigns.com)

First Edition

Printed in the United States

22 21 20 19 18 1 2 3 4 5

To all men and women who prioritize protecting
and caring for their families.

Anyone who does not provide for their relatives,
and especially for their own household, has denied the faith and
is worse than an unbeliever.

1 Timothy 5:8 (NIV)

Acknowledgments

This novel would not be possible without professional editing and proofreading by Jayna Richardson. All the artwork is by our graphic designer, Julie Sullivan. We also thank our reviewers, Leslie Mercer and Marnie Rasche, who read the manuscript and made valuable corrections and suggestions. Jill Rangeley in New Zealand reviewed and helped us in cultural accuracy.

Principal Characters

Dave and Katie Parker • Semi-retired couple from Mobile

Jeremy Parker • Dave and Katie's twenty-six-year-old son

Denyse Larkin Parker • Jeremy's Australian wife

Dingo (Graham) and Beatrice Larkin • Denyse's parents

George and Nikki Ferguson and daughter Holly • sheep farmers

Lena Travnikov • Ukrainian immigrant to New Zealand

Trevor Larkin • Denyse's younger brother

Aarav Kapoor • New Zealand barrister

Malcolm Fraser • New Zealand police sergeant

Rangi and Fetu • Samoans living in New Zealand

Lee Wong • Singaporean

Vocabulary

ankle biter	small child
Aussie	Australian
barbie	outdoor grill
barrister	lawyer
biscuit	cookie
blimey	mild exclamation
bloke's bloke	macho man
boot	car trunk
bushranger	outlaw
cattle drover	cowboy
chai	tea

cockroach	a person from New South Wales
college	high school
corker	something of excellence
crayfish	South Pacific lobster
cuppa	cup of tea or coffee
dairy	convenience store
docking lambs	cutting off the tails of young lambs
Down Under	Australia and New Zealand
fair dinkum	true; genuine
flat	apartment
fresh	chilly
frost	outside temperature below freezing
g'day	hello
galah	an unintelligent parrot-like bird; idiot when applied to a person
garden	yard
gent	gentleman
good on ya	good for you; well done
gum tree	eucalyptus
holiday park	campground
hols	holidays (vacation)
joey	baby kangaroo
kiwi	New Zealand flightless bird
Kiwi	New Zealander (person)

lemonade	Sprite
loo	toilet
lorry	truck
marks	grades
mate	friend
maths	math
motorway	highway
mozzie	mosquito
mum	mother
mutton	sheep meat
never-never	the Outback
no worries	no problem; forget about it
no-hoper	someone who will never do well
OE	overseas experience
oi	expression of uncertainty
pokie	poker played against a machine
Outback	interior of Australia
Oz	Australia
paddock	pasture
petrol	gasoline
pudding	dessert
race	used in sheep handling
reserve	undeveloped park
roos	kangaroos
rooting	intercourse
rugby	sport from which American football evolved

rugger rugby

scone biscuit

sheep station a big farm; grazing property

shit house crude expression for toilet

shrimps shrimp

slice dessert bar

soldier on show persistence

straight-up honest; trustworthy

tap hit

telly television

test international sporting event

trek walk

uni university

ute utility truck

Vegemite yeast-based spread

walkabout solitary bush exploration

wrap jacket

yabbies freshwater crayfish

Darwin
Great
Barrier
Reef
Indian
Ocean
The Never Never
Rottnest
Island
Perth
Blue
Mountains
Sydne
Snowy
Mountains
Tasma
Sea
Melbourne
Southern Ocean
Tasmania

Australia

North Island
Auckland
Lake Taupo
Mt. Ruapeho
(volcano)
Tasman Sea
Cook
Straight
Picton
Wellington
Kaikoura
Range
Kaikoura
Christchurch
Southern
Alps
Timaru
Queenstown
Dunedin
South Island

New Zealand

Prologue

A young man took a seat on a hard, wooden chair at a desk just in front of the nonfiction section—a seat chosen for the convenient view of the library's entrance. *Will she come today?* he asked himself.

Nearly six weeks earlier he had noticed an unbelievably beautiful young woman. Straight, naturally blond hair had been pulled back from her delicate face. She always sat alone at a table turning the pages of various children's books, her lips moving as she read the words. Her clothes appeared worn and certainly not stylish. He guessed that she had little money. *She is like an angel,* he had thought.

His heart jumped when she entered the library. Over a book he held before his face, the young man watched her remove a shabby coat from her thin body, select a children's book, and sit at a table. He had spent many days waiting and hoping for glimpses of the angelic girl. On several previous occasions, he had tried to speak to her. At first, she had merely pretended not to hear him. But the last couple of times, she had acknowledged him with a slight nod or smile without speaking. On this meager encouragement, the young man based his hope. *Today I must try to meet her.* Loneliness forced him to act in spite of a sick feeling of apprehension. *Are you a man or a mouse?* he challenged himself and moved to sit at her table.

It's him again, the girl realized as someone sat down at her table. *Should I try a different library?* Ignoring him, she sighed slightly. She didn't want to walk several kilometers in the chilly spring rain to another library branch. *He looks nice enough. What are you thinking? Remember that your family is depending on you. Just don't acknowledge him. You're safe in a public place.*

The unlikely pair read silently for over an hour. The girl could sense him glancing at her. Several times he cleared his throat as if preparing to speak, but apparently lost his nerve. Despite her apprehension, the girl felt amused. And part of her thrilled that even so bedraggled, she still appeared attractive to someone.

"That's one of my favorite books." His words came as a surprise to her. "I like the way Peter Cottontail outsmarts the farmer."

The girl nodded without looking or speaking. On this slender affirmation, her admirer continued with well-rehearsed words. "You don't know me. But would you consider going with me to McDonald's? It's right down the street. I would buy you anything to eat and drink you liked."

McDonald's? she thought. *That's for rich people.* The girl remembered her only other visit to a McDonald's on a trip from her village to the city. McDonald's had been like another world compared to the farm. The food they had served had been unbelievably delicious. The girl also felt the desperate hunger that accompanies long-term food deprivation. She looked her admirer in the face for the first time. "Da." When her inviter acted confused, she added a heavily accented, "I mean, yes."

The young man felt his heart soar at the same time his tongue froze. He had no follow-on words prepared. Glancing around for inspiration, he saw her coat and held it up for her. The girl hesitated and then comprehended his action. Not used to such courtesy, she sank her right arm into the sleeve all the way to her shoulder. Then she struggled until she could force her left arm into the other sleeve. After that awkward moment, the young man put on his own coat and gestured toward the door.

They walked in a drizzle down a wet sidewalk in silence. He held the door to McDonald's open for her. Inside, the young man pointed to the posted menu. "What would you like?" The girl stared at the listing with incomprehension. *She can't read all the words,* he realized. "Would you like a hamburger with cheese and bacon?" he asked. His guest nodded. "French fries? Milkshake? Chicken tenders? Cookie?" To each offer the girl assented. He ordered two of everything plus soft drinks.

Carrying a tray laden with food, he led the way to a booth where they sat on opposite sides with the tray between them. He was surprised when the girl bowed her head for a moment of silent prayer. He respectfully mimicked her devotion. Once she looked up, he started passing her the items of food.

She really is hungry, he thought as she started to eat in an undignified hurry. After a few minutes, the girl ate more slowly without looking at him directly. "My name is Trevor," he ventured. "What is your name?"

"Lena."

A few more moments passed. Trevor remembered her accent when first answering him. "You're not from New Zealand, are you?" Once Lena had shook her head, he added, "I'm not from here either. I'm from Australia. Where are you from?"

"Ukraine."

"Are you in New Zealand alone?" To her nod, he responded, "I'm here alone too."

After eating everything, Lena seemed in no hurry to leave McDonald's. She relaxed somewhat and answered his questions in halting English. Each time she glanced up at Trevor with deep blue eyes, he thought he might swoon. Speaking slowly, he gradually discovered Lena to be eighteen years old. She had come to New Zealand to find work and hopefully a new home for her mother and younger brothers and sisters. Her father had recently died.

Suddenly Lena noticed twilight outside as the day ended. "I go now," she announced with a tone of alarm. She hurriedly pulled on her coat and headed for the door.

"Wait! Can I walk you home?" When Lena didn't answer or stop he called, "Will you please come to the library tomorrow?"

She stopped then and turned. "Yes." Looking into his eyes Lena continued with a voice that seemed too deep for one so slight. "Thank you, Trevor."

Trevor watched through the window as she disappeared into the deepening darkness. He felt an overwhelming desire to care for and protect Lena. And for the first time in years he didn't feel alone.

Chapter One

Eighteen Months Later

". . . and prepare for landing," the airline pilot finished his instructions as the jetliner approached Sydney.

The fourteen-hour flight from Los Angeles had brought the worst out of Katie Parker. "I can't believe that your son would do such a thing."

Dave, her husband of thirty-five years, checked his seatbelt and raised his tray table. "What thing?"

She looked at him with some disdain. Katie spoke low so that nearby passengers wouldn't hear. "You know very well. Your son Jeremy having to get married because he gets a girl pregnant."

"Why haven't you mentioned your feelings on this before? And Jeremy is your son too."

"You must have known what I was thinking."

Dave spoke lightly, trying to alter her mood. "Do I ever know what you're thinking?"

A deep sigh from Katie communicated her distress. "I'm serious."

Dave changed to a sympathetic tone. "Maybe I did suspect. But why bring this up now when we're just about to meet them?"

Katie returned her seatback and tray table to their original positions. "Maybe I tried to be open-minded. Maybe I hoped they would change their minds about getting married so soon."

"Maybe you're tired. Did you sleep any on the flight?"

"No, I mostly worried. What if he's getting married out of a sense of obligation? Jeremy has your southern honor, you know. And he can be impulsive like me. What if he's hurrying into something?"

Dave attempted a joke. "Apparently, he's already hurried into something." He received a look proving that type of humor was not welcome.

"I wish we could have met the girl. Gotten to know her family. I just think Jeremy might be making the biggest mistake of his life. Aren't you at all concerned?"

Dave sighed. "Of course, I'm concerned. But things are not the same now as when you and I got married in Alabama. Young people do things differently today."

"That doesn't make what they do right or smart," Katie insisted.

The screech of the tires and jerk of the airplane touching down interrupted their conversation.

"We welcome you to Sydney in New South Wales,

Australia," the stewardess announced. "Please remain seated until the captain has turned off the fasten seatbelt sign."

"What if your mum doesn't like me?" Denyse Larkin fretted as she waited just beyond Australian Customs along with Jeremy Parker.

Jeremy gave his fiancée a reassuring hug. "Everyone who knows you likes you."

"I'm not marrying those people's only son. And what will she think when she meets my family?"

"Mom likes everybody. She always regretted not being able to have a daughter. She'll love you as the one she didn't have. And if she loves you, she'll accept your family."

"Do you forget that I'm already pregnant? And didn't you tell me that your parents are rather traditional?"

"Mom and Dad *are* old-fashioned. You're right about that. But they struggled for more than a decade just to have me. They'll be happy that we don't face the same problem."

Denyse's expression remained dubious.

Dave could see anxiety in Katie's face as they waited at the luggage carousel for their bags. "Do you remember when you met my parents?"

"That was different," Katie spoke tersely.

"Yes, that was different. Different by being easier for you than Denyse. But do you remember how you felt then?"

"I was scared to death," Katie admitted.

"Well then, try imagining how Denyse must feel right now."

Katie refused to concede anything in the current situation. "I'm not at all scary."

"Neither was my mother."

Katie considered that as Dave pulled their two bags off the conveyor belt. "Don't worry about me," she promised. "I'll behave."

"You always do. And remember how well you and my mom always got along afterwards."

A large crowd waited at the passenger exit. Jeremy, being over six feet like his father, stood out among the faces. Next to him stood a tall, slender girl with handsome features. She wore little if any makeup. Her chocolate brown hair had been pulled back into a bushy ponytail. Katie recognized her as the girl they had met via Skype calls.

Dave, seeing Denyse, thought despite himself, *Jeremy did alright.* Jeremy and Denyse waved and smiled.

After hugging each of his parents, Jeremy turned and said, "Mom, Dad, this is Denyse Larkin, my fiancée. Denyse, these are my parents, Dave and Katie Parker."

Denyse held out a tentative hand to shake. Dave shook her hand. "Glad to meet you, Denyse."

The girl turned to Katie. "Mrs. Parker, I'm happy to meet you."

"I'm happy to meet you too," she responded and hugged the girl stiffly.

Both Katie and Denyse stepped back in silence. "Let me

get your bag," Denyse offered and reached for Katie's roller suitcase.

"That's okay. I can manage," Katie insisted. The girl quickly withdrew her hand.

"So how was your flight?" Jeremy asked

"Long," Dave admitted.

"You must be exhausted," Denyse sympathized. "I've never been to America. But I spent eighteen hours on a train a couple of times."

"Where was that?" Dave asked.

"Crossing the Outback. And there's nothing to look at but shrubs and red dirt."

Jeremy reached out and took his mother's bag. "The car is this way."

As Jeremy loaded their bags in his car trunk, Dave made strong eye contact with Katie. He tilted his head slightly toward Denyse. His wife grimaced a little and silently nodded.

"You can ride in the front with Jeremy, Mr. Parker. Your long legs must be cramped after that long flight," offered Denyse.

"Thank you, Denyse. And you can call me Dave." Watching Jeremy drive effortlessly on the left side of the road from the right side of the car amazed Dave and Katie.

In the back seat, Katie made an effort. "I understand that you're a teacher, Denyse."

"Yes, ma'am. I teach maths at a college in Sydney."

Katie followed the example Dave had set. "You don't need to say ma'am to me. And my name is Katie."

"Thank you, Katie."

"But I thought you taught teenagers, not at a college."

"College is for fourteen to eighteen-year-olds in Australia," Jeremy explained. "The equivalent of high school in the States. A lot of the best colleges are private. But Denyse teaches at a public college in a Sydney suburb. She's great at bringing the best out of kids from troubled backgrounds. She gives them confidence they can make something of themselves with hard work."

"I was a high school science teacher before Jeremy came," Katie told Denyse.

"Jeremy told me that. I'll stay home with our baby for a couple of months before returning to teaching. We're lucky the birth should come just before the summer hols about six months from now. I won't have to miss teaching much."

"You're going to continue working?" Katie asked.

Before Denyse had to answer, Jeremy broke in to change the topic. "So what have you two been doing in the year since your adventure in Minnesota?"

Dave followed Jeremy's lead. "I've been studying for the forensic accounting exam and took it last month."

"When will you get the results?"

"They should come soon. I'm pretty sure I passed, though."

Jeremy nodded in appreciation. "What will you do with that certification?"

"I've already been getting some requests from police departments. I'm thinking about opening a one-man consulting and expert witness service."

"And what about you, Mom? Your checkups good?" Jeremy asked.

"I'm still cancer-free. And you can see that my hair has grown out."

Dave added for his wife, "Your mother has been helping couples to organize marriage discussion groups all over the Mobile area. You remember the ones that we attended when you were younger?"

"Yeah, I do. And I remember how much more fun you both were afterwards," answered Jeremy.

"I know the two most important things about marriage," Denyse volunteered. "A commitment to a good marriage and a common blueprint. Is that right, Mrs. Parker—I mean, Katie?"

"Yes, that's correct. How did you know?"

"Jeremy told me. And I read that book on marriage you sent to him. Jeremy and I have been talking a lot about our future family. Maybe you could coach us while you're here."

Katie hid her reluctance. "Of course. Sounds like you've made a good start."

Jeremy stopped in front of an apartment building in an older neighborhood. "Denyse and I have an extra bedroom, if you'd like to stay at our flat."

"You two have an apartment?" Katie asked. She restrained herself from adding the word "together."

Jeremy didn't pick up on the subtext to his mother's question. "We want to buy a house as soon as possible. But we really don't have enough saved for a down payment."

The implication of Katie's question wasn't missed by Denyse, though. "We just got the flat together last month. Since we're already expecting, we wanted to save money on housing as soon as possible. Jeremy is rather good with money. He has a long-term financial plan for us already."

Dave interceded, "Staying with you is a generous offer, son. But I think your mother and I would be more comfortable in a hotel."

"Sure. There's one only a kilometer or so down the motorway. Would you come up for a look, though?"

"How about tomorrow? We're both exhausted. And the time in Mobile is about three a.m. right now. We're having trouble keeping our eyes open."

Katie could not help but think, *This afternoon has been plenty eye-opening for me.*

"She doesn't like me!" wailed Denyse after she and Jeremy had left Dave and Katie at the hotel.

"Mom is just tired," Jeremy insisted. "She'll love you when she gets to know you."

"Did you hear how she insinuated that I should stay home after the baby is born? I like teaching kids. I feel like maths is an important subject to my pupils. And you and I can't afford to live in Sydney, pay our debts, take care of a baby, and at the same time save for a house on only your salary."

"Mom has forgotten how she financially supported Dad at first. And that they had been married more than twelve years before I was born. Just give her some time."

"And hadn't you told them before that we got a place together?"

Jeremy admitted having neglected sharing that detail. "Mom and Dad are traditional, even for America. She even calls him 'dinosaur' because of his old-fashioned values. I just didn't have the nerve to tell them."

"Great! I know your mother is thinking, *That's how they got pregnant.*"

Jeremy consoled his fiancée. "I'm sure that Mom and Dad aren't thinking anything like that."

Chapter Two

"I don't like her!" Katie insisted after she and Dave had checked into the hotel. "And living together is why they're in the predicament they're in."

"You mean pregnant?" Dave tried to clarify. "If so, maybe they don't think of that as a predicament."

"What I mean is that Jeremy and Denyse can't afford to have a child. They can barely support themselves right now."

"Do you remember that we wanted children much sooner than the twelve years we had to wait for Jeremy? Have you forgotten all the anxious years and heartfelt prayers we endured before conceiving?"

Dave paused while Katie considered that before he continued, "Sweetheart, we had our personal challenges. Their challenges will be different from ours. But challenges can bond them together."

"Or handicap them from the beginning," Katie pointed out.

"Do you think you could be overreacting, sweetheart? Maybe the result of being tired from the long trip? And it's the situation you don't like, not Denyse."

"You're right, at least partly," Katie conceded. "And I need to acknowledge to myself that I'm jealous. Jeremy was all mine before. I remember him as that precious little boy. Now another woman has taken him away from me. A woman I don't even know."

Dave put his arms around his petite wife and hugged her tightly. He ruffled her salt-and-pepper neck-length hair. "You'll need to get to know her. I'm certain that if your son picked Denyse, she reminded him of you."

"Do you really think so?"

"Yes. And I think we're both tired and need some sleep."

◆

A sharp pain in Dave's foot startled him awake. "Ow!"

"What happened?" Katie asked through her own sleepiness as she turned on the bedside light.

Dave rubbed between his toes. "I kicked the bedpost."

"How did that happen?"

"I had another nightmare. Something creepy followed us on one of our night walks back home. Then the lights on the trail went out. My legs must have tried to run away."

"Would you like a sleeping pill?"

"No. I'm still sleepy from the trip."

Katie turned off the light. "I'm right here with you, big boy."

"We have our own parking garage." Denyse pronounced the word "garage" in a way that rhymed with "carriage." Her pronunciation sounded funny to the Americans. From Jeremy and Denyse's ground floor garage, carpeted steps led to a kitchen and sitting area. Although the entire apartment complex appeared rundown to Dave and Katie, Jeremy and Denyse could not conceal their pride in their first home.

Dave and Katie looked at the sparse furnishings. Dave spoke positively, "This is nicely cozy."

Excitement filled Jeremy's voice. "We picked up the upholstered furniture at a secondhand store. The table and bookcases came from a discount store. The boxes we found behind an appliance shop. Denyse made the curtains herself."

Katie looked at the cardboard box end tables and rubbed her hand over the particle board bookcases.

"This is where I fix dinner," Denyse waved at the tiny kitchen space. "Of course, we can't store much food." The refrigerator stood about four feet tall. "Jeremy cooks sometimes too."

Katie observed where Denyse had decorated the walls with photos of Australian scenery and animals cut from old calendars.

"Come on upstairs," Jeremy offered. The foursome ascended narrow steps to a hallway ending with a linen closet and doors to small bedrooms on either side. One bedroom had an inexpensive tubular bed and a thin mattress. "This is where you would have slept, if you'd stayed with us. We would have slept in the other bedroom." Katie looked across the hall to see the other room had no bed.

"We know we don't have much furniture or other stuff," Denyse explained. "But we'll need money for the baby. And Jeremy has his car loan to pay off. I ride a bicycle to work. Plus, I still have a student loan from my uni."

"Uni?" Dave wondered.

"That's Aussie speak for university," Jeremy explained. "Denyse mostly worked her way through school, but also needed a loan. Her parents couldn't afford to help her. We're already saving a bit toward a house down payment and some more for the baby. When our debts are paid off, we'll put those payments into the house saving account."

"He *is* his father's son," Katie said with pride. "And they are both accountants."

"Well, I'm glad." Denyse looked at Dave with respect. "Jeremy has told me all about Mobile in the province called 'Alabama,' your beautiful home, and your life there. He talked most about fishing in your boat and catching crabs. Mobile sounds wonderful."

"Australia is wonderful too," Jeremy inserted. "Wait until you see the rocky coastline and meet some of the wildlife," he added, speaking to his parents.

Katie forced herself to say, "We're looking forward to you visiting us in Mobile with Jeremy, Denyse."

Denyse smiled at that acknowledgment. "Thank you. I would love that."

Jeremy led the way back downstairs. "Are you ready for lunch?"

"We're going to make you shrimps on the barbie," Denyse explained. "But we'll have to go to the market first. Would you like to come along? The walk is about a kilometer each way."

Dave and Katie looked at each other. A couple of kilometers didn't sound far for a couple used to taking a leisurely hike of several miles. "Sure, we'll walk," Dave answered.

Hand-in-hand Jeremy and Denyse led the way down a street shaded by London plane trees. A few dry leaves fell in a gentle breeze. Katie had to remind herself that even though the month was May, it was autumn Down Under. A sweet, spicy fragrance from nearby eucalyptus trees permeated the air. Katie watched the young couple walk ahead and realized, *Jeremy adores her.*

As they followed, Dave noticed that Katie lagged farther and farther behind. Once Jeremy and Denyse had passed out of hearing range, Katie whispered to Dave, "We should give them some money."

"I thought you didn't like her."

Katie shushed her husband from a fear that Denyse might possibly hear. "I think it's the situation I don't like. You said so yourself. But regardless, I want Jeremy and Denyse to have a successful marriage. We could help them."

Dave gave his wife a harsh look. "No way in . . . heck."

She knew he was thinking something stronger than "heck."

Katie persisted. "With our savings and the buyout you got from the firm, we could easily afford to give our only son some money. Twenty or thirty thousand dollars would get them off to a good start."

"You heard me."

"Why not?"

"Don't you remember when we started out together? Would you take that experience away from them?"

"But you and I started out with nothing. They're starting

out with less than nothing due to debts to pay. In a few months, they'll have a baby to care for. Babies aren't cheap, you know. And money is the biggest source of conflict in most marriages."

"They don't seem to be arguing," Dave returned.

"Wait until the baby comes."

"I'll pay for baby food, if and when they need it."

"Dave . . ."

"I said no."

While Jeremy cooked the shrimp outdoors on a communal barbie behind the apartment building, Denyse made a fruit salad. Used to an open barbeque grill, David and Katie were surprised by the barbie's solid flat plate heated by charcoal underneath.

"I should have asked you to bring some Cajun spices," said Jeremy.

But the shrimp turned out well with Indonesian spices. Denyse's fruit salad featured mango, guava, and papaya flavored with a squirt of lemon. She placed the salad and some mismatched dishes on a shaded picnic table near the barbie. "Would you both like lemonade?"

"Yes, thank you," answered Dave.

Jeremy saw his parents watch Denyse filling glasses from a Sprite bottle. "Aussies call Sprite lemonade," he explained. A group of plumpish gray and pink parrot-like birds landed nearby. Dave and Katie turned to stare at them. "Those are galahs," Jeremy added with heavy accent on the ga. "Australians consider them dumb. Calling somebody a 'galah' here is an insult."

Knowing his parents', especially Dave's, love of wildlife, Jeremy pointed to a bluish-gray bird. "See that fellow in the eucalyptus, or as Aussies say, 'gum' tree? He's hoping we'll leave a shrimp unattended." Jeremy threw a raw shrimp on the ground underneath the gum tree. The bird immediately swooped down to collect it. "That's a kookaburra. They're related to our kingfisher. If you listen, you'll hear them calling almost everywhere." Jeremy mimicked an *ack, ack, ack* sound.

As they ate, Denyse asked about Dave and Katie's experience in Minnesota. "Did you really help solve an old murder?"

Dave took the opportunity to brag on his wife. "Katie is the one who put together the clues. And she saved a policeman's life."

"Dave saved all of our lives," Katie returned.

Denyse stopped eating. "How did he do that?"

An awkward silence followed. Dave looked distressed and wouldn't speak. "He had to shoot a man," Jeremy told his fiancée what his mother had privately told him.

Denyse sat stunned. "You mean with a gun?" When Jeremy nodded she added, "Why didn't you tell me before, Jeremy?"

"That isn't the kind of thing one talks about, especially outside the family."

"But aren't I family?" Denyse asked with a hurt tone of voice. She shifted her gaze from Jeremy to her plate.

Jeremy stammered, "I just thought . . . I mean . . . I didn't think . . ."

"He's telling you the truth, honey," Katie spoke to Denyse. "He just didn't think. You asked me for coaching on marriage. Here is some: young husbands think about food, sex, money, and sometimes catching fish. They rarely think anything else through. Jeremy didn't mean to hurt you or exclude you."

Then Katie turned to Jeremy. "Denyse is right. She is family now. Number one: no secrets between you. Number two: start thinking about how she might feel about everything!"

Sydney Opera House

Both Jeremy and Denyse returned to work the following day. "My students have exams coming up," Denyse had explained. "These kids' marks are really important in determining any future opportunities. Doing well on the exams is what gave me a chance."

Their absence left Dave and Katie free to explore the Sydney area. A nearby metro train could take them into downtown Sydney. From there, ferries could take them all over Sydney's harbor. They visited the famous Opera House roofed with white tiles reminiscent of sea shells, Queen Victoria Market, the zoo, and various museums. Sydney's Royal Botanic Garden featured plants and trees from the South Pacific and huge fox bats squeaking and sleeping in the tropical trees. A group of eighteen-inch sulfur-crested cockatoos on a green lawn attracted Dave's attention. Only a dash of yellow in their topknot prevented the birds from being snow white. Tourists tossed the birds bits of bread. "Don't we have some crackers?" he asked Katie.

After his wife produced the crackers, Dave sat down in the grass. A dozen of the large birds gathered around him as he started throwing out bite-sized pieces. "Take my picture," he urged Katie. As she dug out her cell phone, a cockatoo landed on Dave's knee. Another lit on his shoulder. Dave could not break off pieces of cracker fast enough for the impatient birds. One of them gave him a nip with its beak. "Hurry!" Dave urged as Katie fumbled, trying to line up the camera shot. Other greedy birds started nipping at him. Dave threw the crackers onto the grass and scrambled to his feet. The cockatoos tore apart then consumed all the crackers in just a few seconds.

Katie laughed. "Oh! That's funny."

"What's so funny?"

She showed a photo of Dave covered by white birds with an alarmed look on his face.

"They started biting me," he complained.

"Maybe they only hurried you along." Katie pointed to a tree where a sulfur-crested cockatoo leisurely bit off finger-sized branches, apparently for its entertainment. "Their beaks are strong enough to take a hunk out of you, if they really wanted to."

"Then I'm glad they're vegetarians."

Although infrequent drinkers, Dave and Katie wanted to visit a pub like the ones often depicted in Australian lore.

Finding one turned out to be difficult. Cafés specializing in coffee dominated the city. Finally, they entered an establishment similar to a sports bar in the US. There they enjoyed club sandwiches and tea for lunch.

As they ate, Katie commented, "Denyse hasn't said much about her family. And she's hinted about a difficult upbringing. That could be a reason she's so committed to her students. Have you wondered about her relatives?"

"Yeah, I have," Dave admitted. "I guess we'll find out soon enough."

Chapter Three

"You'll be my best man, of course," Jeremy told his father as the foursome discussed the upcoming wedding.

"I would be honored," Dave responded. Then he asked, "How are we getting to Melbourne for the wedding? Will you drive us there?"

"Denyse and I thought taking the train would be easier," answered Jeremy. "Melbourne is in Victoria, about 500 miles south of here. So considering the petrol cost and wear on the car, the round-trip train ticket for all four of us is less expensive. We'll pay for your tickets. The train is faster, too. And we'll have a good view of the Snowy Mountains."

Dave received an unmistakable look from Katie. "No, let us pay for everybody's ticket," he offered.

"You don't need to do that. You're our guests here."

"Consider this part of your wedding present," Katie offered.

"Okay, sure. And thanks."

"My mum will meet us at the train station in Melbourne," Denyse promised.

"Mum?"

"That means mother," Jeremy explained.

"You can stay at Mum's house, if you like. Jeremy and I are staying at a motel nearby."

"We'll stay at the motel as well," Dave answered.

Katie saw a look of relief on Denyse's face. "That's good because the house will be full of Dad's family. They can be a bit noisy."

"What does your father do for a living, Denyse?" asked Katie.

"Oh, he does a bit of this and some of that, mostly on sheep stations. Springtime, he's a shearer."

"He's rather Australian," Jeremy added.

"Sounds like he's fun," Dave concluded.

Neither Jeremy nor Denyse responded.

The next morning the foursome walked from Jeremy and Denyse's flat to a metro train station, pulling their suitcases.

The train carried them to Sydney's Central Train Station. There Jeremy purchased the tickets from a machine with Dave's credit card.

At a nearby market, each of them purchased snacks and drinks for the eleven-hour trip. Then on the train they took seats facing each other with a table in between them. Whistles announced imminent departure. The train started without a sound or jerk precisely on time.

To make conversation, Denyse brought up the Parkers' home again. "I think Jeremy likes Melbourne because Port Phillip Bay south of the city reminds him of Mobile Bay."

"There are some similarities," Jeremy conceded. "We used to go fishing and crabbing in Dad's boat. Ruthie, our Labrador Retriever, always went along. Did you say that you have a cat now?" he asked.

"Yes, we picked up a cat in Minnesota," said Dave. "Old Yeller made himself part of our family."

"Oh, I love both dogs and cats!" said Denyse. "My mum is an animal lover. I inherited that from her. What does your cat do when you're traveling?"

"Our neighbors the Fogles are caring for him at their house. We had never owned a cat. But this one grew on us and needed a home. He can be quite entertaining," said Katie. "You mother likes animals?"

"Yes, ma'am—I mean, Katie. Mum has always loved animals. She even feeds the possums that come to the house at night."

"Australian possums aren't the same as our opossum," Jeremy clarified. "Although marsupials, they act a lot like raccoons. They love to get into trash cans and gardens."

Denyse continued, "Mum has two spoiled corgi dogs. She says, 'If they're good enough for our queen, they're good enough for me.' "

"Does your . . . mum work?" Katie asked.

"Yes. She's a nurse. Mum came over from the United Kingdom thirty years ago when Australia had a shortage of nurses. She's Welsh. Her name is Beatrice."

"And do you have brothers and sisters?"

"Only one brother, Trevor." Denyse stopped talking, leaving silence in the air.

"So, Dad, how has retirement been?" Jeremy began.

"I never thought I'd get tired of fishing. But I found fishing more fun when I didn't go every day."

"Do you do anything with the firm anymore?" Jeremy explained to Denyse, "Dad started a successful accounting firm with two partners."

"No, they bought out my third. And so I leave them alone. I'm still friendly with everyone, though."

"And you're preparing to be a forensic accountant? You'll be legally qualified to be an expert witness in court?"

Dave looked thoughtful. "Yes, I'm preparing. And I think important clients are out there, especially related to law enforcement. How's your job going?" Dave asked his son. This started the two accountants on a long discussion of the differences between American and Australian reporting requirements and taxes.

As Dave paid rapt attention with genuine interest in Jeremy's descriptions, Katie glanced at Denyse. The girl sat staring at Jeremy with unconcealed admiration. Katie herself felt bored. She looked out the train window to see a hilly landscape of dry grassy spaces broken by groves of eucalyptus trees. Australia's Snowy Mountains lined the eastern skyline.

I shouldn't waste this opportunity, Katie thought. Across the aisle two seats facing each other remained empty. She leaned closer to Denyse and whispered, "Are you following this?" She tilted her head toward the two men.

Denyse looked embarrassed and confessed, "Hardly a word of it."

"Then why don't we move over there and talk?" Katie pointed to the empty seats.

A brief expression of fear flashed over Denyse's face before she answered, "Alright."

The men didn't react to the women's move. Across the aisle, Denyse sat as if about to be interrogated.

"I remember when I first met Dave's mother," Katie shared. "She seemed so prim and proper that I was certain she would think me frivolous. I felt terrified that I would make a mistake and offend her."

"You did?"

"Yes. And later I found out that she had been afraid me."

"Scared of you? Why?"

"She was fearful that I would take her son away from her. Dave and I weren't engaged like you and Jeremy. But she knew Dave wouldn't have brought me home unless he cared for me a lot. But eventually Dave's mother became one of my closest friends. Whenever Dave did something dumb, she always stuck up for me."

"She did?"

"Yes, and she became very grateful for how happy I made her son."

Denyse's voice choked, "Are you afraid I'll take Jeremy away from you?"

"No, because you already have. And I'll confess that I'm a little jealous of you. Dave and I tried to give Jeremy everything in life. He had a happy upbringing. But I've never seen him happier than he is with you. I'd like to thank you for making my son so happy."

"Thank me?" Tears formed in Denyse's eyes. "Well, I want to thank you for raising such a fine son and sharing him with me. Jeremy is the best man in Australia," she finished with conviction.

Katie laughed. "I'm glad you think so. I know Jeremy as being a little stinker." She proceeded to tell a few stories about Jeremy as a teenager. "Jeremy came to me asking for help on his science project. 'When is it due?' I asked him." Katie mimicked a clueless teenager, " 'Tomorrow.' 'Well, how long have you known about it?' I asked him. 'Only a few months.' So I told him, 'Why don't you do a scientific survey on the reasons parents want to kill their teenagers? Your father will have a lot to add when he gets home.' "

Denyse started laughing. Katie continued, "The stinker then spent the evening on the phone talking to his friends' parents. Some of them didn't want to get off the phone, they had so much to say. The worst part is that he got an A for the project. And the school printed his summary in the student newspaper."

Denyse laughed harder. Then she spoke seriously, "Katie, Jeremy says that I remind him of you."

"He does?"

"Yes, but I think Jeremy is more like you than I am."

Katie looked across the aisle to where her husband and son were carrying on an animated conversation about amortization rates. "He's also a lot like his father though."

"Yes, I can see that. You must have married the best man in America."

Katie laughed then. "Dave is a stinker sometimes too." She smiled at Denyse, who had visibly relaxed. "How did you and Jeremy meet?"

"We met playing on a church co-ed volleyball team. I had seen Jeremy sitting in church and thought he was so handsome. When he showed up for the first volleyball meeting, my heart nearly stopped. Then he said something with that beautiful southern accent. I was so nervous that I couldn't speak to him for weeks except to say, 'Coming to you.' I set the ball for Jeremy to spike. Then one Sunday he started talking to me after church. Finally, he asked me to go for ice cream after a volleyball game. The next week he invited me to a movie."

Katie felt her heart softening toward Denyse. She smiled and touched Denyse's hand. "I can see why. You are so pretty and smart and energetic."

"No, I'm not."

"Yes, you are. Approaching you must have been hard for Jeremy. He always acted bashful around girls."

"I believe that. He didn't even hold my hand until our fourth date. But we could talk nearly all night. Jeremy told me stories about growing up. My childhood wasn't so nice." Denyse hesitated. "My family is different from yours, Katie. My father is a bloke's bloke from the Outback and not very responsible. Please don't judge Australia by him. My mother earned most of the money to take care of Trevor and me. Mum loves Dad, but being married to him has been tough.

Most days she seemed to be just trying to survive. Once she told me to work hard to get an education and to become somebody that a good man would want to marry. I never expected anyone as good as Jeremy."

"I never expected Jeremy to marry a girl as resourceful as you. One who would work her way through university and make a home without much money."

The women sat quietly for a minute. Across the aisle the men had moved on to long-term depreciation. "Katie," Denyse began, "I know that you must be disappointed that I'm already pregnant."

"I was surprised," Katie acknowledged.

The girl sighed. "We didn't mean to get pregnant already. We didn't mean to have sex. I was the happiest girl on Earth after Jeremy asked me to marry him. As we planned our future one night, I loved him so much that I wanted to give him something special. That was the first time for both of us. Then we found I had gotten pregnant. It was my fault."

"No, it's never just one person's fault," said Katie. Then she asked, "But are you telling me that you were already engaged before you had sex or started living together?"

"Yes, Jeremy had even given me this ring." Denyse showed a thin band with a minuscule diamond. "But we made a big mistake."

Katie thought, *This is a responsible girl willing to acknowledge an error. And she truly loves Jeremy. She'll make a good wife for our son.*

She smiled kindly at Denyse. "Dave and I do think that being legally married is important, and by a pastor if possible. But what has happened has happened. Dave and

I are delighted that God is giving Jeremy such a wonderful wife. We hope you'll consider yourself our daughter."

Denyse stood up, leaned over, and hugged Katie. "Thank you so much. Jeremy and I hoped you'd feel that way. And you know about us taking our honeymoon early?"

"You've already had your honeymoon?"

"Yes, we both need to be back at work after the wedding. And when the baby comes, we'll be busy for years. So Jeremy suggested we take our honeymoon in advance. Last month we went for three nights to an ocean-side town up north."

Katie rolled her eyes and laughed. "Well, that's his father's careful planning side coming out. When is your baby due?"

"Twenty-three more weeks."

"How has your pregnancy gone?"

Denyse shrugged. "Well, I don't have any experience to compare to. But I haven't been sick in a couple of weeks. And the obstetrician says I'm doing fine."

"Did the doctor tell you the baby's sex?"

"No, we both wanted to be surprised."

Chapter Four

"G'day, mates!"

A stocky, balding man with a broad mustache greeted Dave and Katie. He wore shorts and had sharp facial features that showed evidence of brawls and a life outdoors. The man switched his bottle of beer to his left hand and extended a tattooed right arm. "I'm Dingo Larkin. Glad to meet ya."

"This is my dad," Denyse explained as he and Dave shook hands.

Dave noticed a rock-hard grip. "Glad to meet you. I'm Dave Parker. This is my wife, Katie."

"Come on in." Dingo invited them into a modest older house in the suburbs on the east side of Melbourne. "Would you like a cold one?" He gestured toward the drink in his left hand.

"Maybe some hot tea would be nice."

Denyse's mother, Beatrice, had not mentioned Dingo during the short car ride from the train station. She stood nervously behind the Parkers during Denyse's introductions. "I'll get cuppas for you," she offered and hurried toward the kitchen.

Katie could not help but observe differences between Denyse's parents. His lean body with darkly tanned skin contrasted with her plumpness and almost pasty complexion. She stood an inch or two taller than her husband. Her manner seemed deferential—almost apologetic. His manner felt confrontational.

Dingo confirmed her latter observation by shrugging and turning to Jeremy. "So you got my daughter preggers, huh?" He sat down in a hard-backed chair.

Jeremy's face turned ashen. "Uh . . ."

"Dad, we've told you that we had already gotten engaged." Denyse stepped toward her father in defiance. She spoke with firmness and even seemed menacing. "We're getting married on Saturday."

"Well, ya better." Dingo eyed Jeremy before choosing to ignore him. Turning back to Dave and Katie, he waved toward a worn couch. "Sit down. Is this your first time Down Under?"

"Yes, we've never been in Australia before," Dave answered as he and Katie took places close together on one end of the couch.

"You have a beautiful country," Katie added.

"You think that 'cause you haven't seen much of it," Dingo responded. "Oz is like a moss-covered rock. The outside, by the ocean, is soft. The inside is hard."

Interesting comparison, Katie thought. *Just like Beatrice and Dingo—soft and hard.*

Dave gently petted two corgis that had come to sit by his feet. "You mean the Outback?"

"Yeeah. The never-never gets temperatures reaching 45 degrees a lot of days. Some days 50."

Katie took a moment to think. "That would be 113 or 122 degrees to us."

Dingo nodded in confirmation. "Yeeah. And it's a dry heat. I've seen a man drink three gallons of water in a day and still not piss."

Beatrice returned with a large teapot and several cups. "Oh, and I have some Anzac biscuits. Would you get them, luv," she said to Denyse. "Sit down by your parents, Jeremy," she added as Denyse left to retrieve the biscuits. "I presume everybody wants milk?" She proceeded to pour tea.

"Yes, I'll take milk. Thank you," said Katie.

"Uh . . . do you have a little lemon?" Dave asked.

"Whatta ya want lemon for?" Dingo wanted to know.

Dave picked up his teacup. "I use a little lemon in my tea."

Dingo rolled his eyes. But before he could say anything, Beatrice directed him, "Dingo, you go over to the neighbors' garden and get a lemon from their tree." Without comment, Dingo stood and shuffled out the door.

"Dingo is a bit rough toward men," Beatrice explained in his absence. "He acts like each man is a challenger. He's better toward women, though."

Denyse returned with some round brown cookies. "These biscuits are what our ANZAC soldiers ate during the Gallipoli campaign in 1918. ANZAC stands for Australian and New Zealand Army Corps."

The historian in Dave came out. "That was Winston Churchill's strategy to invade Europe from the sea through Turkey. If I remember correctly, the campaign turned into a disaster. After eight months of fighting and over 300,000 casualties, the Allies evacuated without capturing Istanbul or accomplishing anything really."

"That's right. Every April 25th the Aussies and Kiwis celebrate ANZAC Day to honor and remember our men's heartbreaking sacrifice," Denyse added and sat on the couch with Jeremy.

Dingo slouched in with a large green lemon. "Cut a piece for Dave," Beatrice told him. He pulled out a big pocket knife and sliced off a piece. Then he extended it, balanced on the blade, to Dave.

Beatrice sat down in an easy chair. "It's so good to get to know one another. In just three days we'll all be family."

Dave squeezed the lemon into his tea. "Well, yes. We've only known your daughter a couple of days. But we can see how much Jeremy and Denyse love each other."

"What have you done in Australia?" asked Beatrice.

While Dave told about the sights they had seen in Sydney, Katie took a closer look at Beatrice. Obviously, she had once been very pretty. Then she had put on pounds, a lot of them. Her graying hair appeared unkempt. And her face had a tired look. *I guess living with Dingo might age anyone,* Katie thought to herself.

"Do your Forest Gump imitation, Jeremy," Beatrice urged after Dave had described the Sydney harbor.

Jeremy declined until he received a slight nudge from Denyse. "I heared Aus-tra-lia was on the bottom of the world. I come to see people standin' upside down. That must not be true, 'cause everybody here stands the same way as me," Jeremy mimicked with a deep southern drawl.

"What have you seen in Oz, Forest?" Denyse prompted.

"Wal, I don't know much, but you all sure do have some big rabbits here. And they hop along on their hind legs. I tried to give one a carrot. I guess they don't like carrots 'cause he kicked me."

All the Aussies laughed. Beatrice asked, "What else is there, Forest?"

"Wal, we got al-le-gators, back in Al-a-ba-ma. But here I seed a croc-o-dile. They's like an al-le-gator with a bad attitude."

"There's plenty here to kill you, fair dinkum," Dingo agreed. "Have you heard about the snakes?"

"Yeeah," Jeremy's Forest persona mimicked Dingo. "Of the ten most poisonous snakes in the world, thirteen live in Aus-tra-lia." Dingo laughed the hardest.

Denyse joined in, "The brown snake can kill you in a minute with a bite. And unfortunately, they like to hide in lawns. So when we put up a sign saying 'Stay off the grass,' we really mean it."

"Don't forget the death adder," Dingo chimed in. "They burrow just under the sand. Think about that on the beach."

Beatrice got serious for a moment. "If you do go to the beach, watch out for box jellyfish, riptides, and sharks. A prime minister disappeared in the ocean not far from here."

The Forest Gump persona returned. "Wal, it sounds like Aus-tra-lia is a good place for a workaholic to go a swimming. If a man comes out of the water alive, he feels like he's really accomplished something."

They all roared. Dingo got up, went to the fridge, and returned with a cold beer. He handed the bottle to Jeremy in a bloke's tribute of acceptance. "Good on ya, mate."

Jeremy really inherited his mother's storytelling ability, Dave thought to himself.

Friends of Denyse's started arriving the next morning. All of them wanted to meet Jeremy and spend a little time with the happy couple. Two of Dingo's brothers arrived from the Outback. They proposed a tour of various local drinking establishments. Dingo invited Dave and Katie to accompany them.

"I've got a better idea," Beatrice offered. "I could take Dave and Katie on a tour of Morningside Peninsula." She explained to her guests, "That's south of Melbourne along the bay."

Both Dingo and Dave looked at her with gratitude. "Would you?" Katie relieved either man of making a verbal commitment. "I would really love that."

On the ensuing day trip, Dave and Katie found the area remarkably similar to Mobile and the Alabama south coast, yet with a few differences. They appreciated Port Phillip Bay's crystal-clear water and light-colored sandy bottom compared to Mobile Bay's waters made murky brown from incoming rivers. And they saw grape vineyards growing east of Port Phillip Bay compared to the pecan orchards east of Mobile Bay.

Dave and Katie commented that both bays had small picturesque coastal towns, an entrance from the south, and ocean beyond. But Australia's Southern Ocean crashed violently onto a rocky coastline with bits of secluded beach hidden among the rocks. The Gulf of Mexico lapping onto flat beaches south of Mobile Bay was relatively placid by comparison. Dave and Katie kicked off their shoes and spent hours exploring Australia's southern seacoast. Tidal pools, each one like a fancy saltwater aquarium, held exotic marine life. The Alabamians marveled at star fish, sea urchins, sea cucumbers, and brightly colored little fish. An octopus darted under a rock, leaving a smear of black ink.

Beatrice urged them on. "Listen carefully and you can sometimes hear seals barking. And penguins come ashore near here. Just remember that the water has riptides that can pull you offshore in a minute."

The trio stopped for a late lunch in a charming bayside village. At a café, Katie attempted to get to know Beatrice better. "Denyse told us that you're from Wales. How did you come here and meet Dingo?"

"Thirty years ago, Australia had a big shortage of nurses. I came here to get a good job. Australia being a commonwealth country, there was no problem getting a work visa." Beatrice lowered her voice a little. "And I had heard about Australian men, their manliness and all. Plus, the weather back home alternates between dreary and miserable.

"I met Dingo in a pub. I had never seen a more handsome, virile man. We . . . well, we didn't get married before Denyse came. But when Dingo saw the babe, his daughter, he agreed to marry.

"Living with him hasn't been easy. When we did live together, that is. Sometimes we would get tired of each other. He would leave for months, once for nearly two years.

"He always showed back up though, usually with a pocketful of money from working on some sheep station. Then it would be fun times for everybody 'til he ran outta money. He's alright as long as he's sober. And God help me, I still think he's handsome."

"Denyse seems to have turned out well," Katie suggested as they enjoyed sandwiches and soft drinks.

"Well, no thanks to Dingo." Beatrice paused and sighed. "Nor much thanks to me either. I wasn't much of a mother myself. When Dingo was home, we were arguing. When Dingo was gone, I was moping.

"Denyse, she's different. She always wanted something better than the life we offered. She never acted like she was better or deserved anything. No, Denyse was willing to work toward somethin' better. She made good marks in school, worked her way through uni, even went to church. She's quality, like your son, Jeremy. He's a gent. You should be proud of him."

"We are proud of him. And we're starting to love your daughter." Katie reached out to clasp Beatrice's hand. "Jeremy and Denyse can be very happy together."

Katie and Beatrice looked at each other in quiet appreciation for a long moment.

Dave had finished his sandwich and broke the women's silence. "Did I hear Denyse say that she had a brother?"

Beatrice broke eye contact with Katie. "You mean Trevor. He's three years younger than Denyse. She practically raised him while Dingo stayed away and I worked. Once Denyse left for uni, Trevor felt alone. He took it hard, acted out, got arrested once, and fought with his dad."

"All young men have conflict with their fathers," Dave suggested. "Jeremy and I argued about plenty when he was a teenager."

"I don't mean they argued," Beatrice clarified. "No, Dingo and Trevor fought. To his credit, Dingo never laid a hand on me or Denyse. But he hit Trevor plenty. I think Dingo only knows how to deal with men by conflict. Before she went off to uni, Denyse protected Trevor. But once she was gone and Trevor grew taller than his dad, Dingo didn't hold up on him any. Dingo wanted Trevor to stick up for himself with other men. But Trevor just didn't seem to have the stomach for fightin'. Took after me, I guess."

"Where is Trevor now?" Katie asked.

"Trevor disappeared when he was eighteen after Dingo beat him up extra bad. Dingo had been drinking . . ." Beatrice trailed off. Tears came down her cheeks.

Katie broke the silence. "I think Denyse is hoping Trevor will come to the wedding."

"I'd like that too. But I doubt he'll come. We haven't heard from him in almost three years. We didn't even know where to send a wedding invitation. Although he would never admit it, Dingo is hoping he comes too. Dingo won't ever talk about Trevor. He feels to blame. But men like him just can't admit wrong."

Chapter Five

A muscular man waited in a dark spot just outside of an inexpensive extended-stay motel in Dunedin, New Zealand. He had been there nearly all night. Finally, he saw his quarry approaching room 125. The man started moving, timing his pass by room 125 to be just after the younger man had unlocked the door and stepped in.

As the thin young man turned to close the door, the man pushed it into him with great force, knocking him back and to the floor. "What . . .?" Trevor began, but something heavy hitting his forehead interrupted his words. In confusion and pain, he didn't see a second man slip into the room and close the door.

Rough hands pulled his hands behind his back and secured them together with a zip tie used in electric connections. Someone lifted his feet and secured them as well. A cloth stuffed into his mouth stopped him from calling out.

Words penetrated his daze. "You're in a bit late, kid. Been out hustling somebody else? You thought you were smart.

We're here to collect our boss's money. Give us the sixteen thousand dollars you took from Mr. Wong, and add an extra thousand each for my partner and me."

Trevor struggled to focus his eyes. The smell of alcohol and tobacco filled the room. He saw two dark-complexioned barrel-chested men standing over him. The men appeared to be descendants of native South Pacific islanders.

"You can make this easy or hard," one of the men said in a guttural English. "Just give us the money, and we'll leave you alone."

The young man shook his head. One of the two men opened a drawer in the hotel room's mini-kitchen. He selected a knife and started heating the blade tip on the motel room's tiny stove. "Hard, then."

⸻

That night Dave invited Jeremy and Denyse to meet with him and Katie in their motel room. There he asked them to sit on the bed. He paced back and forth while Katie watched with curiosity from a chair. "We have a wedding present for you," he announced.

What is Dave doing? Katie wondered.

The young couple could not hide a brightness of expectation. "Jeremy, how much do you owe on your car?" Dave asked.

"Twelve thousand dollars."

"Your mother and I will pay that off so you can save toward buying a house."

Jeremy and Denyse looked at each other with a mixture of shock and joy. But Katie looked at her husband with amazement. He avoided her open-mouthed stare.

"And Denyse, how much do you owe on your student loan?"

Denyse couldn't believe what was happening. "Fourteen thousand dollars."

"We'll pay that off as well."

Katie's mouth opened wider.

"No," Denyse insisted. "That's too much."

"We paid a lot more than that toward our son's education. You're our daughter now. We'll help pay for your education too."

Jeremy and Denyse sat dumbfounded. Katie went with the flow. "This will give you and our grandbaby a fair start on life together. Your father and I started with nothing. This will bring you to where we started."

Denyse started to cry and hugged both Dave and Katie's necks. "I love you."

"We love you too."

"Could I ask one favor?" Denyse said through her tears. "Please don't tell my family about this. They already feel intimidated by you. Your generosity would leave them feeling inadequate too."

"Okay, we'll also give you a nice towel set for them to see."

"Thank you so much."

Ever the accountant, Jeremy added, "This will make you happy, Dad. Four Australian dollars only cost three American dollars." Being himself, Dave had already realized that.

"Is that all? A set of towels?" Dingo interrupted the enthralled couple as they opened some of the early wedding gifts the next day. The family was sitting in a circle in Dingo and Beatrice's living room with opened boxes and wrapping paper strewn across the floor as on a Christmas morning. "We expect more than that from our future in-laws."

Dingo's outburst had caught Dave off-guard. "Uh . . ."

"They flew all the way from America," Denyse broke in. "That's expensive."

"Then they should be able to afford a nicer gift."

"Dad, there's something you need to know," she started again.

"No, Denyse, Dingo is right," Dave intervened. "How about a thousand-dollar gift certificate for a baby stroller, bassinet, car seat, all that baby stuff?"

"That's more like it!" Dingo settled back in his chair. "Between that and the diapers and baby clothes from Beatrice and me, they should be ready for the little ankle biter."

"A good idea, Dingo," Dave concluded and winked at Denyse.

She smiled back and said, "Thank you, Dave," with genuine feeling.

". . . and I pronounce Jeremy and Denyse husband and wife. You may kiss the bride," the Anglican minister intoned. "All rise."

The heavy music of a pipe organ filled the church chapel as Jeremy and Denyse walked down the center aisle smiling and nodding to well-wishers.

"A reception has been arranged at the park across the street. Please join the bride and groom and their families," invited the minister.

"Meet me at the open bar!" shouted Dingo above the music.

Dave and Katie along with Beatrice joined Jeremy and Denyse in a reception line. Dingo, his brothers, and a few drinking mates held court at the bar surrounded by a crowd of Aussie blokes.

Most of those passing through the line introduced themselves as friends of Denyse or work associates of Beatrice. The well-wishers soon petered out while the group around Dingo grew both in number and noise.

Dave and Katie stood nearby while a photographer posed the happy couple in front of the wedding cake. Dave heard a voice say, "Excuse me, sir."

Dave turned to find a well-groomed and sharply dressed middle-aged Asian man. "I'm looking for Trevor Larkin. Have you seen him?"

"I'm sorry, I don't know Trevor," Dave returned. "But I don't think he's here."

"That's unfortunate. I owe Trevor some money. My conscience demands that I repay him," the man explained. "Would you point out his family who might know how I could contact Trevor?"

"Your best bet could be his mother." Dave pointed out Beatrice, who hovered near the photographer making suggestions.

"Ah, yes. The bride's mother and Trevor's. Thank you very much." The man moved away.

"Who was that?" Katie asked.

"A man looking for Trevor. I directed him to Beatrice."

"He didn't take your advice, then." Katie pointed out the man approaching another group of wedding guests.

"That's odd."

Louder voices from the direction of the bar drew their attention. "What business do you have with Trevor?" Dingo demanded from a beefy rough-looking man a head taller than himself.

"I'm just looking for him, that's all," the man returned.

"He's not here! So why don't you stop drinking our liquor."

"We attended the wedding. That entitles us to drink at the bar." Several other burly-looking men backed up the one confronting Dingo.

"Not without telling me why you're looking for Trevor." Dingo's brothers and mates moved behind him as the other bar patrons started to back away.

"If you must know, your worthless son cheated me and my mates in cards. We're here to find him and get our money back."

At this, Katie looked for the Asian man who had also inquired about Trevor. She saw him standing unobtrusively, observing from a distance. An unexplained chill went through her when he produced a camera and surreptitiously took photos of Denyse, Jeremy, Beatrice, and Dingo. When he turned the camera toward her and Dave, the man saw Katie looking at him and slipped into the crowd that was watching the disturbance by the bar.

"Why don't you look for Trevor in the shit house," Dingo

challenged. "Even if you don't find him, your own relatives are certain to be there."

"Maybe we'll make you pay the money for your no-hoper, cockroach."

Unexpectedly to those watching, Dave stepped between the belligerent men. "Does anybody know where I can see some kangaroos?" He grinned foolishly.

Something blurred before Dave's eyes and impacted his nose. He felt searing pain and instant dizziness.

Dave opened his eyes to see ankles dancing around him as standing men exchanged blows with their fists and curses with their mouths. *I'm on the ground,* Dave realized through his pain. He struggled to his knees, only to be pushed back to the ground and held down. Somebody lay on top of him. Despite the blood flowing from his nosc, Dave could smell something sweet—perfume.

"Stay on the ground, Mr. Parker!" Dave turned his head slightly to see Denyse's face only inches from his own. "You'll be safe on the ground!" she shouted into his face. "Understand?"

Dave nodded slightly and felt Denyse release him. From his position on the ground, he watched Denyse stand and move to where two men wrestled on the ground. She stood over a young man who had restrained a much larger and older man in a double-armed rear head lock.

The young man appeared to be holding on for dear life. The larger man flailed around trying to free himself. *Is that Jeremy holding the big man?* Dave thought.

Seeing her husband of an hour to be in no imminent danger, Denyse moved to insert herself between the men exchanging blows. They continued to hit at each other around her.

Where is Katie? Dave suddenly thought. From his prone position, he looked around. *There she is.* He saw Beatrice holding diminutive Katie in a bear hug to prevent her from endangering herself. The wedding photographer continued taking shots of the fracas from a safe distance.

Chapter Six

"At my wedding!" Denyse stormed in front of Dingo, Dave, and Jeremy after their opponents had departed. "You got into a fight on my day-of-all-days! How many brides do you know who have ever had to break up a fight at their own wedding?"

She stood glaring at the three men. Nearby Beatrice and Katie stood in support of Denyse. The wedding guests who had not participated in the fight looked on in silence. Denyse focused on her father. "Dad, this wouldn't have happened without you. Can't you behave for just one day?"

"They started it by insulting Trevor," Dingo protested.

"Who cares? Trevor isn't here."

"Well, they—"

"I don't care! This was my wedding day!" Denyse softened her tone a little. "Dad, I know you feel bad about what happened with Trevor. But this didn't help that situation any."

"I don't feel bad . . ." Dingo protested.

Denyse's harsh tone returned. "Yes, you do. Now shut your trap." Dingo remained silent but could not disguise a remorseful look.

Denyse turned to Dave. "Mr. Parker, why did you get involved?"

Katie spoke up, "Dave thought he could prevent a fight by providing a distraction."

"Is that so, Mr. Parker?"

Dave nodded while still holding a napkin under his nose to stop the bleeding. "You can call me Dave."

"Maybe calling you Mr. Parker will remind you who you are—not some ruffian." Denyse's tone softened again. "Dave, those galahs on both sides had already decided to fight." She gestured toward Dingo and his brothers. "They were just going through the pre-fight insult ritual. You couldn't have stopped them."

Finally, Denyse turned to her new husband. Jeremy had released his opponent after Denyse had separated the groups of men by pushing and shoving them. The man he had been holding then hit Jeremy in the face in frustration. Jeremy now stood with a hand over the welt.

Denyse considered berating him and then decided on a different approach. "Jeremy, what do you think your company would have done if their accountant had been arrested for public fighting?"

Jeremy realized the real danger to him the fight had posed. Horror showed on his face. "They would have fired me," he answered.

"And you would have had a criminal record. How would that have helped with getting a new job?"

"Was I supposed to let them beat up my father?"

"Dave wasn't in any danger as long as he stayed on the ground. You could have protected him better by lying on him, rather than by fighting yourself."

Denyse paused before continuing, "You're married now, and we're going to have a baby. You need to think about the baby and about me first. That's the kind of man I want to be married to. The kind of man you are."

"I'm sorry, Denyse. I just didn't think. It won't happen again."

"I'm counting on that." Denyse approached her husband and gave him a big kiss. Then she picked off debris and dirt he had gotten on his tux while grappling on the ground. "Try remembering that this tux is only rented, alright?"

Denyse turned to the unscathed wedding guests who had watched her corrective performance with awe. "We still need to cut the cake, I think."

"How does your nose feel?" Katie asked her husband back at their motel room.

"Really sore. And I have a splitting headache."

"Do you think you should see a doctor?"

Dave gingerly felt around his nose. "No, I don't think that'll be necessary. I'm just bruised."

Katie had collected some ice into a damp towel. "Here, hold this on your face. Maybe the swelling will go down. And here are some aspirin for your headache. Would you like a sleeping pill?"

After swallowing the aspirin, Dave lay on the bed and gently placed the towel over his eyes and nose, leaving his mouth free to breathe. "Yes, I'll take the sleeping pill. Thanks, sweetheart."

"You tried to do the right thing, dinosaur. I'm proud of you. I don't think many Australians are like Dingo. But, regardless of what we expected, Denyse's family is our family now."

Dave grunted acknowledgment and lay quietly for a few minutes. Then he asked, "So then, what do you think of Denyse now?"

"If Jeremy and Denyse ever try to split up, I'm keeping Denyse," Katie said.

In spite of the pain, Katie's quip made Dave laugh. "Don't joke!" he ordered. "Laughing hurts."

"I wouldn't look in the mirror then. You're going to have two black eyes. I'll be calling you 'raccoon' tomorrow."

"I said stop being funny," Dave said between teeth clenched to avoid chuckling.

Katie changed the subject. "What do you think about Trevor?"

"He sounds like trouble."

"Well, a lot of people are apparently looking for him."

Dave's headache persisted the next morning, albeit slightly diminished. With aspirin, he could tolerate the discomfort. His nose, although swollen and congested with coagulated blood, functioned. A tapping at their door told Dave and Katie that Jeremy and Denyse had arrived to take them in a taxi to the train station.

Katie invited them into the hotel room. "We've got plenty of time to catch the train. Could we sit and talk a bit first?"

"Of course. I apologize for being rough with the men yesterday," said Denyse.

"No, you were wonderful." Dave repeated Katie's quip about keeping Denyse in the event of a breakup.

Jeremy smiled in appreciation. Denyse looked at her mother-in-law with affection. "Thanks, Katie."

Katie noticed that Jeremy had one black eye himself. "Nice shiner," she commented.

Denyse took a long look at Dave. "Nothing like his though. I'll put a little makeup on Jeremy before he goes to his office tomorrow. Nobody will notice. But you . . ."

"Beatrice told us that Dingo and Trevor had a fight," Katie told Jeremy and Denyse. "Is that why he left?"

Denyse sighed. "Partly. Well, that was the final straw. Dad treated him pretty rough, like his father had treated him. Trevor couldn't fight Dingo physically, so he developed into a trickster—someone able to deceive and manipulate people."

Katie shook her head in sympathy. "Beatrice said you two were close."

"We had each other in a difficult situation. I shouldn't have left him alone when I left home for uni."

"How old were you then?"

"Eighteen."

"That's pretty young to have responsibility for a teenage brother. What happened isn't your fault," Katie reassured.

Denyse slumped back in her seat. "My head tells me that. My heart breaks thinking about my little brother out there alone. I've tried to get him to communicate. He doesn't answer. There's no telling what sort of trouble he's in. I have no doubt he hustled those men who came looking for him. Even as a teenager, Trevor took advantage of schoolmates and neighbors, and even family, all except me. I'd give anything to find him."

"Maybe Mom and Dad could help you," Jeremy suggested.

Katie looked incredulous. "What do you mean?"

Jeremy gave the winsome smile he had used as a youngster when trying to convince his parents of something. "Aren't you two detectives, of a sort, after solving that big mystery at the mansion in Minnesota? You could follow up on some of Trevor's last known places. Maybe somebody knows where he is. And you'd get to see some more of Australia at the same time."

Dave protested, "We're fish out of water here in Australia. We wouldn't know how to start."

Denyse spoke up, "Jeremy, have you forgotten what happened at the wedding? Look at your Dad's face!"

"No, wait. I wasn't saying they should endanger themselves by getting involved with any thugs. Just some mild sleuthing work. You know, kind of like accounting—collecting information."

Katie looked at Denyse and recognized hope in her eyes. She could tell that simply trying to find out more about Trevor's whereabouts would mean so much to her new daughter-in-law. *What could it hurt?* she thought. The challenge even sounded adventurous. She turned her head to her husband. "Dave, I'd like to at least try."

Dave could see in Katie's expression the importance

to her of helping Denyse. And after Minnesota, they had agreed to not shy away from new adventures. "Okay then," her husband agreed.

A few hours later, the foursome waited on the platform at the train station. Obvious to Dave and Katie, Denyse and Jeremy had resolved any lingering negative emotions between them in the night. "I told Tarzan here that if he ever wanted to play with gorillas again, he'd be making love to Chita sooner than he would to Jane," said Denyse. Jeremy grinned.

"Please don't make me laugh," pleaded Dave.

"What's wrong with laughin'?" a familiar male voice asked.

The foursome turned to see Beatrice and Dingo. Denyse smiled. "Mum and Dad! You came."

"We wanted to see you off and say goodbye," Beatrice explained.

Dingo, looking unaffected by the previous day's fracas, added, "I had to see my mates again." He took a close look at Dave and winced. "Oh booger! You don't look so good. Ya got to keep your guard up."

Dingo inspected Jeremy in turn. "Looks like you got a tap there, lad."

Denyse looked stern. "Dad, you heard what I said yesterday."

Sober again, Dingo answered, "Yeeah, I heard. I'm just a bloke like my father before me. I don't know how to be any different. But I do know that I screwed up yesterday and led these two gentlemen into trouble. It's just that Trevor and me . . . we . . . I . . ." Dingo's words trailed off.

Denyse gave her father a little hug. "I know, Dad. We all miss him." Dingo nodded.

Beatrice looked at her husband with admiration and touched his arm for reassurance.

Final boarding whistles blew. Denyse and Jeremy started to climb onto the train, leaving Dave and Katie on the platform.

Dingo pointed to Dave and Katie. "What about them?"

Denyse turned partially around. "They're staying in Melbourne, Dad. Dave and Katie are going to help us find Trevor. You take care of them, now."

Chapter Seven

"What makes you two think you can find Trevor?" Dingo blurted out as the train left the platform.

Katie raised her hands to a palms out position and smiled. "All we can do is try."

Beatrice placed a hand on her husband's shoulder. "Don't be so fast, Dingo. The Parkers are some sort of detectives. Just after she and Jeremy got engaged, Denyse told me Dave and Katie had solved an old murder."

Before Dingo could comment, Dave made a proposal. "How about us having lunch together? Katie and I will treat you to any restaurant you pick. Do you like seafood?"

Beatrice's face lit up with a smile. "That would be lovely. There's a nice place down by the bay I've always wanted to try." She turned to her husband. "No drinkin', Dingo. These folks are taking us to a nice, respectable restaurant."

Dingo made a sour expression and then looked at Dave. "Two beers?"

"Sure."

Katie watched the exchange and thought, *Dave is maneuvering them onto his turf now. He's used to taking clients out to nice lunches.*

"Let me drive us all," Beatrice offered. "You can put your bags into my boot. Dingo left his ute out at the station where he works during shearing season."

Dave and Katie watched as Dingo picked up their bags, carried them to her car, and put them in Beatrice's trunk.

The restaurant rested on pilings driven into the bay shore sand. Large picture windows looked out over tranquil Port Phillip Bay. A freighter slowly approached Melbourne's harbor under a cloudless blue sky. A hostess guided them to a table for four by the windows. Smells of butter, garlic, and spices made them hungry.

"This is so nice," Beatrice gushed and looked reproachfully at her husband. "The only seafood I ever get is fish and chips."

Dingo appeared ill at ease in the unfamiliar environment. "Just you look at the prices," he whispered to Beatrice.

"This is on us," Dave reminded his guests.

Katie helped Beatrice to order a grilled Chilean Sea Bass with artichokes. Dave ordered Dingo's first beer and one for himself. Then he suggested the Alaska salmon, which came with asparagus and roast potatoes.

An energetic waiter took their orders. Dave added several appetizers: freshly baked bread, calamari, grilled scallops, and fried cheese sticks for all to share. As they nibbled at the appetizers, Dave kicked off the conversation. "Do you favor any sports, Dingo?"

"I used to play a little rugger."

"Rugger?"

"That's like American football except without any padding."

"Oh, you mean rugby? That's growing in popularity in the US." Soon Dave had Dingo talking about his experiences playing rugby. Then they talked about America's and Australia's other favorite sports.

Dingo, not surprisingly, was a fan of mixed martial arts fighting. "Your son Jeremy might be pretty good on the ground game and submission," he explained. "If he had lowered his arm he could have gotten a deep choke-hold on that bloke."

"Jeremy wrestled some in high school," Dave explained without taking issue with the use of choke-holds.

Katie looked across the table at Beatrice. "I hear you're an animal lover."

Beatrice was happy to talk about Australia's iconic wildlife. She became animated describing wombats, koalas, platypuses, possums, wallabies, brumbies (or wild horses), and even feral camels. She looked distressed when Dingo inserted some comments on killing roos for meat.

Their dinners arrived. As they ate, Dave turned the conversation. "Finding Trevor is going to be difficult. We'll need your help."

"We'll do anything," Beatrice promised. "What do you need?"

"We've heard about the family conflicts already," said Katie, wishing not to embarrass them. "What else could you tell us about Trevor? What did he like to do? Where did he hang out?"

Dingo and Beatrice looked at each other and seemed to visibly relax when not required to talk about their family problems. Beatrice spoke first, "Trevor would eat pizza for every meal, if you let him. He was a quiet boy. His head always stuck in some book. Trevor never expressed much interest in sports."

"He was always interested in games though," Dingo added. "Card games. Board games. Mind games. Some of his teachers called him a genius, whenever something interested him."

Trevor's parents continued telling stories about their son. Gradually, Dave and Katie felt like they knew a little about Denyse's brother.

"This is really good, mate," Dingo said of the grilled salmon.

Dave looked sympathetic. "It's not a very big portion, though. Would you like another?"

"Yeeah!"

Dave ordered an extra portion of salmon and another beer for Dingo. Beatrice declined more sea bass but nibbled at another order of calamari.

Dingo had nursed just two beers over a two-hour lunch, which showed them all that he didn't need booze to be engaging. He started telling tales of working in the Outback and of Australia's criminal heritage. "England used to send their prisoners here never to return home."

"Tell them about our greatest folk hero," Beatrice urged.

"Ned Kelly was what we call a bushranger. That's somebody who escapes authorities by hiding in the Outback. But he was a real-life Robin Hood born not far from here," claimed Dingo. "He and his mates stood up against corrupt politicians. Once the police cornered them, Ned came back to fight for his mates wearing a metal suit of armor. Too bad his legs weren't protected from the bullets. They hung him here in Melbourne." Regret tinged Dingo's voice.

They all sat silently a moment thinking about Ned. "Do you want to go to the loo, luv?" Beatrice invited Katie.

"She means the lady's room," Dingo explained to Katie's confusion.

In Katie and Beatrice's absence, the waiter brought the bill. As Dave figured a 20% tip, Dingo spoke up, "A big tip isn't necessary here, mate. The restaurant pays waiters and waitresses well. Minimum wage in Oz is $18.29 an hour."

"Thanks! That sounds better than our voluntary system in the US." Dave left a couple of dollars instead.

"How will you start looking for Trevor?" Dingo asked.

"Did your son have any close friends we could talk to?"

"The boy was a bit of a loner. But I wasn't around all the time either," Dingo confessed. "You might go to his school and ask."

"That's a good idea. Did Trevor leave behind much in the way of records or documents when he left?"

"There's a big pile of papers and stuff in his room at the house. You're welcome to look at it. We haven't touched anything. He spent a lot of time on the computer. After Denyse left for uni, we moved all that electronic gear into his room for him to use anytime. What he did, I don't know. But his light might have been on at any hour."

The women returned. “Beatrice has asked us to stay with her and Dingo. She says the house is empty of guests now.” Katie’s eye contact and look told Dave, *Your decision.*

Dave decided quickly. “That’s very generous. And that would be convenient considering we’re working together to find Trevor. Dingo has offered to let us look at Trevor’s belongings.”

The two corgis greeted Dave and Katie by jumping against their legs as they entered the Larkin home. Both Alabamians leaned over to pet the excited animals. Beatrice smiled. “They’re happy to see you again. You must be dog people.”

“Actually, we have a cat right now,” Katie answered. “But up until a year ago, we always had dogs.”

Beatrice pulled her pets away. “We have three bedrooms. Me and Dingo are in one. Then we still have Denyse’s and Trevor’s rooms. Denyse’s is nicer.” Beatrice nodded toward Katie.

“I think we’ll try Trevor’s room. Better to get to know him,” Dave responded.

Inside Trevor’s old bedroom, the Parkers found bunk beds, a lot of books, various games, and an older desktop computer. “Do you have a password for the computer?” Dave called out.

“Denyse wrote it on the side of the monitor so that the whole family could use it. Me and Dingo hardly ever touch the thing though,” Beatrice answered. “Would you like tea?”

Katie returned to the living room to chat some more and drink tea with Beatrice. Dingo had disappeared somewhere. “He’s probably at McGinty’s Pub just down the road,” Beatrice explained.

Dave started to look around Trevor's room. He found lots of games and cards plus typical male teenager stuff: posters of attractive women, some beat-up looking clothes, and various mementos from school days. Non-typical for most teenage boys, piles of books and paperback novels also remained in the room. Trevor favored science fiction and action adventures. Unlike the décor in Jeremy's old room, no sports memorabilia was on display. The room confirmed Beatrice and Dingo's description of their son.

Next Dave turned on the computer. Sorting through someone else's computer wasn't as easy as depicted on TV detective stories. While fictional sleuths frequently turned on a suspect's computer and immediately found incriminating evidence, Dave quickly realized reality would be much more challenging. School assignments and directories from both Trevor and Denyse cluttered the hard drive of the Larkins' computer. Dave settled in for a systematic search.

Beatrice and Katie continued sipping tea and chatting in the living room as the hours ticked by. "Won't he ever come out of there?" Beatrice asked.

Katie answered while stroking the corgis' heads. "No. Dave is in his element now. He won't give up until he finds out all about Trevor."

"I wish I could help."

"You will eventually." Katie thought another minute. "There is one thing you could help with right now. Dave and I will need to rent a car. Could you teach me how to drive on the left?"

"What's to teach?"

"Well, we drive on the right."

"Let's take my car for a practice."

A few hours later the women returned laughing and relieved. "How many times did you shout out, 'Not that side!'?" Katie teased Beatrice.

"Nearly one too few. That lorry driver gave us a nasty look, didn't he?" To Katie's confused look Beatrice added, "The truck driver."

Katie nodded understanding. "Maybe we could practice again tomorrow?"

"I'd like that. Now if you'll excuse me, I need to get ready to leave for my shift at the hospital."

Katie decided to check on Dave and found him still staring at the computer screen. "What have you found?"

"A lot of what you'd expect: music, YouTube links, and school assignments. Trevor also apparently did extensive online research. Several web sites of poker tips are bookmarked. His website choices also reveal a lot of interest in con games and hustles."

Katie shook her head. "That sounds ominous."

"Unfortunately, that's not the worst. Look at this." Dave opened a file titled "Enterprises." A simple bookkeeping spreadsheet documented Trevor's effort to collect easy money by several schemes. "I think this shows that Trevor had found practical ways to put his skills to work."

Katie nodded. "This also tells us something important about Trevor. Hustling is more than a way to get money. It's a game or contest to him."

"Well, he kept thorough records. If this is accurate, he left home with nearly ten thousand dollars cash in his pocket,"

Dave observed. "I'll bet he had built a stake in preparation for striking out on his own."

Katie pointed to a series of entries. "He's documented the names of those he took money from."

"Maybe he didn't want to try the same trick again on anyone."

Katie shook her head. "No, see how the names are all males? This means that Trevor and Dingo aren't as different from each other as everybody thinks. Dingo fights men with his fists. Trevor fights men with cunning and deception. This is his list of victories."

Chapter Eight

A gentle rapping on the bedroom door woke Dave and Katie the next morning. They heard Beatrice through the door. "Breakfast is almost ready." They could smell sausage cooking.

Cold air of early winter surrounded them as they left their respective bunk beds and reported to the kitchen. "I never expected to be cold in Australia," whispered Katie.

Beatrice noticed them shivering. "Melbourne being farther south is fresher than Sydney. You'll need wraps today. Tonight, it should frost according to the weather reporter. I'll have Dingo build us a fire in the wood stove before tomorrow morning." She pulled two worn jackets from a closet. "Try these on."

Katie's fingers barely reached the sleeves of Beatrice's coat. Dave's arms protruded out of Dingo's jacket, leaving his wrists exposed. "Oh dear," said Beatrice. "Maybe you'll want to get your own wraps later."

Dingo already sat at the breakfast table ready to eat. He looked odd sipping hot coffee rather than beer. "So, what have you found in Trevor's room?" he demanded.

Dave remembered Dingo's belligerence when Trevor had been accused of chicanery at the wedding. He answered the question about discoveries evasively. "Trevor did a lot of research online and in books. Curiosity is a sign of intelligence."

"Yeeah, the kid was smart. Maybe too smart for his own good," said Dingo.

Beatrice had risen early to make a traditional English breakfast for her guests: eggs, sausage, mushrooms, beans, a cooked tomato, and toast with jam. She placed laden plates before them and her husband. "Let them eat, luv," she instructed Dingo. To Dave and Katie, she said, "I'm on shift at the hospital today. But before I go, I'll make some nice fresh scones to go with your afternoon tea."

Dingo immediately started spreading a brownish paste on a piece of toast. "Try a bit of this here, mate," he suggested and pushed a jar across the table.

Vegemite, Dave read on the label. Dave watched Dingo eating the toast and Vegemite with gusto and covered his piece of toast with the paste. The first bite filled his mouth with bitterness. He resisted the urge to spit the mouthful out and swallowed. "That's strong."

Dingo grinned. "Yeeah, they make it with brewer's yeast. It'll wake your mouth up. Mostly just blokes eat it."

Dave pushed the jar to Katie. "Try this."

She had seen his reaction. "Didn't you hear that this is bloke food? I'll stick with the jam, thanks."

After enjoying the other parts of breakfast, Dave and Katie sipped tea while Beatrice made the scones. Katie saw that the scones were like southern biscuits with raisins mixed in.

"Do you have a photo of Trevor we could use?" Katie asked.

"The most recent I have is a school picture that they used in the yearbook his final year at the college."

"That would be perfect. Thanks."

Beatrice put the scones in the oven to bake and brought them a photo revealing a tall, skinny teenager. Dave and Katie saw that Trevor's round face and light complexion did resemble his mother. "And what will you two do today?" she asked.

"I'm still studying Trevor's computer and papers. But we'll need a break later. What do you suggest?"

"Do you like to walk? If you go out to the main road and turn left, you'll find a shopping center in a kilometer or two. You can find wraps there to your liking. Turn right and you'll find a reserve. They have walking trails through some bush. Our reserve has a few kangaroos, if you keep a sharp eye."

By midday, the Australian sun had warmed the air to a bracing chill. The Alabamians enjoyed a brisk walk to the shopping center. In a discount store, they each selected a jacket. Afterwards, Dave noticed his wife loitering in front of a bakery window. Odors of fried dough and sugar invited them inside. "Would you like a treat and tea?"

Katie smiled at her husband. "I think I would." Inside

the shop she pointed to a flaky pastry in the display case. "I'll have one of those and tea," she told the girl behind the counter.

Dave ordered tea plus a slice of lemon and a plate of shortbread filled with chocolate chips. "Maybe these will help me forget the taste of Vegemite," he joked. The couple took seats at a small round table.

"What fruits do you suppose they use for fillings here?" Katie wondered aloud.

The girl brought out a tray with two pots of tea, milk, lemon, Dave's shortbread, and Katie's pastry the girl had warmed in a microwave. Katie bit into her choice. "Ugh! What's this?" She placed the pastry back on her plate. Warm bits of beef mixed with carrots and potatoes in gravy spilled out.

"That must be what they call a 'meat pie.'" Dave reached over to scoop up a forkful. "It's not bad, though. A bit overcooked to my taste."

"Then you eat it." Katie pushed her plate over to Dave and pulled his shortbread to herself.

"What about venomous snakes?" Katie fretted as she and Dave entered the reserve Beatrice had mentioned.

"I've been watching for snakes all my life. This path is wide and smooth. And anyway, snakes hole up in cold weather."

"What do you know about Australian snakes? Maybe they like cold weather."

"All snakes are cold-blooded. We'll be fine," Dave assured his wife.

Katie wasn't so certain but followed Dave's lead into the bush. Quickly she started enjoying their walk. Cool, dry air made them both comfortable in their exertion. A breeze rustled eucalyptus and other trees shading the path. Picturesque foot bridges crossed over several small streams of clear water. Brightly colored birds fluttered in the trees. "This is lovely," she commented.

"It's about to get better. Look over there." Dave spoke in a whisper and pointed to an open space off the trail. There several kangaroos dozed in the warm sunlight. "Let's get closer to the herd."

Katie returned his whisper, "They call a group of kangaroos a mob. And I don't think they're safe, Dave."

"What are they going to do besides run away?"

"Remember when curiosity led you to break through the ice in Minnesota? See those huge hind legs? Kangaroos can lean back on their tail and kick you with both feet into next week."

But Dave had already started edging closer. He got to within a few feet when suddenly the mob scrambled to their feet. A large buck kangaroo stood erect and stared into Dave's face at eye level. The animal's ears towered above him. *This thing is big,* Dave thought. From inside the animal came an unmistakable grrr. Dave quickly stepped back and returned to the trail.

"Smart move," said Katie.

The buck leaned forward to rest on its front feet but continued watching Dave. Behind the buck a wakened joey's head appeared from its mother's pouch. "I can see them fine from here," replied Dave. "Did you know kangaroos can growl?"

"This is United Kingdom's traditional roast dinner," Beatrice explained as she served supper. Dave and Katie saw a large piece of well-baked beef plus peeled oven-roasted potatoes and a few parsnips. "Dingo cooked it for you while I was at work." She smiled at her husband.

Dingo looked away with apparent embarrassment. "Sometimes we use mutton instead of beef, especially on a sheep station. You learn to cook or go hungry in the never-never."

Dave personally loved meat and potatoes. Katie, although less enamored with the plain food, managed to compliment, "You've made the beef tender."

"Will you have room for pudding?" Beatrice asked after the roast dinner.

To Dave and Katie's agreement, Beatrice brought out a dish she had picked up at the bakery. Katie saw a meringue dessert with a crisp crust and soft, light inside topped with fruit and whipped cream. "What's this?" she asked. "I thought we were having pudding."

"This is pudding, luv. It's a pavlova, part of Australia's national cuisine," Beatrice answered.

"At home, we would call that dessert," Katie explained.

After supper, Katie helped Beatrice with the dishes. Dave found Dingo holding a beer and watching a sporting event on TV, or as Dingo referred to it, the "telly." Tall, thin men seemed to be running around a field in a random fashion. They leaped high in the air to catch a kicked ball. "What are they playing?"

"This is Australian-rules football, mate. The Melbourne area is a hotbed for the sport. When a player catches a kicked ball without it touching the ground, he gets a free kick. The object is to get the ball close enough to kick it through those goal posts."

Just then one player kicked a goal. A dapper umpire wearing a hat signaled "good" with two arms bent at the elbow pointing away from him.

"Did you ever play this?"

"Nah. This is a sissy sport. It's the only game on the telly right now, though."

Dave watched a couple of men collide as they jumped high for the ball. *They don't look like sissies to me,* he thought. He sat down to watch with Dingo. "Which team are you rooting for?"

Dingo looked at Dave strangely. "Whattaya mean, rooting?"

"The team you want to win?"

"Ah! I'd be careful how you use that word Down Under. Root is what men and women do in private."

"Ooh, sorry!" Dave thought silently a few minutes about Aussie culture versus his native South. The regions seemed to share at least one item: a male fondness for pickup trucks. "On the street, we've being seeing the pickup trucks you call utes with pipes coming out of the engine. What are those about?" he asked.

Without taking his eyes from the TV, Dingo answered, "Those are snorkels, mate. So that they can roll up the windows and run through deep water."

"The snorkels are often higher than the cab. I thought Australia is mostly desert. Do you have floods that deep around here?"

"Nah. The floods are during the rainy season way up north toward Darwin. City blokes down south have snorkels to look rugged, like they spend a lot of time in the bush."

"Dave, I've got something you might like to see," Beatrice said, interrupting his study of the game on the TV.

Beatrice led him to a dark window where Katie already waited. The window overlooked a small deck at the rear of her home. "Now watch this." She then turned on a spotlight to reveal several raccoon-sized animals. "These are brushtail possums," she explained. "I put out bread for them. They'll get into the rubbish cans, if you don't keep the lids on tight."

Dave saw yellowish-brown animals with soft fur, bright eyes, and long furry tails. One mother carried a baby possum looking a bit like a North American flying squirrel on her back. Two of the animals became involved in a squabble over a piece of the bread. "They *are* like raccoons," he said, "except cuddlier looking."

⁂

In Trevor's bedroom, Katie's cell phone rang. "Hello."

"Katie, this is Denyse. How are you and Dave doing?"

"We're okay. Dave's face is starting to look better."

"That's good. Where are you staying?"

"We're at your parents' house. Dave is watching some sport on TV with your dad now."

"You're staying with Mum and Dad?"

"Yes, Beatrice invited us to stay here. And this is very convenient for learning about Trevor. We're staying in his room in the bunk beds."

Katie heard Denyse yell to her husband, "Your parents are staying with Mum and Dad!" Katie heard Jeremy's laughter in the background.

Denyse came back on the phone. "Well, how is the search going?"

"We're learning a lot about Trevor. Denyse, did you know that Trevor had established an address separate from your parents by using a post box?'

"How could he do that?" asked Denyse.

"He was eighteen. That's more than legal age in Australia, isn't it? He also had plenty of money."

"How much money did he have?"

"Maybe ten thousand dollars."

"Where did he get that much money?"

Katie evaded a direct answer. "He had some schemes."

"I can imagine. You don't need to tell me more."

"Trevor had also gotten a passport. The evidence shows

he had prepared to leave home for years before he actually left. This started about the time you left for university."

"How did you find out these things?"

"Dave found records and receipts in his room."

"Did my mum and dad know?"

"No, I'm sure they were clueless as to what Trevor planned."

"What's next?"

"We're going to try asking questions at Trevor's school tomorrow."

Chapter Nine

Mr. Broadmoor met Dave and Katie outside his office at picturesque Canterbury College near Melbourne. "Wow! What happened to you?" Trevor's former headmaster reacted upon seeing Dave's face.

"I made a mistake," replied Dave to the distinguished gray-haired man, who looked to be about their age.

"Oh, no! You're not that guy in the video who gets cold cocked at the wedding? When he tries to get up, a woman in white—she must have been the bride—knocks him back down. It's all over YouTube. We know someone took the video locally because we can see St. Marks in the background."

"That could be me," Dave temporized. "But we're here today to ask about Trevor Larkin. I believe he was a student of yours."

"Certainly." The headmaster led them into his office. An odor of old pipe smoke lingered there. He indicated two leather-covered chairs to sit on. He sat in a third chair behind a mahogany desk from the Victorian era. "We average around eighteen hundred students here. Most of them are forgettable. But I'll never forget Trevor. He graduated, just barely, three years ago."

"We've been retained by the Larkin family to locate Trevor. Do you have any idea where he might be?"

"I know Trevor had come from a difficult family situation, like his sister Denyse. But I don't know where he might be now."

"Did Trevor have any particular friends who might know his whereabouts?"

"I'm sorry, but I don't know that either. Trevor was somewhat of a loner. I'm certain he had acquaintances. I just don't recall any."

"Mr. Broadmoor," Katie asked, "why is Trevor so memorable to you?"

"Because of the complaint."

"The complaint?"

"Yes, some parents filed a complaint that the school had allowed Trevor to run a type of con game."

The headmaster saw that Dave and Katie appeared confused. "Let me explain."

"Please do."

"Someone, we suspect it was Trevor, introduced to our student body a game using lines of circles. Someone would draw several lines of circles on a piece of paper. Then two players would take turns marking off circles on a row until the last. Depending on prior agreement the winner could be the contestant who took the last circle or forced their opponent to take it."

"I've heard of that game," commented Dave.

"We didn't know any of this was going on until afterwards. The game had become a rage among the male students. Bets of a dollar or two made the game more exciting. Trevor won and lost like everybody. Then Trevor organized a tournament. Sixteen boys put in five dollars each. The kids drew to determine the brackets. The ultimate winner pocketed eighty dollars.

"Did Trevor win?" asked Katie.

"No, apparently Trevor didn't enter himself. But the tournaments organized by Trevor became very popular. Various boys won. Trevor did enter one tournament and won." Regret tinged the headmaster's voice as he looked at the ceiling and spoke slowly. "Next, Trevor proposed a tournament of champions. Eight boys entered the eighty dollars they had won to determine the grand champion. Trevor won that tournament and collected six hundred and forty dollars."

"Do you think Trevor somehow fixed the game?" Katie persisted.

Mr. Broadmoor sighed and looked back at Dave and Katie. "The captain of the chess team, who had been one of the favorites to win, thought so. He challenged Trevor to a head-to-head match. Trevor put up the six hundred and forty dollars and insisted the other boy front the same amount. Trevor let the other boy design the circle pattern and gave him the first move. After looking at the pattern, Trevor chose that the winner would leave the last circle.

"Trevor won the match and had apparently also won a lot of side bets on himself made through an accomplice. The chess captain's parents complained after they found out their son had lost money set aside for his university education. We investigated but couldn't prove Trevor cheated. The game is now banned on campus."

"That's an old con man's gambit," Dave told the headmaster. "Trevor could hardly lose. It involves paring up the eights, fours, twos, and ones into binary numbers. Trevor probably discovered it online."

"If we had known anything, we would have stopped the betting, or tried to. Hiding rule-breaking activity is great sport to teenage students."

"What else can you tell us about Trevor?" Katie asked.

"Well, he was undeniably bright," the principal said. "He sometimes astounded his teachers with what he knew. But he wasn't really interested in schoolwork. He barely graduated. I got the impression that even graduating wasn't important to him."

"Anything else?"

"Actually, yes. Trevor had a true gift for acting. The drama teacher cast him as Inspector Javert in the stage play of *Les Misérables.* He depicted Javert's inner agony so vividly that by the end of the play, the audience favored Javert over Jean Valjean."

Dave stood to go. "Thanks for your help, Headmaster Broadmoor. If our investigation determines that Trevor defrauded the students and that compensation is in order, how would we contact those needed?"

"I can give you the Campbells' number. Their son, Rick, was the chess captain. I don't know who else would qualify.

Most of the kids wouldn't talk about the circle tournaments."

"Would you object if we interviewed other students and teachers who might know about Trevor or his . . . activities?"

"Certainly not. I, many of us at the school, always thought Trevor had great potential. His older sister, Denyse, had been an excellent student and a delightful girl. I hope you can find Trevor and somehow get him on the right track."

As they left the headmaster's office, Katie asked Dave, "How did you know about the circle game?"

"Part of an accountant's training is to recognize Ponzi schemes, chain letter schemes, and other cons. Professor Wilson used the circle game as an example at Auburn."

"Taking advantage or deceiving people to get their money could land Trevor in a lot of trouble."

"You're right. Especially if he cheats the wrong people."

"Thank you for meeting with us, Mr. Rutherford," said Dave an hour later as they met in Canterbury College's teachers' lounge. The man appeared to be two decades younger than Mr. Broadmoor and slovenly by comparison. Dave and Katie sat with him at a conference table.

The teacher replied with an English accent, "My pleasure."

Katie started, "You know that we're investigating Trevor Larkin?"

"Of course. Headmaster Broadmoor told me. Trevor attended several of my classes."

"What can you tell us about Trevor?"

"He's a genius, if you count cunning as intelligence."

"Can you give examples?"

"I think you've already heard about the circle tournaments." Both Dave and Katie nodded. Trevor's former teacher continued, "Trevor also wrote papers for other students. He usually charged a hundred dollars. We first caught him when he sold the same paper to two different kids. The headmaster suspended him for a week. The next time we caught him was by examining writing style. After that Trevor would study his client's writing style first and then mimic it. He was simply determined to beat us. And he nearly always did. The funny thing is that the papers he wrote for others usually deserved very high marks. But Trevor's papers for his own assignments barely passed. I think the kid wanted people, especially the teachers, to think him unintelligent."

Better to disguise his trickery, thought Katie.

"Trevor also became quite adept at poker. We knew the boys played poker using five-cent coins or small candies as chips. No significant money exchanged hands. At first, we didn't mind. Poker made the boys think and assess odds. Trevor played with anyone who would participate and won a few dollars. He taunted some of those who lost consistently. He claimed that poker wasn't gambling but a test of wits. Some of the kids' older brothers or even dads became determined to teach Trevor a lesson by winning the money back. That's when Trevor won some significant money.

"Once, Trevor got arrested for shoplifting. That must have put a scare into him because afterwards Trevor shifted into daring other kids to shoplift for him. They took all the risk for a ridiculously low reward. He could also taunt kids into making bets at poor odds, usually by playing on their emotions."

"Sounds like Trevor was quite a troublemaker," said Dave.

"That's an understatement. I felt relieved when he graduated. I even suspect a couple of teachers fudged his marks to get rid of him. But Headmaster Broadmoor must have really disliked Trevor. The superintendent of schools censured him after the circle-tournament fiasco. He claimed that Broadmoor had let Trevor get out of hand."

Upon returning to the Larkin home, Dave and Katie found Beatrice and Dingo sitting together at the dining room table. Before them nearly a hundred photos covered the table.

"What's this?" Katie asked.

Beatrice looked around with a smile. "These are the wedding pictures. See what a beautiful bride Denyse made." She held up a picture for the Parkers to see. "Jeremy is rather handsome too."

Katie picked up another picture. "And look at the handsome parents of the bride." Indeed, Beatrice and Dingo looked well together.

"Oh, you Americans. Always somethin' nice to say."

Dingo concentrated on sorting a different set of photos.

"What have you got there . . . mate?" Dave inquired.

"The photographer took pictures of our fight. Look at these!" Dingo handed Dave photos showing men standing erect punching at each other.

Dave recognized himself on the ground behind them with Denyse on top of him. Two other men not recognizable wrestled nearby. *That must be Jeremy,* he thought.

Dingo passed another photo. "I like this one." The photo showed an enlargement of Dingo landing a punch to the jaw of a much taller man. "One rule I try to live by is to avoid hitting men smaller than me."

Katie reached out and picked up another photo which included the crowd of spectators in the background.

"Who is that man?" She pointed to the well-dressed Asian man who had spoken to Dave at the wedding.

Dingo looked at the photo. "Blimey if I know. Beatrice?" His wife shook her head.

"Could we make a copy of this?" Dave asked.

Beatrice had returned to admiring the photos of her daughter. "Sure. The photographer put the files into something called Dropbox. You access it through the computer. I had a photo shop make the prints. Here's the link and the password the photographer gave me."

Dave and Katie prepared for bed in Trevor's room.

"Sleeping in bunk beds reminds me of summer camp," Katie giggled.

"Is that why you took the top?"

"I just didn't want to take the chance on you falling out."

"Thanks."

The couple settled into their chosen beds. "Dave, I like this."

"What? Sleeping in bunk beds?"

"No, us working together again, as a team. When we got back to Mobile, we seemed to go our own ways. Now we're cooperating on a project like last year in Minnesota. I feel like we're doing something more than ordinary again."

"At least there's no danger this time."

"Have you forgotten what your face looks like?"

Dave chuckled in agreement. "Hey, I can laugh without pain."

"Congratulations."

"It is rather nice working together again," Dave added. "You did well picking out the man at the wedding. Photographers' pictures have a lot of resolution. I'll bet we can blow that up and crop it to make a pretty good close-up."

"Thanks. I also emailed the Fogles. I asked them to take care of Old Yeller and watch over everything for an additional two weeks."

"Good. We'll certainly be home by then."

Chapter Ten

A fluorescent light illuminated a dingy, windowless basement. Trevor heard the lock turn and the door open. He propped himself up with his elbows on a filthy cot. He saw an Asian man and two stocky islanders, the same pair that had taken him from his extended-stay motel.

"Ready to pay the $16,000 you cheated from me?" asked the Asian.

Trevor rattled the chain connecting his wrist to a cast-iron drain pipe. "Let me loose. I'll get the money for you."

"Good news for you. That's exactly what we have in mind." The Asian gestured to one of the islanders who proceeded to unlock the shackles. "But how do I know you won't disappear before your debt is paid?"

Trevor swung his feet to the floor and sat up. "I've learned my lesson."

The Asian man threw a photograph onto his captive's lap. "Then, who is this?"

Trevor saw the picture of Lena he had been carrying. When he remained silent, the islander named Fetu spoke up. "Rangi and I have tried to find that out, Mr. Wong. The maggot won't talk."

Wong stared at Trevor. He saw burn marks and bruises on his arms and face. "She's your girlfriend, isn't she? She's somewhere in central Auckland by the address we found on you. We can find her if we need to. How would you like to see her locked in this basement and taken care of by my associates?"

To this, Trevor only shook his head. "Then you'd better not take off until you've paid back every last cent with interest plus my associates' finder fee of a thousand each. And we now have more to motivate you to stay put," continued Wong. He threw some more photos onto Trevor that showed Denyse in a wedding dress. "Recognize your sister? We can get to her even in Australia. We'll make her pay your debt if you don't."

Tears formed in Trevor's eyes. "I'll pay you."

"Then we understand each other?"

Trevor nodded.

"Alright, you're good at cards. We're going to set you up in a little joint business venture. You'll do exactly as my associates tell you." Wong then instructed Fetu and Rangi, "Clean him up. He's no good to us looking and smelling like a vagrant."

After another hearty breakfast the following morning, Beatrice suggested, "You two need to take a day off. You've spent days searching Trevor's room. Then more days talking to people who knew him. Katie has learned to drive on our roads. Why don't you take my car someplace for fun, like the Healesville Sanctuary? I know you like animals."

"Is that like a zoo?" Dave asked.

"Partly. But the sanctuary only has Australian animals. And you can get up close to them."

Remembering the buck kangaroo, Dave wanted to know, "How close?"

"As close as you want to some gentle creatures like the koala and wombat. You're allowed to go into their enclosures. They're used to people being nearby. You can touch them."

Koala

True to Beatrice's promise, a couple of hours later Dave and Katie stood next to a sleeping koala that clung to a post. Katie tentatively reached out to rub it. "Its fur is rough." The koala didn't stir. Looking at a descriptive plaque, she reported, "Says here koalas aren't even related to bears and sleep twenty hours a day."

"Since eucalyptus leaves are its only food, koalas probably don't get enough nourishment for a lot of activity," suggested Dave. "Look at those claws." Long black claws seemed out of place for such a gentle animal. "A koala must need them to hold on to trees while sleeping."

Katie continued reading the plaque, "Koalas are marsupials like the kangaroo. A young koala lives about seven months in the mother's pouch and is called a 'joey' just like kangaroo babies."

Next Dave and Katie visited an animal that appeared unable to stop moving. A dark walk-through tunnel next to an aquarium revealed habitat provided for the nocturnal duckbilled platypus. Dave and Katie had expected webbed feet, a beaver-like tail, and bill-like snout. But pictures of the platypus had not revealed its river-otter-like playfulness and ceaseless energy. Reading from a plaque again, Katie reported, "The platypus is carnivorous and eats about twenty percent of its body weight a day. Mostly worms and yabbies it finds in the water. They're common in streams around the Melbourne area."

"What are yabbies?"

"That's the Australian name for crayfish. I'll bet platypuses could thrive in south Alabama."

"I don't think we want them though." Dave looked at the

descriptive plaque himself. "They have venomous spurs on their legs." His face reflected a look of amazement. "The platypus digs a burrow in a river bank then reproduces by laying eggs. After hatching, the young are nursed by the mother. Platypuses locate their prey in part by detecting minuscule electric fields generated by muscular contractions. The ability is very rare in the animal kingdom and is called eloctrolocation."

After the platypus, Dave and Katie saw many other fascinating Australian animals: the sugar glider, a tree-kangaroo, wombats, echidnas, Tasmanian devils, and a plethora of exotic birds including the bower bird and elegant black swan. In the reptile house, the couple marveled at the lizards and shuddered at deadly snakes, including the brown snake and death adder Dingo had mentioned.

As Katie drove them back to the Larkin residence, Dave summed up their sanctuary experience, "Science fiction can hardly dream up stranger creatures than those that actually live in Australia."

Katie agreed, "As a science teacher I had read about some of these. But actually seeing them makes me marvel at God's creativity."

Dave somewhat reluctantly turned their conversation back to their search. "What's our next step for finding Trevor?"

"We've learned a lot about Trevor. I feel like I know him. But we're not getting any leads on where he might be," Katie complained.

"You're right. All the people we've talked to are from his high school—I mean college—years. Maybe we need to talk to someone after he graduated and closer to the time he disappeared."

"Aren't the records you found of Trevor's victories dated?"

"Good idea! I'll check," answered Dave.

Once back at Beatrice and Dingo's home, Dave reopened the Larkin computer and found Trevor's "Enterprises" file. "Yes, here's the last entry with 'Poker,' 'Hogan,' and '$1,256' listed. The date is a month after his graduation and only a week before his disappearance."

"Who is Hogan?"

"I have no idea. Let's try asking Dingo and Beatrice."

Although Beatrice had left for the hospital, the Parkers found Dingo watching a different type of sporting event on TV. Dave couldn't help glancing at the screen. "What's this?"

"This is Rugby League, mate. It's the type of rugger I used to play. Notice that they don't waste time with rucks and scrums like Rugby Union. League is all running and rough tackling. I once scored a try from eighty-three meters out."

Dave stood transfixed by the violence and fast action on the screen. Katie nudged him without receiving a response. She finally spoke to Dingo herself, "Do you know anybody named Hogan? Apparently, Trevor had some dealing with him not long before he left home."

"Hogan?" Dingo turned to look at her.

"Yes, do you know him?" Katie jerked on Dave's arm to get this attention away from the screen.

"Yeeah. Hogan is the bloke who did the work on your husband's nose." Dingo thought a minute. "I couldn't figure out why Hogan acted so riled that day. Usually he's a straight-up bloke."

Dave forced himself to not look at the TV screen. "Where could we find Hogan?"

"Hogan runs an auto body shop over near the train station. I'd better go with ya, though."

"Thanks, but let us try first. We'll go tomorrow," Katie answered.

"Suit yourself."

Dave's eyes had returned to the screen. "Come on, Dave," Katie prompted.

"I think I'll join Dingo for a bit," Dave replied as he sat down. Katie shook her head and headed back to the bedroom.

"Get yourself a brew from the fridge, mate. You haven't missed much," said Dingo.

"This must be the place." Katie parked their rental car in front of a dilapidated dent and body shop on a back street. A sign outside promised, *Top quality repair work. Free estimates.*

Nobody attended the front desk. Following the sound of an electric motor, they found a large man in the auto bay using a sanding wheel on a fender. "Excuse me," Dave spoke over the noise.

The startled repairman looked up. His face showed uncertain recognition of Dave and Katie. "What do you want?" he demanded.

Dave noticed that the man had formed fists. Muscles stood out in his neck. "We don't want any trouble. Could you please answer some questions about Trevor Larkin?"

"Who are you?"

"My name is Dave Parker. This is my wife, Katie. We've been retained by the Larkin family to investigate legitimate claims against Trevor's . . . uh . . . activities."

"You mean hustling?"

"Maybe."

"Aren't you the man I saw at the wedding of Dingo's daughter? You look different now."

"Yes, they say you punched me."

"Oh! I sorta remember that." He took a closer look at Dave. "You came up and said something about a kangaroo. I put it on your nose. That way there wouldn't be any permanent damage like a broke tooth or somethin'."

Dave noticed that the man's own nose was bent and deformed. "Uh . . . thanks!"

"No worries, mate. You'd have done the same for me.

And a bloke can break his hand if he hits somebody in a bony spot."

"Is Hogan your first or last name?"

"Just Hogan." The man extended a grimy hand. "You're a Yank, aren't you?"

Dave, being from Alabama, thought to correct the Yank title then decided not to. "We're from the US." He shook Hogan's hand as firmly as he could grip.

"My father fought in the Vietnam War with Americans. He said that you Yanks are straight-up. You're a lot like us Aussies."

"My brother fought in Vietnam," Dave responded without elaborating.

Hogan reached for a rag to wipe his hands. "You bein' a Yank and your brother a mate with my dad and all, I'll talk to you. So what about Trevor?"

"Why were you looking for him?"

"Me and a bunch of mates have a card game every month. The kid showed up and told us Dingo sent him to learn poker. That was maybe . . . three years ago. The kid was so nervous that he dropped his wallet. All of us could see that he had a couple hundred. So we let him in . . . as a favor to Dingo."

Dave could see indignation on Katie's face at the men's willingness to take advantage of a teenager. She started, "As a favor to Dingo? You—"

"So how did Trevor do?" Dave interrupted his wife.

"Well, the kid played for 'bout three hours losing his money steadily. Mostly he folded before making a bet. All of us could see his tells when he played a hand. Nobody cared. He was adding five dollars to each pot just on the ante." Hogan smiled.

"Later in the night as everyone gets drunker, the pots tend to get bigger. Then the kid's luck changes. He starts winning pot after pot, big ones. A couple of the guys got mad and vowed to win their money back. But the harder they tried, the more money the kid raked in. All of a sudden, the kid said something about being somewhere, grabbed his pile of cash, and was out the door. Later we figured he must have cheated somehow."

Katie could remain silent no longer. "Please help me understand you, Mr. Hogan."

"Sure."

"You and your mates were content to take money from Trevor?"

Hogan only shrugged and grinned.

"And most of you got drunk during the game. Did Trevor drink?"

"Only a little beer."

"You said you all noticed his tells. Have you ever heard of planting tells?"

"Of course." But Hogan's tone made those words seem doubtful.

"Okay, then let me tell you what happened. Trevor watched all of you for three hours learning your tells and faking some of his own. Then when everybody but him was drunk, he used what he had learned and took your money. Is that possible?"

The big man hung his head without answering like one

of Katie's high school students found guilty of a school rules infraction.

"You may have been hustled. But Trevor didn't cheat you. Poker is all about trickery." Katie let that sink into Hogan. "Could I give you some poker advice?" The big man nodded.

"The real game of poker takes place watching the other players during the preliminary rounds and between hands. I'll bet Trevor talked about not having any luck, didn't he?"

"Yeeah."

"That proves you were hustled. Because real poker players know that the cards even out luck. The best players learn to play the other players more than the cards. Face-to-face poker is a contest more than gambling."

Hogan looked dumbfounded. He turned to Dave for understanding. "Who is she?" he asked, pointing at Katie.

"That's my wife and partner. And I've learned to listen to her." Dave gave Hogan a sympathetic male-to-male look. "Hogan, do you know where Trevor might have gone? Did he say anything?"

"Oi. That's been a few years now. I do remember the kid talked a lot, especially during his losing streak. He asked a lot of questions about Perth."

"Thanks, Hogan. We've got a present for you from Dingo."

Hogan's voice revealed suspicion. "What's that?"

Dave handed him a photo taken by the wedding photographer showing Hogan and Dingo exchanging blows, both men featuring grim expressions.

"Wow! This is great. Thanks, mate."

Chapter Eleven

As they drove back to the Larkin home, Dave asked his wife, "How do you know so much about poker?"

"Have you forgotten that my father was a poker enthusiast? He always knew that he didn't have the aptitude to be a consistent winner. But he loved trying to match his skills with the others. His group had a one-dollar limit on bets. Some weeks Dad won five or even ten dollars. But most weeks he lost a few dollars. He used to practice with me and told me all about poker."

"And you've never told me this during all of the times we've played?"

Katie grinned. "Beating you was more fun that way. And part of winning is to disguise yourself."

"Trevor isn't the only hustler."

Katie picked up her cell phone and dialed. Her daughter-in-law answered. "Hello."

"Denyse, this is Katie."

"Katie! How are you getting on with Mum and Dad?"

"Well, when I anticipated future in-laws, they didn't exactly come to mind," Katie admitted. "But Beatrice is a dear. Dave and Dingo are getting along rather well watching rugger and drinking beer together."

"They're not the parents I would have chosen either," Denyse came back. "But I love them."

"Here's a little more coaching for you, Denyse. Life doesn't always give you what you hoped it would. Then you have a decision to make. Are you going to fret and complain about what could have been? Or are you going to make the best of what you do have? Thankfully for me and Dave, you are the daughter-in-law we would have chosen."

Both women laughed. Then Denyse asked, "How's the search for Trevor going?"

"So far nobody knows where he is, but a lot of people would like to find him. Tomorrow Dave and I are heading to Perth. We think Trevor could have gone there."

"Perth? How would Trevor get to Perth?"

"You're still thinking of him like the fifteen-year-old he was when you left for university. Remember that he had grown into an adult and had plenty of money. Plus, he had reasons to leave."

The three-hour flight from Melbourne to Perth passed quickly compared to the fourteen-hour flight Dave and Katie had endured traveling to Sydney. Dave and Katie emerged from the airport to a balmy ocean breeze and a sense of being at the end of the world. "The only other city in the world as isolated as Perth is Honolulu," claimed Dave. "And Honolulu is in the middle of the Pacific Ocean."

Katie looked at him in amusement. "Where do you get this stuff?"

"I read it in the airline's magazine."

"Did it say anything about Trevor?"

"Afraid not."

"Too bad. The car rental pickup is this way."

Once in the rental car, the couple drove around sightseeing. But unlike the rocky coastline south and west of Melbourne, miles and miles of broad sandy beaches, mostly deserted, extended both north and south of the city. They found Perth itself to be a thoroughly modern, well-managed city. High-rise buildings on the Swan River dominated the skyline. "Perth is bigger than I expected," commented Katie.

"Nearly two million people live in the area, about the same size as Nashville," reported Dave.

"The airline magazine again?" asked Katie. After Dave merely grinned, she added, "You like this, don't you?"

"Like what?"

"Me chauffeuring you around."

"You're the one who knows how to drive on the left."

"I'll teach you."

"That's okay. You're doing fine."

Katie pulled over on a more remote stretch of road. "Time for a driving lesson for you."

"Aaah!"

The anguished scream wakened Katie in the night. She shook her husband hard. "Wake up. Wake up. It's just a bad dream."

Dave sat up, shook himself, and then lay down, still breathing hard. He could feel his heart pounding. "Thanks."

Katie snuggled up to him. She knew her presence would help to relax him. "Was it another dream about the shooting in Minnesota?"

Dave didn't answer for a minute. He sighed and hugged his wife close. "Not specifically. I dreamed someone or something was looking for us. We hid in the woods in the dark. I could see dark shapes like shadows moving among the trees. Suddenly, one was right in front of us."

"That doesn't sound like our experience."

"No, it was just an anxiety dream. No worse than normal."

"Need a sleeping pill?"

Dave declined the sleeping aid. But Katie could tell by his breathing that he took a full hour to fall back asleep. Then she too slept.

"Where should we begin?" Katie asked over breakfast at their hotel the next morning.

"Let's try the police," Dave suggested. "After all, Trevor is a missing person."

Two hours later the couple inquired at Perth's central police station. The police officer looked suspicious as Dave began, "We're looking for a young man, Trevor Larkin, who disappeared from Melbourne." Dave offered Trevor's photo plus driver's license and passport numbers.

"And who are you?" asked the officer. He then looked at the American passports Dave handed him. "Why are two Americans looking for an Australian citizen?"

"Our son married Trevor's sister," Katie explained. "She asked us to find him."

"Then you're some sort of investigators?"

Katie and Dave both nodded affirmation.

"Can you confirm this?" the officer asked.

"You could phone our daughter-in-law." The policeman dialed Denyse's number that Katie provided. No answer. "Denyse is probably teaching school at this hour," she said. "Could you try Trevor's mother, Beatrice, instead?"

Someone answered the call. The policeman lapsed into an Outback Australian dialect. Dave picked up the words "Yanks," "Larkin," "YouTube," and "bloody hell," but not much else. The man looked up at Dave's healing face and smiled, then laughed. He ended with, "Thanks, mate," and hung up.

"You're the one I saw on that video of the wedding party fracas. The one rescued by the bride."

Dave hid his irritation. "Yes, that's me. Did you talk to Beatrice?"

"No, that was the boy's father, Dingo. He doesn't take much stock in your finding his son. But he says you're straight-up and having a go at it." The policeman looked at Dave's face again and shook his head. "I'll be back in a few minutes."

Twenty minutes later the policeman returned with a grim look. Katie could not help blurting out, "Did you find anything?"

"Yes, but you're not going to like it. Your lad is mentioned in our computer on a hospital report." The date the policeman provided was about six months after Trevor had left Melbourne.

"Does the report say why he was at the hospital?" Dave asked.

"Apparently someone found him punch drunk near the casino and called an ambulance. Your Trevor gave his address at the hospital as an extended-stay hotel nearby. Here's that address." The policeman held his hands palm up. "I'm afraid that's all we have. He hasn't been arrested in the Perth area."

After thanking the policeman, Dave and Katie walked toward their rental car. Katie could not conceal her excitement. "This is a solid lead. He might still be at that hotel."

Dave tried to tone down her expectations. "Or maybe not. This lead is still more than two years old."

Katie controlled her irritation by walking ahead of Dave to the car. When he arrived, she had firmly ensconced herself in the passenger seat. "Your turn to drive."

They didn't find Trevor staying at the hotel. None of the staff could remember him either. "We get a lot of turnover here, both residents and staff," the manager explained. But the hotel records proved that a Trevor Larkin had stayed at the hotel for several months prior to the date of the hospital report. "The statements show that he always paid in cash," the manager added.

Back inside the car, Dave sat listlessly. "Dead ended."

Katie also felt despondent but refused to give up. "We

know Trevor stayed here. Where would he have gone? What might he have done from here?"

"I have no idea."

Katie continued thinking out loud. "Pizza."

"You want lunch?"

"No, Trevor loved pizza. If he lived here, I'll bet he frequented pizza places in the area."

The fifth pizza place they tried showing Trevor's photo paid off. The middle eastern owner of a pizzeria responded, "I remember him. A good customer. Almost every day he came in by himself. He always ordered extra cheese and sausage. He seemed lonely. Asked about my home and family."

"Where are you from?" Katie asked.

"We immigrated here from Iraq. You know, during the wars." The owner paused a few seconds before continuing. "The last time this man came in he looked like somebody had beat him up. Left me a fifty-dollar tip and asked me to do something special for my family. We all went to an American movie and ate popcorn."

"Do you have any idea where Trevor might have gone?" Dave asked.

"No. And I never even knew his name." Dave and Katie felt the downside of the roller coaster ride of expectations. "Why don't you try the place he worked?" the pizzeria owner asked.

Up again! "Where did he work?"

"I saw him sometimes at a used car lot two or three kilometers from here. He must have worked there."

"Sure, he worked for me. He was just a kid. And he didn't know a bloody thing about cars," the car lot owner explained. "But nearly everyone who came onto the lot left with a car. The kid knew how to make them love the car he showed. Sometimes they brought the car back after a few days. I always bought the car back minus five hundred for expenses and depreciation. Trevor sold one piece of junk four times. We had a money machine going. I paid him two hundred dollars in cash for each car he sold. I could see a bright future for us; me buying, him selling. I don't know where he is now."

Katie felt the downside of roller-coaster emotions again. "What happened?"

"He came in one day and settled up. Said he needed to leave town. I think he did need to." The dealer gestured toward Dave. "His face looked like—well, like yours, only worse."

"Do you have any idea where he went?" asked Dave.

The car dealer sat quietly for a full minute. "No, but maybe I could find out. What's it worth to you?"

Katie saw Dave's jaw muscles tighten. She heard him say, "A hundred dollars."

"I'll have to split with my source. Fifty dollars isn't worth my time and trouble. I think a thousand dollars would be fairer."

"Forget it," Dave reacted.

Katie put her hand on his arm to calm him. "Could we have a few minutes, please?" she said to the car dealer. Once they had stepped outside, she implored Dave, "We can afford a thousand dollars to find Trevor. Remember how much money we gave Denyse and Jeremy."

"That was your idea," Dave reminded her. "And I can't stand being extorted."

"True to both. But think about how actually finding Trevor would be a gift to all the Larkins. I feel for Beatrice who has lost her son," she persisted.

Dave grimaced. "Would I get to go home to Mobile as soon as we locate Trevor?"

"Absolutely!" she promised.

Dave turned and stalked back into the car dealer's office. There he said, "Six hundred, if you can tell us where he is."

The car dealer gestured a lack of enthusiasm with a shrug. He paused as if thinking before proposing, "I'll go halfway. Eight hundred sends you to the kid."

"Alright," Dave managed to force out.

"You bring the money here day after tomorrow in cash. By then, I'll see what I can dig up for you."

"Dave, I know you didn't like doing that," Katie sympathized in their rental car. "You did what you had to do to make the best of a difficult situation."

"That guy is a crook. Trevor and he deserve each other." Dave sighed and shook his head. "As long as we're making the best, we have some idle time. We aren't likely to be in Perth again. What should we do?"

"I read about Fremantle, only twelve miles away at the mouth of the Swan River. They have a fishing boat harbor. Let's go there," Katie proposed.

"I know about Fremantle. It's on the Indian Ocean. The US submarine fleet was based there during World War II."

Fishing boats and history. What could be better for Dave? thought Katie.

Chapter Twelve

Two unshaven men of European descent approached the slight girl sitting on a park bench cradling a baby. A cup holding several coins sat on the ground before her.

"Where's your boyfriend?" one of the men sneered.

Lena remained silent and covered the baby's face as if to protect him.

"He's run off and left you, hasn't he?" the man continued. He waited for a response, but received none. "Well, no matter. You owe us another four thousand dollars."

"We paid you already," the girl spoke slowly with an accent. She didn't raise her head.

"We forgot to charge interest," the other man claimed. "And now the interest is drawing interest. You'll owe us five thousand dollars next week."

"I don't have any money," the girl insisted.

"That we know," said the first man looking down at the cup. "But if you'll come work for us, you'll have money. You'll be able to keep a roof over your head and take care of your kid. A pretty white girl with blond hair and blue eyes like yours can make plenty of money."

"No!"

Both men laughed. "Then what are you going to do?" the second asked. "Will you be able to rent a room with this change?" he pointed to the cup. "Can you buy food for yourself so that you can feed this brat?" To the girl's silence, he added, "And it's not like you're a virgin." He pointed down at the baby.

The girl remained silent. The first man reached down to lift her chin, but she turned her face away. "The weather is getting colder and rain will fall every day. You'll soon come crawling to us. If not, we'll report you. The government will put you in jail for being here illegally and give your baby to someone else."

The second man looked around to see that nobody was watching, then picked up her cup and emptied the meager collection of coins into his pocket. "We'll just apply this to your interest."

"That's the biggest rat I've ever seen," Dave marveled out loud while looking at a rabbit-sized animal begging for food on its hind legs. Katie looked at the informational brochure provided by Australia's Rottnest Island Nature Reserve a few miles' boat ride from Fremantle. "That's not a rat," she said of the chocolate-brown creature with little rounded ears. "It's a quokka. Another marsupial like a tiny kangaroo. But others have made the same mistake. The island's original name was Rat's Nest."

Dave stood looking out at the tranquil Indian ocean under a clear blue sky. "Well, the quokkas sure have a nice place to live. Have you ever seen such beautiful waters?"

Katie admired the view with him. "You enjoyed the boat ride over, didn't you?" Katie took her husband's hand. "Take it in while you can. Tomorrow we'll need to deal with that shyster car dealer again."

"Don't remind me. I woke up last night after dreaming someone had cheated us out of our retirement fund and savings."

Katie put her arm around Dave and spoke playfully, "Then we turned out even. Because I dreamed that I won the lottery."

Dave hugged his wife back. "Too bad you didn't dream we found Trevor."

⁂

"Let's see the money," demanded the car dealer. Dave laid eight one-hundred-dollar bills on the desk. The dealer picked up the bills with one hand and passed a sheet of paper with the other.

Dave and Katie saw the printout of an airline ticket purchase. The ticket for Trevor Larkin showed an itinerary from Perth to Wellington, New Zealand.

"Where in Wellington?"

The car dealer shrugged. "I said that I'd send you to him. He's in New Zealand."

Dave and Katie turned to go without speaking. "By the way," the car dealer added, "my source at the airport says that someone else has been asking about Trevor and his family."

Dave turned back. "Who?"

"My source didn't know the man. Only said he was Asian, maybe from Singapore."

"Thanks for that."

"Just thought you should know."

⁂

"Guess where your mum and dad are going now," Denyse challenged her husband.

Jeremy looked up from washing the dishes. "I don't know. Darwin?"

"Farther than that. They've traced Trevor to New Zealand. Apparently, they discovered he ran into some trouble in Perth and escaped to Wellington."

"How did they figure that out?" He tossed his wife a towel to dry the dishes.

Denyse caught the towel and picked up a damp plate. "Your mother didn't explain. But she did say something rather odd."

"Odd?"

Denyse elaborated, "Katie told me that Dave felt better after taking a boat ride out of Fremantle."

"Oh, Mom and Dad got on a boat. Where did they go?"

Denyse gave Jeremy an *are-you-listening* look. "Who cares where they took the boat? Why did your father need to feel better?"

Jeremy didn't answer while he put away the dishes. "Jeremy, you're not supposed to keep secrets from me, remember?" Denyse insisted.

"Dad has had periodic nightmares and sleeplessness since he was a pre-teen. They mostly went away after I was born. Since the problems they had in Minnesota, his anxiety has returned. Mom carries sleeping pills for when he needs them."

"You still haven't told me much about what happened there." Denyse followed Jeremy to where he sat down on their couch. "About all I know is that he shot a man to save someone's life. That's terrible. But didn't he do the right thing?"

Jeremy looked at her. "Even Dad would admit that he did the right thing. Maybe it would have been better if the man had died. But the shotgun blast really crippled him. He's close to an invalid now and in constant pain without drugs. Intruders broke into the mansion where Mom and

Dad housesat. The criminals started to kill a policeman who came to rescue them. Mom told me that Dad came out of hiding to save the policeman and went berserk. He would have shot a second man if his shotgun had still been loaded. Dad didn't want to believe that side of him existed."

Denyse sat down beside Jeremy and faced him. "What side?"

Jeremy sighed. "Dad had a much older brother named Chuck. Our family has always been pretty patriotic. Chuck took ROTC and volunteered for the Vietnam War. As a green lieutenant, Chuck led his platoon on patrol into an ambush. The Viet Cong killed six of his men and severely injured some others. Chuck blamed himself. My grandmother told Mom about this a year or so after she and Dad had been married."

"Why would that give your father nightmares?"

"You haven't heard the worst. In the months after the ambush, Chuck went kind of crazy trying to get back at the Viet Cong. He killed a lot of Vietnamese who may or may not have been combatants. The army hushed it up and gave Chuck a medical discharge.

"Uncle Chuck came home to Mobile haunted by his experiences. Sentiment in the US had turned against the war in 1969. People were much more likely to ostracize Vietnam veterans than listen to them. Chuck needed somebody to listen to him as he struggled with his experiences. Unfortunately, my grandparents thought that talking would only make Chuck worse. Granddad had never talked about World War II. But Dad loved and admired his older brother.

Without anybody else to talk to, Chuck told Dad all about the war. He warned Dad that we Parkers have a demon lurking inside. Later Chuck couldn't live with himself and committed suicide. Dad found his body."

Denyse shook her head. "That's horrible!"

"Mom noticed how Dad could become completely fixated on details other people would consider tediously dull: accounting, history, animals, fishing. She thought that occupying his mind with details kept Dad from thinking about the things Chuck had told him. After he shot the man in Minnesota, Dad's nightmares returned."

Denyse sat transfixed. "Is that the reason your dad is reluctant to talk about what happened? He's afraid his trauma might affect others like Chuck's affected him?"

"Maybe. Dad may also be concerned that Chuck was right. He's afraid he does have a demon inside himself just like his brother."

Denyse took Jeremy's hand. "You're a Parker, too. Are you afraid you have a demon?"

Jeremy laughed. "No, I'm more like my mother." Then he grew more serious. "I think desperate circumstances can bring terrible violence out of nearly anyone. Sometimes the violence is necessary. Even then, the circumstances can change people, like they did Uncle Chuck."

Wellington's high-rise buildings funneled wind from the South Pole into a gale-like blow mixed with cold rain. "Where should we begin?" Katie asked as she and Dave walked down Victoria Street after leaving the airport.

Dave pulled his jacket hood over his head. "I'm glad we bought these coats in Melbourne. Let's try the police like we did in Perth. Then let's look for some stocking hats and gloves."

Katie could not restrain a snicker. "I'll feel funny buying winter wear in late June."

"Maybe we should just go home to get warm instead," her husband returned.

"Great idea. We could come back in their summer to look for Trevor."

"Don't tempt me."

"Sorry, mate. We don't have anything on a Trevor Larkin in our files," the New Zealand police officer reported.

After that, Dave and Katie spent three days approaching owners of pizza restaurants. No luck. The couple tried used car lots. No luck again.

"This is like finding a needle in a haystack," Katie complained. "We're out of ideas."

"Remember where they found Trevor punch drunk in Perth? Near a casino. I'll bet he hung around gambling places, looking for marks."

But Wellington had no casino. As much as Katie didn't want to admit that this was the end, she felt defeated. She imagined calling Denyse and admitting that the search was over. She hung her head and shivered. "I guess this is the end," she said sadly. "We failed. There's nothing left to do but go back to Mobile. At least we'll be warm there."

Dave didn't appear to have heard. "Didn't you say that

Trevor wasn't really a gambler? Hustling was more a battle of wits for him?" Dave thought out loud, "Trevor's teacher told us he would take advantage of kids by getting them to bet on emotions rather than sense."

Katie wrapped her arms around herself, trying to stay warm. "So?"

"What do men bet on with strong emotions? Let's try some sports bars."

"Sure, I remember the arsehole," a man sitting at the bar told Dave over a beer. "Our All Blacks were playing the Wallabies in the annual Rugby Championship between New Zealand, Australia, Argentina, and South Africa. The Wallabies are the Australians. The test was here in Wellington."

Dave's bar buddy pointed to the picture of Trevor Katie held. "This guy shows up wearing Australia's gold and green colors in a section of All Blacks supporters. He talked big with an Aussie accent and made all kinds of predictions. Everybody around wanted to deck him. But the jerk was so drunk, it wouldn't be fair."

Or he acted so drunk, thought Katie.

The man took a swig of beer before continuing, "Do you know what we Kiwis call an uncouth idiot?"

Dave shook his head.

"An Australian." The man laughed at his own joke. Dave and Katie forced themselves to laugh with him. "Anyway, I wanted to hurt the guy in a way that he'd remember when he got sober. I bet him a hundred dollars that the All Blacks would score a try the next time they got the ball. And they didn't. Other Kiwis bet him too, especially since the game was close. Maybe we weren't too careful about the chances. The bloody Aussie won nearly all the bets.

"When the All Blacks eventually won, I thought we'd had the last laugh. Then I saw him at a Wellington Lions game wearing Auckland Blues colors. He was drunk again and talking down the Lions. That's when I knew he was a hustler. Our Kiwi blokes couldn't stop betting for our team. Even knowing he was a hustler, I lost another fifty dollars to the jerk."

"Is he still around?" Dave asked.

"No, I haven't seen him in more than a year. Some of my mates had started talking about teaching him a more personal lesson, when he disappeared. I hoped that a lorry had run him over. But one bloke told me that he saw the same guy playing poker down in Queenstown."

Chapter Thirteen

Once warmed up in their hotel room, Katie looked at a New Zealand map over her husband's shoulder. "Where is Queenstown?"

"On the South Island. That's where they filmed most of the panoramic scenes for the *Lord of the Rings* movies. We'll need to catch a ferry across the Cook Strait. Then we can take Highway 1 south from Picton."

Katie wrapped her arms around Dave's neck and hugged him. "I never thought I'd be traveling around New Zealand looking for an Australian scoundrel."

Dave leaned over to give his wife a kiss. "I never imagined that I'd be related by marriage to an Australian scoundrel. Have you given any thought as to what we'll do if we *can* find Trevor?"

Katie shook her head. "Let's just find him first."

Driving onto the ferry was a new experience for the Parkers. After following a line of cars onto the ship, they left the rental car on the lowest level. Upstairs they found the decks of the boat to be warm and comfortable with huge windows for passengers to enjoy the scenery. Wind and waves from the Tasman Sea rocked the ferry while crossing over to the South Island. Sleet pinged against windows. Dave and Katie each purchased tea and a bakery treat from the cafeteria-like concession and settled in to enjoy the storm.

The inclement weather lessened once the ferry passed behind Arapaoa Island and entered Queen Charlotte Sound of the South Island. There brushy hills towered above the boat in the narrow fjord-like passage. Waves broke over the narrow edge between water and steep hillsides. Occasional houses provided their occupants with nearly inaccessible solitude. Floats attached to nets indicated the location of a commercial salmon farm.

In Picton, Dave and Katie found a cluster of small shops. A café featured pumpkin soup made from winter squash along with various sandwiches and meat pies. "Picton isn't much of a town, is it?" whispered Katie over the soup and a ham sandwich.

"No, but it has a certain charm. With only just over a million people on the entire South Island, I think New Zealand has a lot of little country towns. I'm going to enjoy being out of the city."

A middle-aged woman wearing a turban over a bald head passed the Parkers as they strolled idly, looking into shop windows. Dave noticed his wife looking at the woman. He knew Katie was thinking about the cancer she had endured. A few steps later a young woman pushing a baby stroller passed, going the other way. Dave saw Katie turn to watch the mother with her baby. "You were a wonderful mother, sweetheart," he volunteered.

Katie turned back to resume walking with him. "Do you ever wish we could do it all again?"

"You mean have a baby? If so, there are parts I wouldn't want to repeat."

"No, I meant life in general, including a baby."

"Sure. I can think of things I'd do differently, though."

Katie looked up at Dave. "What?"

"I'd marry you earlier."

"We weren't mature enough when we did get married."

"We had a lot of fun together, though." Dave took Katie's hand. "Anything you would change?"

"I just think about all of the time we wasted on things that didn't really matter. And now there's not much time left."

"We've got plenty of time."

"What if my cancer comes back? Maybe I won't see Jeremy and Denyse's baby, our grandchild, grow up. I've been thinking about that a lot lately."

"Could I say something, sweetheart?" asked Dave.

"You will regardless of what I say. So go ahead," she quipped.

Dave smiled. "Your concern reminds us to make each day count. Remember you created our motto, 'Every day is our last best day.' " Dave put his arms around Katie. "I've got an idea. Let's you and I take a few days of pure vacation."

His proposal surprised Katie. "You mean now?"

"When would be a better time? And our Fourth of July is tomorrow. Our search for Trevor can wait for a few days."

"One thing I wouldn't change in my life is marrying you, dinosaur."

Kaikoura Range

The road south of Picton turned into farm country with many fruit crops. A roadside produce stand encouraged the couple to pull over. Gala apples from the fall crop filled baskets. A quarter bushel could be purchased for three dollars. Paper bags of fuzzy brown kiwi fruits could be had for a dollar.

"Why are these called 'kiwi fruits'?" Dave asked the proprietor.

"Just because we raise so many here," she answered. "They originally came from China. We grow them like grapes on trellises." The woman pointed toward an orchard. There the Parkers saw kiwi fruit hung from vines on arbors, though not in clusters like grapes.

"What is a kiwi?" Katie wanted to know.

"The kiwi is a brown flightless bird indigenous to New Zealand. I've never seen one in the bush. But someone started calling New Zealanders 'Kiwis' after the war. The name stuck to us and transferred to the fruit."

Southwards the road hugged the east coast of New Zealand. Turbulent cold water from the lower Pacific Ocean crashed against rocky beaches. Another roadside stand advertised "Cooked Crayfish."

Dave and Katie looked at each other. Their eyes asked, *Crayfish?*

Katie pulled the car over. Inside, they found New Zealand "crayfish" to be South Pacific lobsters twelve to eighteen inches long, albeit without the massive claws of Maine lobsters. Despite recently having had lunch, Dave and Katie each enjoyed a Kiwi crayfish at a picnic table nearby. Seagulls hovered, prepared to swallow anything left unattended.

Inland from the coast, snow-covered mountains of the Kaikoura Ranges roughly paralleled the turbulent ocean. Under the mountains, a seaside town—also named Kaikoura—welcomed the Alabamians. Dave pointed out a holiday park on the ocean. There they rented a cabin with a sitting area/kitchen combo, a single bedroom, and a bathroom. Although the evening had turned chilly, they walked a hundred yards to see pounding waves, then turned around to watch the sun set over the snowy peaks. Back in the cabin, they fell asleep snuggled together and listening to the heavy surf.

Dave stumbled toward the shower stall early the next morning. Waking up always challenged him. He stood enjoying the hot water with his forehead pressed against the shower's side. To his surprise, the shower door opened. "Want to save some water, lover?" said Katie and slipped in beside him.

Later the couple visited a market and returned to the cabin with eggs, sausage, and potatoes. Together they created a breakfast that could discourage hunger all day. By noon they headed farther south through orchard country toward Christchurch.

A rare sunny day warmed them walking along the Avon River, which meandered through the center of the city. They admired Tudor-style buildings. The first daffodils bloomed in green lawns. "I never thought I'd see a place that appears more English than England," Katie remarked.

"Does this mean that I don't need to take you to London?" Dave returned.

"Were you planning a trip there for us?"

"No. But going *any* place would be fun with you."

"Are those Christmas decorations in July I see in the shop windows?" wondered Katie.

A storekeeper explained after being asked, "The decorations are for a mid-winter Christmas. December will be summertime here. Most people go to the beach then. The southern hemisphere celebrates a July yule season during the cold, dark months, just like most of our ancestors knew in Europe."

After spending the night at a mom-and-pop hotel in Christchurch, Dave and Katie drove south through the sparsely populated region called Canterbury. Unlike England, the rugged and snow-covered Southern Alps loomed to their west. Numerous snow-melt rivers rushing to the South Atlantic crossed the highway.

Near Timaru, they found a charming restaurant with a deck on a bluff overlooking the ocean. Seated on the deck in the sun, the Parkers ordered a seafood platter with shrimp, scallops, and various fishes. Once again, seagulls hovered overhead. Nearby, a family of tourists speaking French stepped away from their table to pose in front of the ocean for a photo. Instantly, dozens of seagulls swarmed down on the unattended table. Dave could see nothing but squabbling birds where the tourists' food had momentarily been neglected. The family turned to see him shooing the birds away from what little remained of their lunch. Dave shrugged in sympathy as he sat down again with Katie.

"Let's wait until after finishing lunch to use the toilet," she suggested. Dave nodded and continued watching the hovering birds.

After lunch, the couple followed a two-lane road westward toward the mountains. The road climbed and wound to the skiing and outdoor sports center of Queenstown. The town rested on Lake Wakatipu surrounded by mountains covered by snow. Nearby bungee jumpers leapt 141 feet off the Kawarau Bridge. The cord length had been adjusted by body weight to dip their heads in the river before rebounding.

"Would you take a leap like that?" Dave asked his wife.

"I married you, didn't I?"

He chuckled in response. "So, do you want to try this?"

"No. Life with you has been thrill enough."

Dave sighed in resignation. "Nice little vacation we've had. I guess since we're in Queenstown we'll need to start looking for Trevor again."

Dave and Katie first tried the police headquarters. That turned out to be fruitless like in Wellington.

"We know he liked beating men at poker," Dave reasoned. "Where would he find poker players? The casino?"

That made sense to Katie. "Although they play on machines or 'pokie poker' in the casino, that could be a place to recruit rubes for a face-to-face game. Machine players would be easy marks for Trevor. They think they know poker but don't understand the nuances of reading opponents."

"The casinos watch their floors pretty carefully, though. They aren't going to allow us to simply walk around showing Trevor's photo. Katie, are you up for a little gambling? You'll need to play a pokie machine. And strike up conversations with fellow players."

"Why don't you play yourself?"

"I'm not prepared to lose that much money."

Katie had to privately acknowledge that she looked right at place among the late-middle-aged to older women patronizing the casino. Mostly they sat in grim solitude at slot machines. The large hall containing hundreds of gambling machines smelled of alcohol and stale tobacco. Colorful lights from the machines made the interior lighting seem drab.

Playing poker against a machine felt odd to her. For players able to assess odds, machine poker simply depended on luck. The house had a built-in advantage on luck. The casino management set the machines so that virtually all players would lose gradually and thereby not quit in discouragement. Those not able to figure odds, otherwise called "heavy losers," became discouraged more quickly.

Striking up conversations with fellow patrons wasn't difficult, though. Most of the Kiwis there seemed friendly. And Katie, despite being in her early sixties, still drew men's attention. But nobody had seen Trevor.

While Katie played pokie poker, Dave pursued pizza places, used car lots, and sports bars all over Queenstown. Nobody remembered Trevor.

On the fourth day and over two hundred dollars down, Katie finally got a little real luck. She had noticed an older man playing nearby and glancing her way. He looked like a regular patron. She acted frustrated and somewhat loudly complained about her luck.

"Some days are just like that," the man commented.

After playing a few more hands, Katie asked, "Do you come here often?"

"My wife thinks too often," he returned.

"So does my husband."

"Are you an American?"

"Yes, my husband went fishing or something. He left me here." Katie gave the man a disarming smile. "Say, I've been looking for my nephew Trevor. He's supposed to live somewhere around here. I don't suppose you've ever seen him?"

The man took the photo of Trevor that Katie held out to him. His head tilted back in recognition. "I remember him. He played at a nearby machine. I heard him say that playing poker against a machine was like playing tennis against a wall. Then he asked if I would be interested in a real game. He said all of the players would have a better chance because the house can't build in an edge for themselves.

"So, I played in a live game with him. We met with three other guys in a casino hotel room for an unsanctioned game. I felt like a criminal hiding like that. It was fun. Somebody had brought some bottles of booze. And at first, I won more than I lost. Then about two hours in, my luck went bad at the same time your nephew's luck went through the roof. In an hour, I lost more than six hundred dollars. I could have played machine poker for a week without losing that much. The other three guys all lost money too. We dropped out of the game one by one. For weeks afterwards, I saw him here recruiting players for more private games. Although he invited me, I never tried that again."

Katie thought, *Bad luck didn't have anything to do with your losing.* But she only asked, "Do you know where Trevor might be?"

"I heard that some patrons complained to the hotel. They banned him from the premises. I don't know where your nephew is now. Hey, how about you and I get a drink?"

Katie picked up her purse to leave. "Maybe another time. I'm late to dinner with some friends."

"How about tomorrow?"

"Look for me here tomorrow."

Chapter Fourteen

"Trevor isn't here. He's banned from the hotel and casino." Katie told Dave about her encounter.

"And your contact didn't have any idea where he went?"

"No, he didn't."

Dave pondered that and sighed. "We must be at the real dead end, then."

"Trevor did have a hotel room, though. And the front desk would have checked his passport," Katie suggested. "So the room would have been in his own name."

"How would they know where he went?"

"Asking them won't cost anything."

"Maybe it will." Dave led Katie to the reception desk. There a bored-looking clerk stood with nothing to do. "Did a Trevor Larkin stay here, maybe even a year or more ago?"

The clerk, glad for any diversion, punched the name into the computer records. "Yes, Mr. Larkin stayed with us for several weeks last year. Uh-oh. The records show that Mr.

Larkin is forbidden any services at this facility. That's all I can tell you."

Dave felt like a character in a cheap detective novel. He laid a hundred-dollar bill on the front desk. "Isn't there something else you could tell us?"

The clerk rolled his eyes and looked down at the bill. "We don't sell chips at the front desk, sir. You'll need to get them in the casino."

Dave pulled the bill back in humiliation. Katie broke in, "Is there anything at all you could tell us, please? We're really trying to find my nephew."

With a dismissive look at Dave, the clerk returned, "Funny that he would be an Australian while the two of you appear to be Americans."

Katie then started on the long story about Denyse and Jeremy, Trevor and Dingo, the wedding fight, Melbourne, Perth, Wellington . . .

"Never mind," the clerk interrupted. "The only thing I have here is that Mr. Larkin requested an airport shuttle the morning of his final departure. Honestly, that's all I have."

After thanking him, Dave and Katie conferred in the hotel lobby. "The airport means he was flying somewhere," Katie started. "He was doing well in New Zealand. I'll bet he tried another city here. Any ideas?"

"Auckland has the most people and several casinos. Let's at least try there."

"I'd better email the Fogles about Old Yeller again."

The South Island of New Zealand had been so wild

and beautiful that Dave and Katie regretted the necessity to drive north. To add some variety to the long drive, they crossed over the Southern Alps and followed the highway up the remote western side of the island. Small towns looking dreary in the frequent rain hugged the fog-enshrouded coast.

A highway sign advertised a "Tea Room" near one such town. Katie, fancying little old ladies, ruffled doilies, lots of fine china, and cucumber sandwiches, instructed Dave, "Turn in here." Inside she found sausage rolls, quiche of different types, packaged sandwiches, pumpkin soup, baked potatoes, meat pies, and an eating area with simple wooden tables. "This tea room isn't what I had imagined," she said.

"Give it a chance. Look, they offer hamburgers and fries," said Dave. He approached the counter to order.

In the glass display case, Katie spotted something that reminded her of the dessert bars she had bought from Hansen's bakery in Minnesota. "I'll try that bar and tea, please," she told the girl behind the counter and pointed.

"We call that a lemon slice," the girl answered as she collected the one Katie had indicated. She placed it on a tray along with a teapot, teacup, and silverware.

A taste revealed the slice to be tart without being overly sweet—the perfect companion to tea in the chilly, wet weather. Katie noticed Dave looking inside his burger. "What's wrong?"

"Nothing really. It's just not what I expected." He showed Katie a thick, round slice of dark-red pickled beet instead of a tomato.

Katie smiled. "Well, that's consistent. Nothing on this trip is what we expected. But this slice is wonderful. I think

I'll order a few to take with us. And their carrot cake looks good too."

From Picton they took the ferry back to Wellington and without delay started toward Auckland. Several hours north, an arid landscape surprised the couple after all the rains. As Dave drove, Katie examined the guide book. "Kiwis call this the 'Desert Road.' Apparently, mountains to the west collect most of the moisture."

"Those mountains can't be *too* damp. There's a forest fire near the top of one," Dave observed through his side window.

Katie leaned over to look past him and then back at the guide book. "Uh, that's Mt. Ruapehu, an active volcano." She continued to read for a minute. "Near here a volcanic mudflow of melted snow mixed with ash overtook a passenger train on Christmas Eve in 1953. A hundred and fifty-one people died."

Mt. Ruapehu

Dave shook his head in horror before he commented, "New Zealand has amazingly varied geological features for such a small space."

An hour farther north, the countryside turned greener with gently rolling grass-covered hills. "Have you ever seen so many sheep?" Dave rhetorically asked. "Look at all the little newborn lambs. They seem whiter than their mothers."

"That's because the lambs haven't gotten dirty yet. They sure are adorable, though."

Katie then pointed to a sign for a country B&B. "I'm tired of the car. Let's see if we can stay there."

Up a long driveway bordered on both sides by cherry trees flowering in the North Island's early spring, they found a sprawling farm house. No sign indicated a B&B office. Dave led the way to the front door. Before they could knock, the door opened. "I thought I heard someone come up the drive," a late-middle-aged woman greeted them. She looked strong and practical. Dave could imagine her on a farm in Oklahoma.

"We saw your sign for a Bed and Breakfast—" Katie started.

"Come on in," the woman interrupted. Her voice sounded like rural Ireland. "My name is Nikki Ferguson. We don't get many guests this time of year." She led the way through a dimly-lit foyer and living area and down a composite sheet-paneled hallway to a door. She opened the door to reveal a high-ceilinged bedroom with plain, old-fashioned wooden furniture, including two twin beds. "This was our sons' room before they left home. One of them is in the army; the other is studying to be a vet at uni. Are you Canadians?"

"We're Americans," returned Katie as she looked at various athletic and fishing items in the room.

"Wonderful. We don't get many Yanks here. Most of them stay in tour groups. Are you hungry? I've got plenty of soup ready."

"Let me guess," ventured Katie. "Pumpkin?"

"How did you know?" Without waiting for an answer, Nikki directed them back down the hall to a farm kitchen with a metal-legged Formica-topped table. The smell of cooked squash and yeast bread filled the room. "Have a seat."

"Thanks. Uh, could I ask your room charge?" Dave asked.

"Oh, I don't know. This is off season. I'm just glad for some company. What would you like to pay?"

"A hundred dollars?"

"Alright." Nikki placed a basket of freshly baked bread on the table and ladled out two large bowls of soup. "My husband is docking lambs today. Eat up."

"Docking lambs?"

"They cut their tails off for hygiene. Otherwise the sheep soil themselves."

"Oh."

The front door opening drew their attention. "I'm home, Mum. Whose car is that?" A cute girl of about fifteen wearing a school uniform with neck tie and short plaid skirt came in and saw Dave and Katie.

"This is . . . I forgot to ask your names."

"We're Dave and Katie Parker," Katie told the girl.

"They're Americans staying with us tonight. This is Holly," Nikki introduced her daughter as she placed a fresh kettle of tea on the table. "Would you like some soup, dear?"

"No, but I'll have tea." The girl dropped her book satchel on a chair and sat down at the table. "I'm hoping to do my OE in Canada," she told Dave and Katie.

"What's an OE?" Dave asked.

"That's 'Overseas Experience.' Most New Zealanders take a year or two in their early twenties to work and travel. I can get a job in Canada because it's a Commonwealth country."

"You'll have to collect enough money to pay for your airline ticket first, though," her mother reminded. "And you won't be old enough for another five years."

Holly grimaced a little but nodded agreement. She then rattled on about Canada and started asking questions about visiting the US from Canada. Whenever Holly paused, Nikki asked about the Parkers' home and life in Alabama as she cooked supper.

The conversation continued for an hour until an outside door to the kitchen opened, revealing twilight outside. Dave and Katie hadn't noticed the sun setting. A weather-beaten man wearing a long-sleeved wool shirt and khaki shorts entered. "This is my husband, George," introduced Nikki. "George, meet Dave and Katie Parker from Alabama in America."

The Parkers stood up to shake hands. "Glad to meet ya," said George with a hearty smile. He kicked off dirty boots into a box near the door and sat down at the table. He appeared exhausted.

Nikki placed a plate with mashed potatoes, boiled carrots, and two lamb chops in front of her husband. Without asking, she also placed a full plate in front of her guests and daughter. Dave and Katie followed the Fergusons' example by bowing their heads to say grace.

George slumped over his food as he started to eat. "How did the docking go?" asked Nikki.

"Awful. Spencer didn't show up again. And the lambs are getting bigger and faster every day. I sure miss our boys on the farm," George lamented and looked up. "I'll need your help tomorrow, Nikki."

"I can't. My mum has that doctor's appointment. You know she can't drive herself."

George turned his eyes to his daughter. "Holly will need to miss school then."

The teenager rolled her eyes. "Dad, I have a big test tomorrow. They deduct points unless you have a doctor's excuse."

"Maybe we could help," offered Dave.

All the Kiwis looked at the Americans in surprise. "You'd have a go at it?" said George.

Katie nodded for both of them.

At sunrise, Dave and Katie followed George's all-terrain vehicle into a paddock. A dog of some Shetland ancestry ran alongside him. Nikki had found jeans, sweatshirts, rain jackets, gloves, and boots for the Parkers. George and Holly's clothes fit Dave and Katie respectively.

Tranquil scenes of sheep grazing peacefully in green pastures surrounded them. George stopped to explain, “In general, field-raised sheep fear humans. The last time a human caught them, they felt cold for weeks afterwards because somebody sheared them. Genetic memory of wolves tells sheep that dogs aren’t their friends either.” George then assigned Dave and Katie to stand on either side of a gate to direct the sheep into a corral.

Next, George on his four-wheeler and the dog disturbed the tranquil scene by herding the sheep toward the Parkers. The dog hardly measured up to the precise border collies depicted in sheepdog trials. He mostly just ran around barking and biting at the hindmost sheep. Dave and Katie attempted to force groups of ewes and lambs to enter the gate by waving their arms, shouting, and jumping in front of those trying to veer off path.

The sheep weren’t very smart. But some suspected that no good waited for them in the corral. Both the ewes and lambs were amazingly fast. Groups of the ewes followed by their lambs attempted to dodge by Dave and Katie, jinking and juking, in an effort for freedom. Those who succeeded had to be re-rounded up. One lamb eluded everyone until the Parkers cornered him against a fence. Still Katie had to dive to catch him by one foot as he tried to dart past.

Finally, 180 sheep with lambs had been corralled into a pool of wooly backs. The next step was to separate the adult ewes from the lambs. Dave and Katie, assisted by the dubious dog, tried to funnel them into a “race” with a swinging gate controlled by George. The ewes went to the left and back to pasture. The lambs went into a holding pen on the right.

That's how the division was *supposed* to work. The lambs hadn't been around very long and didn't know much. But they knew that the holding pen contained nothing looking remotely like mom. They put up quite a fight to avoid going that way.

At this point, the dog caused twenty sheep to panic and charge the race at once. Each adult ewe was a 150-pound battering ram mounted on four powerful legs. Their plan of escape was to smash through. Lambs were separated from their mothers in the chaos. But, in a crisis, any mom would do. Lost lambs tried to follow other ewes into the race. The result was a tremendous tangle of wool, hooves, and trampled lambs. Bleating and barking filled the air so that nothing else could be heard.

As Dave and Katie tried to untangle the mess, some of the first ewes who had made it through the race realized they had lost something. Their lambs! In the only noble act of this species of idiots, some mothers tried to force their way back up the race to find their lambs. There they met the next group of dog-panicked sheep head on. Ewes cried for their lambs and lambs cried for their moms. The chaos ebbed and flowed until the flock was separated. At some point, Katie found her clothes soaked. She realized a rainstorm had passed over without her even noticing. But at last the lambs had been isolated for docking.

The ten to fifteen-pound lambs had already been frightened witless. Then Dave had to pick up each lamb, turn it onto its back, and spread-eagle pinion it for treatment. This was not a natural position for the lambs. The strong, dirty little beasts struggled and kicked. Once the lambs were pinned on their backs, Dave slid the animals on rollers to where Katie inoculated them for scabby mouth disease and George cut off and cauterized the tails with a propane-heated wedge. George then released the lambs to heart-warming reunions with their moms. Within seconds, each lamb grazed or nursed, showing no trauma from their ordeal. Dave and Katie helped George dock five paddocks of lambs, about 700, that day.

As the sun set, Dave and Katie trudged wearily back into the Fergusons' home. Nikki had roast beef and roasted potatoes ready. She had also made a cherry pie. George was jubilant. "We got the early birth all done. I kept an eye on the Parkers to see how they'd hold up. There was no quitting in them," he told Nikki and Holly over the dinner table. He turned to Dave and Katie. "Even with Spencer that would have taken three days. Thank you kindly, mates!"

Dave, who had done most of the lamb lifting, nodded a tired acknowledgment. "Thanks for giving us that experience."

George went on, "In truth, sheep are greedy animals. They eat all day long. They don't even raise their heads to swallow. In winter and spring, New Zealand's fifty million sheep nearly doubles with newly born lambs. They're cute, until you have to handle them. Field lambs are dirty, wild little animals. They eat so much and grow so fast that they're ready for the meat market in just four months." George leaned forward. "I don't know what you're doing here in New Zealand, but you could stay on here at the farm as long as you liked. Without our boys, I'm only raising half the herd the land could sustain. We have a cottage you could stay in, and I could pay a little salary."

Dave and Katie looked at each other.

Lamb

Chapter Fifteen

Katie smiled at the thought of them becoming sheep hands. Her look told Dave, *Maybe looking for Trevor isn't so bad.* Before Dave could politely decline George's offer, Katie began to explain their search for Trevor. Being family oriented themselves, the Kiwis appreciated the priority of finding Trevor.

The Parkers felt sadness and soreness leaving the Ferguson farm the next morning. Dave took out two one-hundred-dollar bills to pay for their room. "Oh no! You've more than earned your keep," Nikki insisted.

"Then do you mind if we . . ." he nodded toward Holly, who had her back turned while clearing the breakfast table.

Nikki considered a moment and whispered, "Can you make her promise to earn it?"

"Can she visit us in Alabama on her OE?" Katie responded with her own whisper.

"If she wants to."

Katie took the bills from Dave and approached Holly. "Holly, we'd like to hire you to do some painting and other work if you'll visit us during your OE."

Holly glanced to her mother, who nodded approval. "Could I? I'd love to."

"Okay, here are two hundred dollars in advance to help you pay for your airline ticket."

The girl's eyes widened. "This is the first part of my travel money. Thank you heaps!"

"This is the biggest haystack to find Trevor in yet," Dave said to Katie as he stood on top of Mt. Eden and surveyed the panorama of Auckland in every direction.

Katie held a guidebook, reading about the city. "We're standing on the rim of a dormant volcano and an old Maori fortress. The caldera is the hole in the middle. The Maori populated New Zealand by outrigger canoe and built stockades around their villages for protection against other tribes. They lived on several of the fifty inactive volcanos in the city." She looked up. Green grass-covered hills dotted the metropolis in every direction. "I'll bet those hills are the old volcanos. The big island to the east of the harbor entrance is a volcano that formed just 15,000 years ago."

Dave shaded his eyes as he looked. "I've heard about volcanos growing out of the ocean."

"In this case, no. The sea level was 300 feet lower then. That's when continental glaciers covered most of North

America and Europe," Katie, ever the science teacher, explained.

Dave pointed to the north. "Look at that harbor. I've heard they call Auckland 'The City of Sails.' Shall we go look?"

"Do you think Trevor frequented the harbor? Remember that we're here to find him."

"Probably not," Dave admitted as he looked wistfully at the harbor. "Maybe we should take a few more days of vacation."

Katie shook her head. "Let's keep looking first. We could be getting close. I'd hate to just miss him."

"Okay, where's the casino? Maybe we'll find him there."

"The biggest is called Sky City." Katie waved toward something in the distance. "See the Sky Tower? The casino is at its base."

Sky Tower

The third cold rainstorm that morning drove the couple to their rental car. "Now I know why New Zealand is so green. I've never seen such frequent rain," said Dave. "Why don't you work the casino again while I hoof around showing Trevor's picture."

"Your job sounds like more fun than mine."

"Maybe so. But I can't do your job."

Driving down Queen Street toward the casino, Katie spotted a baby shop. "Look at those cute baby clothes. We're going to have a grandbaby soon. In all the excitement, I haven't let that thought sink in."

"We are going to be grandparents," Dave conceded.

"But Dave, Australia is a long way from Mobile. We'll never get to see them. Our grandchild won't even know who we are."

"Don't worry. At this rate we'll still be here for the baby's birth."

"Very funny. I'm serious. Let's go into the shop and look around. I want to pick something out for an early shower present."

How do I get rid of this leech? Katie thought. Several men had approached her during three tedious days of playing pokie poker. None of them had recognized the picture of Trevor. The last one—a single, somewhat corpulent older tourist from Germany—had followed her around for most of the day. His persistent offers to buy her drinks and show her the attractions of New Zealand had become an irritant.

"Oops, that's my husband," she said after seeing Dave looking for her among the rows of gambling machines. She hurried to him without another glance at her admirer.

Dave grinned bigger than normal when he saw her coming. "Sometimes you just get lucky," he started. "I went into a library to get out of the rain. While waiting for the rain to stop, I remembered the books in Trevor's bedroom. So I showed the librarian his picture. She recognized him."

Katie couldn't restrain her eagerness. The long search had become tiresome. "Well, where is he?"

"The librarian didn't know that. But she said that Trevor used to frequently meet a girl there. And the librarian said that she had recently been seeing the same girl sitting in a city park not far from the library."

"Thc girl might know where he is!" Katie's face showed anticipation.

"Now, don't get your hopes up. You know that—"

But Katie wasn't listening. "What does the girl look like?"

Dave froze. "I forgot to ask. In my excitement, I just wanted to tell you."

Katie rolled her eyes. "Let's go back and talk to the librarian."

Katie and Dave walked a couple of blocks through a light drizzle to the library. They found the librarian pushing a cart of books into the non-fiction section to be re-shelved. She greeted Dave and Katie warmly, and when asked for details about the girl Trevor had been meeting, she told them as much as she could remember.

"I was curious," the librarian explained after describing the girl. "She appeared homeless. So one day before—his name was Trevor, right?—before Trevor came in, I asked the girl about their meetings. She told me that she was alone in New Zealand and that he had befriended her. She appeared smitten with him." The librarian concluded with, "She had a heavy foreign accent. Occasionally I see her alone now in the park."

Why are they looking at me? Lena wondered. An older couple had several times walked by the park bench where she sat. Now they stood together fifty meters away furtively glancing in her direction. *Could they be the authorities?* But their dress and mannerisms made them look more like tourists than government officials. And the couple looked nervous. Police or immigration officials wouldn't be nervous. They look kindly. *Maybe they are concerned about the baby and will put something in my cup.*

Finally, the couple approached her. To Lena's joy, the man folded a hundred-dollar bill and placed it in her cup. *Food for us tonight and maybe a dry place to sleep.* She looked up and smiled a little in response.

The woman's voice revealed her to be an American or a Canadian. "Excuse me, but could we ask you a question, please?"

A hundred dollars should entitle them to a question. The girl nodded.

"My name is Katie Parker. This is my husband, Dave. We are looking for a young Australian man. Do you recognize the man in this picture?"

The woman handed a photo to her. Lena's heart soared. The picture showed Trevor. Younger, but unmistakably her

Trevor. An inner voice said to her, *You don't know why they want Trevor. Protect him.* "Why you want this man?"

"Our son married his sister. She is worried about her younger brother, who left home unexpectedly and hasn't been heard from in several years. His family asked us to look for him." The American woman crouched down to look eye level at Lena. "Do you know Trevor Larkin?"

Lena looked back and forth between the woman and the man with her. *You need to trust somebody.* "I am his wife."

Her statement visibly startled the woman crouching before her. The woman looked up at the man and then back at Lena. She indicated the baby with her hand. "Is this Trevor Larkin's baby?"

"Da, I mean yes. My English is not so good."

"Do you know where Trevor is?"

"He went to get money to pay hospital bill. The baby came early and needed much care. We had to find money for the baby."

"I mean where is he right now?"

"I do not know."

Katie stood erect again. She motioned for Dave to step a few yards away with her. She whispered, "Now what do we do? Has Trevor conned this girl and then abandoned her?"

Dave's face assumed his professional accountant posture. "I don't know. In fact, we don't *know* anything yet. Certainly not that she and Trevor are married."

"What if they are actually married? That would make her Denyse's sister-in-law."

Dave nodded in agreement. "That's true. But even if she's not, this young woman is obviously in trouble. And the baby is probably Trevor's. We need to help them regardless."

A splatter of rain interrupted Katie's response. She turned to see the girl pocket the hundred dollars and wrap up the baby, preparing to move out of the weather. "Wait!" Katie pleaded. "We need to talk to you. Is there a place we can go?"

The girl returned a blank look. Dave pointed across the street. "How about that café?"

Lena shook her head. "It costs much." The baby started to cry.

"Don't worry about that. I'll pay. Hurry now, or your child will be soaked." Dave took off his jacket and draped it over the young mother's head and back. Katie picked up her carry bag. The girl cradled her baby in both arms and hurried across the street to the café.

Inside the café, Dave got a table for them. Katie lifted Dave's jacket off the girl and grabbed a handful of napkins to help her dry and quiet the baby. Then she asked, "What is your baby's name?"

"Vladimir."

"And your name?"

"Lena Travnikov; now Lena Larkin."

Katie smiled. "Where are you from, Lena?"

"Ukraine. My mother, brothers, and sisters run from war. They live in a camp with nothing. Some men from my country pay my way here to work as a nanny. I hope to send money home. Then the Ukrainians take money from New Zealand men and tell me to work for them. These men do not want a nanny. They want me to do bad things for money. I run away and hide until I meet Trevor."

A waiter appeared. "Lena, what would you like to drink? Do you like coffee?" Dave asked.

"Chai."

To Dave's confused look, the waiter explained, "Chai is hot tea outside the commonwealth countries."

"Then bring us three pots of chai with milk and lemon and sugar."

"Would you like something to eat, Lena?" Katie asked. The girl nodded. "Would you like a hot soup? Do you like quiche?" Lena nodded again. Katie ordered hot soup (pumpkin the only choice) and bacon-tomato quiche for three.

After the waiter departed, Dave began, "We did not know Trevor had gotten married. When was that?"

Lena reached for her carry bag. After a few moments of fumbling, she produced a folded piece of damp paper and handed it to Dave. The words "Marriage Certificate" were emblazoned on top with the date twelve months previous and the seal of a New Zealand civil court. Dave passed the paper to Katie. She looked at the paper and then at Dave with her eyebrows arched. "But you don't know where Trevor is right now?"

"I no hear from him for a month. Before he sent me this." Lena pulled another piece of paper from her bag and handed it to Dave. He saw a stub from a cashier's check for sixteen thousand dollars. Then she produced several pictures of her and Trevor together. The last had the young couple standing smiling beside a prenatal crib. A birth certificate documented the baby's name as Vladimir Larkin with Trevor and Lena listed as the parents. "I give this money he send to the hospital. Then no more money come from Trevor. I know he is in trouble."

The warmth of the café started to relax Lena. The waiter brought their tea and food on a tray. Lena, although obviously eager to eat, bowed her head for a silent prayer first. Dave noticed that she used lemon in her hot tea in the Russian fashion. Katie caught Dave's eye, then tilted her head toward the toilet and announced, "I need to use the restroom."

Her husband had gotten the message. "Me too."

"Why would Trevor send her so much money, then abandon her?" Katie asked Dave out of Lena's hearing.

"I don't know. Maybe he hasn't abandoned her. This whole situation is completely confusing."

"What are we going to do?" Katie persisted.

Dave shrugged and returned to the table. "Lena, where are you staying?"

"We had a room, part of a house. No money. Six days ago, they make me leave."

Katie could not believe what she had heard. "You've been homeless with a newborn baby since then?"

"Yes. The New Zealand men find me again. They want to make me to do the bad things for money. I say, 'No. I'm a Baptist.' We hide in the trees at night. I know Trevor will come back for me and Vladimir."

"Why didn't you go to a women's shelter?"

"The police could put me in jail and take my baby away."

Dave deliberately breathed slowly. Katie saw his determined look coming on. "God has sent us here to help you on behalf of Trevor, Lena. We'll pay for a hotel room for you and Vladimir. Then we'll start figuring out what to do next."

Lena started to softly cry. "My milk for the baby. It is not enough."

"More food will help you, honey," answered Katie. "And we'll buy some formula as a supplement." She turned to Dave and said, "First, we'll need to take Lena and Vladimir to a market. I think Lena and the baby need a few things."

Having been a young mother herself, Katie knew the items Lena needed. She let Lena choose formulas, a bottle, disposable diapers, any food she wanted for the hotel room, and dry clothes. Together the Parkers checked Lena into the same hotel where they were staying.

"Lock the door behind us," Dave told Lena. "If you need anything, we're in room 142."

Back in their own hotel room, Dave and Katie collapsed on the bed in emotional exhaustion. "That's not what I expected when we woke up this morning," Dave admitted.

"Well, we found something. Just not Trevor," returned Katie.

Dave covered his eyes with his forearm and groaned. "What are we going to do now?"

Katie groaned herself. "Remember Beatrice talking about the riptides?"

"Yes. So what?"

"I feel one is pulling us into an ocean of trouble."

Galah

Chapter Sixteen

After lying quietly for a while, Katie picked up the hotel phone. "I know what we need to do first," she said to Dave as she dialed Jeremy and Denyse's number.

Jeremy answered. "Hi, Mom! How's New Zealand?"

"New Zealand is interesting. Could I speak to Denyse, please?"

Denyse came on. "Katie! Any news about Trevor?"

"We've got important news. But it's not what you expect."

"Bloody, 'ell! Trevor has a wife?" Dingo turned off a Rugby League match between rival clubs in Melbourne and Sydney. He waited for Beatrice to continue.

"You heard right. The Parkers found her in Auckland. Denyse talked to her over the phone. She knows all about Trevor and has pictures of them together. Her name is Lena. She's nineteen years old and a Ukrainian. After her father died, she agreed to take a nanny job in New Zealand to send money home. But instead they wanted her to do other things, wrong things. So she ran away from them and hid. Later Lena met Trevor in a public library."

Dingo rubbed his face. "So then where is Trevor?"

"Now get ready, Dingo. What you're about to hear is like a movie or something. Trevor fell in love with Lena and married her, all legal like. She's a religious girl, a Baptist. Then Trevor paid the men who said Lena owed them eleven thousand dollars. It took all the money he had saved. Isn't that romantic? My son, Trevor."

"Where did Trevor get the money?" Dingo asked.

Beatrice raised her voice. "Who cares where he got the money? Are you daft? I'm telling you our son has a young wife. And that's not all he has—"

Dingo broke in, "You still haven't told me where Trevor is."

"He's in New Zealand, you galah. Let me finish telling you what happened!"

Dingo fumed but remained silent.

Beatrice waited a moment to make certain she had her husband's full attention. "About a year after Trevor and Lena got married, she gave birth to a baby boy."

Dingo rose to his feet. "Trevor's got a son? I have a grandson?"

"That's what I've been trying to tell you. But you keep interrupting. Now be quiet." Beatrice delayed a few seconds to enjoy keeping Dingo in suspense. Then she continued, "But the baby came a little early, a preemie. Neither Trevor nor Lena are eligible for government healthcare in New Zealand, so they needed money. Trevor went away to get more money and a week later sent Lena sixteen thousand dollars to pay the baby's medical bills."

Dingo paced back and forth with impatience. He wondered where Trevor had gotten the sixteen thousand dollars, but didn't interrupt Beatrice again.

"After that, the money stopped coming. Lena is afraid Trevor is in trouble somewhere."

Dingo stopped pacing and sat back down. "So then where are Trevor's wife and baby now?"

"That's the best part. Dave and Katie are bringing Lena and the baby to Sydney as soon as they can arrange her entry into Australia. She's legally married to Trevor, an Aussie, but he's not with her. They should arrive there day after tomorrow. Dingo, I want to be there to see my grandchild, Trevor's son." Beatrice continued to repeatedly whisper aloud to herself as a tear formed on her cheek, "Trevor's son."

"What's the boy's name?" Dingo asked softly.

"Vladimir. Lena named her first son after her deceased father."

"See if you can get us on tonight's sleeper train to Sydney."

Two days later, Jeremy and Denyse waited for Dave and Katie outside of Australian customs again. Alongside of them fidgeted Dingo and Beatrice. Denyse imagined Lena's trepidation at meeting her mother-in-law for the first time.

Passengers from the Auckland flight to Sydney came pouring out of customs. Greetings and reunions took place everywhere. The passengers slowed to a trickle, then ceased entirely. Still no Parkers or Lena emerged. Finally, Denyse saw

Dave and Katie walking out on either side of an emaciated-looking teenage girl. She looked only about fourteen years old rather than her actual nineteen. Even so thin and without makeup, there was no denying the girl's wholesome Slavic beauty. She carried a bundle in her arms. Katie pointed toward the Larkins and whispered something to her. The girl nodded and smiled at Katie in appreciation.

Before anybody could say anything, Lena walked directly to Dingo and placed her baby in his arms. "Vladimir Larkin, your grandson," she said and curtseyed.

Dinge stood speechless for a long moment. "Yeeah. Uh, welcome to Australia," he managed, not knowing how else to respond.

Lena nodded acknowledgment and held out her arms for the baby. Dingo gladly relinquished the infant. Whereupon, Lena turned to Beatrice and repeated the gesture. Unlike Dingo, Beatrice clutched the baby to her bosom. Joyful tears ran down her cheeks.

After being astounded by Lena's ancient village custom, nearly everybody started to talk at once.

"I can see Trevor's eyes in Vladimir," Denyse claimed.

Katie went around introducing Lena to each of them.

Dave apologized for their long wait. "Immigration had to sort out a Ukrainian without a visa married to an Aussie not present and escorted by Americans. Then they dealt with a baby born in New Zealand to a Ukrainian and an absent Australian."

Jeremy admired how his father's face had healed.

Katie gave Denyse a hug, took a look at her tummy, and asked about her pregnancy.

Dingo gave Dave an ungentle but affirming punch in the

arm for finding Lena. "Good on ya, mate."

Beatrice continued to cry.

"Our car wouldn't hold everybody. So we rented a minivan," Jeremy announced. He drove them all to his and Denyse's flat. There Katie felt gratified to see that the cardboard boxes had been replaced with used end tables. And the spare bedroom now included a new mattress on the floor.

Beatrice had yet to relinquish the baby. Katie prepared a bottle of formula for Vladimir. While Beatrice fed the baby, the Larkins asked Lena questions about meeting and marrying Trevor. Despite being among strangers, the Ukrainian girl wasn't timid. They all laughed as Lena described Trevor's clumsy efforts to meet her at the library. And through Lena's eyes everyone saw a different side of him. "Trevor is a good man," she reported. "I never saw him drink alcohol. Men in my country . . . drink causes many problems."

A few eyes glanced at Dingo. If he noticed, he made no sign.

Lena continued, "Because I had no money and slept in the park, Trevor paid for a small room for me. I made him sleep someplace else. 'No marriage, no sex,' I tell him. And I didn't marry him until I knew that he truly loved me and wanted a family. Trevor talked a lot about his mother and sister. Until now, I didn't know he had a father." Lena didn't see a reproving look Beatrice gave her husband. "I am happy to know you all."

Vladimir started fussing a little in discomfort. While still talking about Trevor, Lena casually took the infant from

Beatrice, burped him on her shoulder, and handed him back. "Since I was seven years, I care for brothers and sisters," she shared. "He'll be ready for sleep now."

Jeremy cut down one of the boxes that had previously served as their end tables to make a crib. He put a soft cotton blanket in the box and placed it in the spare bedroom. Beatrice, having gently cradled her grandson to sleep in her arms, laid him on his stomach in the box. "No, on his back is better," said Lena. "And not too hot." She cracked a window to let in cool winter air. Then she inserted a pacifier in her son's mouth. "I'll mind him while he sleeps." Lena closed the door and lay down on the mattress.

"So what happens now?" asked Dingo downstairs.

"I vote for supper," Jeremy suggested.

Denyse gave her husband the *I-don't-have-anything-to-fix* look.

"Denyse and I will need to go to the market," Jeremy added.

"Katie and I can go to the market for you," Dave suggested. "What should we get?"

Denyse looked at her father-in-law gratefully. "How about we have a seafood chowder with fresh bread?" She named several ingredients for the chowder. "I can make the bread while you're gone."

"You can use my car," Jeremy offered.

"Dingo asked a good question that we need to ask ourselves.

What's next for us?" Katie asked Dave in the car.

"How about Mobile?"

"Home sounds wonderful. I'm sick and tired of this trip. Even though I never expected to miss a cat, I want to see Old Yeller. I'm sure he misses us too. But do you want to give up on finding Trevor?"

"Oh, I want to give up. I just hate to disappoint Denyse and her parents," Dave answered reluctantly as he parked the car by the market. "This trip has morphed into something I never anticipated. We came here for two weeks to attend a wedding, remember? A wedding you had even hoped wouldn't happen."

Katie made no move to leave the car. "I know. And I want to go home too. But we came so close to finding Trevor."

"Don't you want to feel more than ordinary anymore?" Dave teased.

"I'd settle for ordinary right now."

"Well, now we truly are at a dead end. Even Lena has no idea where Trevor might be." Dave opened the car door. "Let's not keep them waiting for supper."

"Okay."

In Dave and Katie's absence, Dingo repeated to Beatrice, Denyse, and Jeremy, "What I meant was, what happens now in the search for Trevor?"

Denyse looked at Jeremy. "Do you think your parents would soldier on?"

Jeremy shrugged. "They've been away from home a long time. But both of them are pretty persistent, each in their own way. Together, I wouldn't want to try stopping them."

Denyse measured out flour for the bread, then added salt and baker's yeast. "I'm worried that Trevor might be in trouble. Lena thinks so. And maybe she knows the real Trevor better than any of us."

"If there's going to be trouble, I could go along and help," Dingo suggested from the couch. "I owe it to the lad."

Denyse shook her head. "Dad, I know you want to help, but this calls for a different approach than knocking somebody's teeth out."

Dingo stood up and answered with some hostility. "And you think that Yank is better able to deal with trouble than me? We saw how inept he would be in the fight at your wedding."

Jeremy started to respond, but waited when Denyse reached out to squeeze his forearm. She answered, "Dad, that Yank came back into a gun battle and shot a man with a shotgun a year ago. He saved a policeman's life and Katie's. Dave just avoids fights when they aren't necessary."

"Parker shot a man?" Dingo pondered that improbability. "He came back for a mate, like Ned Kelly?"

Jeremy nodded. "Don't make him talk about it though, Dingo. I won't tell you the entire story, but my father has nightmares about what he had to do."

Dingo settled back onto the couch. "What about Lena?"

"What, 'What about Lena?' " Denyse responded. "Jeremy and I will take care of her and the baby here."

Beatrice spoke up for the first time. "No, your father and I will take them back to Melbourne."

Chapter Seventeen

Dave and Katie returned to the flat with the groceries to find the sweet smell of bread baking and an undeniable atmosphere of tension.

"Beatrice insists on taking Lena and the baby back to Melbourne," Jeremy whispered when letting them in the door. "I had offered to let them stay here with Denyse and me."

Katie saw Beatrice and Denyse standing facing one another. Dingo sat in sullen silence on the couch. "You're expecting your own baby," repeated Beatrice. "And you both have careers. You live in a small flat. Meanwhile our house in Melbourne is practically empty in a quiet neighborhood."

"We'll manage, Mum," promised Denyse.

Beatrice lost her normal demeanor of deference. "I'm taking my son's wife and my grandson home."

"Should I remind you that Vladimir is a male? You and Dad aren't very good with girl children. But compared to Dad with boys . . ." Denyse's voice trailed off. She resumed more softly, almost in a whisper, "You heard what Lena said about alcohol and men."

Pain showed on Dingo's face. He would have rather been pounded unconscious in a bar fight a thousand times than hear those words. He cleared his throat. They all turned, expecting to hear a confrontational outburst. "I can change," said Dingo. "I can change for little Vlady."

Denyse sat down beside her father. "I'm sorry, Dad. We all know you mean well."

Dingo looked up and into Dave's face to ask, "Maybe you and I could have a talk together outside, man-to-man, eh?" After Dave nodded, Dingo stood up and opened the flat's front door for them to exit.

"Blimey, my daughter is a tough one," Dingo stated outside. "Sorry about all I've thought about you as a Yank and all. You're straight up, Dave. Let's you and I walk someplace and get a brew."

"Forget about it. Denyse is a fireball," Dave agreed. "I think she takes after you." He pointed in the direction of the market. "This way, mate."

Dingo started in a determined trudge. "Yeeah. She's smarter than me, though." He walked in silence for several minutes. "The frustrating thing is that I've gotten into fights over nothin' all my life. Now, when there's real trouble, I'm useless."

"I think there are just different ways of fighting. Sometimes the toughest fights are won using your head and maintaining self-discipline," said Dave. "My wife is small and not very strong, but she's a fighter. Two years ago, I watched her battle cancer. She actually helped me through the ordeal."

"What about Jeremy? He a fighter like his mother?"

Dave laughed. "You saw him in Melbourne."

"Yeeah, the lad did alright."

"But Denyse was smarter. Jeremy could have done a lot better by staying out of that fight. His most important fight is to take care of Denyse and their baby."

Dingo stopped walking and looked at Dave. "That's the fight I should have fought and didn't." He resumed walking. "Not fighting when you should have fought is worse than fighting and losing. I wish I could start over."

Dave extended his stride to catch up. "Maybe it's not too late."

"What do you mean?"

"My family wasn't always very happy with me either. I became obsessed with work for years after Jeremy was born. Having a baby in the house can be stressful. Probably I worked so hard to avoid the stress, which brought back memories of troubles my older brother experienced. Eventually, I lived a separate life from Katie and Jeremy even in the same house. Katie recognized the problem and helped me to fight for the things that counted most—our family."

"What makes you think I can take care of a family?"

"You're here, aren't you? And there's another little boy who needs you."

"You mean little Vlady?"

"Sure."

Dave and Dingo had reached the market. Inside, Dingo selected a bottle of Foster's beer from the cooler. Dave picked out a Coca-Cola. The two men stood drinking their choices outside under a tree.

Dave started the conversation again. "How did you get the nickname 'Dingo'?"

"My father worked as a sheep man and a cattle drover. A bit of a bushman himself, he was. Hiding from a couple of drunk and disorderly charges for certain. He started calling me Dingo after the wild dog to encourage me to be wild and unpredictable. I grew up thinking about myself like a wild dog."

"What's your real name?

"My mother named me Graham." Dingo went into the market to buy another beer for the trek back. Rejoining Dave he asked, "Do you really think I could put up a good family fight?"

Dave mimicked the Aussie, "Yeeah." When Dingo smiled, Dave took another chance. "But you know that Lena was also right. Men and a lot of alcohol . . . 'many problems.' "

Dingo looked at the bottle he carried. "Two regular-sized beers a day? Not a drop more?" He looked to Dave for affirmation.

"Sounds reasonable. And you don't have the luxury of

disappearing for months into the Outback."

"Fair dinkum, mate."

"The chowder is ready," Denyse announced. "Are Dave and Dad back yet?"

Jeremy looked out the window. "I see them coming."

"Somebody please see if Lena is awake. If she is, tell her we're about to have supper."

Both Beatrice and Katie went upstairs. "Tea time, luv," Beatrice called. Lena came out of the bedroom blinking away sleep. "I'll watch over Vladimir," Beatrice offered.

"No. Let's wake him up," Lena said. "Otherwise he might stay up all night. Would you bring him, Mama?"

Beatrice had brightened at being called Mama. She collected the baby, who whimpered just a bit and then relaxed in Beatrice's arms.

Katie carried Jeremy's makeshift crib downstairs after Lena.

Everybody crowded around Jeremy and Denyse's small kitchen table. While Denyse ladled out bowls of steaming chowder, Katie remembered Lena's prayer at the café. "Could we start with a family prayer over dinner?" she suggested. Nobody objected. "Dave?" He prayed for all of them.

"This is a wonderful chowder, Denyse," said Dave a few minutes later. "And the bread turned out perfectly."

"It's an easy recipe," she responded, then described the process.

After a period of small talk, Dave addressed Lena. "What would you like to do next?"

The girl didn't need to think. "I go back to Auckland with Vladimir. Otherwise when Trevor comes back, he won't find us."

No one spoke, but nobody liked the idea of Lena returning to that environment alone, especially with the baby. "I've got another idea," Katie suggested. "You can stay in Australia. Dave and I will go back to New Zealand to look for Trevor."

"But he will think I have left him."

"The librarian where you met Trevor will recognize him. We'll leave a message at the library. He is certain to go there looking for you if we don't find him first."

Lena quietly pondered that offer. She looked toward her baby, who rested peacefully in Beatrice's arms. "I will do. Thank you, Katie."

Dave looked at Katie, who had just made a major promise for both of them. When she looked back, he gave a small, albeit resigned, nod. She slightly shrugged.

"There is another question, Lena," resumed Dave. "Where will you live in Australia? You could live with Denyse and Jeremy and have the room upstairs where you napped, or you could go to Melbourne where Graham and Beatrice have a house and more space."

The others, including Dingo himself, wondered about Dave's subtle change of Dingo's name to Graham. Dave went on, "You should know before you decide that Graham drinks two bottles of beer a day, but he has promised that he won't drink more or get drunk."

"No getting drunk?" Lena questioned.

"No getting drunk," Dingo promised. "And I'll tell the sheep station to get another shearer this spring. I'll be getting a job in Melbourne. I'm pretty sure Hogan will take me on at his body shop. He and I were mates on a farm a few years back. He knows I can work. I'll take care of you and Vlady." Beatrice and Denyse exchanged cautiously optimistic looks across the table.

Dave returned the discussion to the young mother. "Lena, both places would love to have you and little Vlady. Do you have anything to add, Denyse or Beatrice?" Neither did. "Then Lena, do you have a preference about where to go?"

"Grandparents are very important in my village." She looked at Jeremy and Denyse. "Could I go with Mama and Poppa?"

"Whatever you would like," responded Denyse without any hint of disagreement.

That decision made, everybody relaxed. Dingo gave Dave a respectful nod across the table. Beatrice started to cry quietly again.

"Let's take a family picture," Jeremy proposed.

After supper, Jeremy used the rented minivan to convey the out-of-town guests to the nearby hotel. Dave put all their room charges on his credit card.

In their room, Katie said, "That was amazing diplomacy you did tonight. You brought them all together."

"Thanks, sweetheart. Frequently at the firm I had to

get several parties of the same client to work together."

"But how in the world did you get Dingo—I mean Graham—to agree to only two beers a day?"

"I just repeated the things you said fifteen years ago when my priorities needed adjustment. He suggested the limit of two."

Katie continued, "Did you mention that we struggled for a while longer? That people don't change lifetime habits overnight?"

"No, Dingo had enough to think about," Dave answered.

After a pause, Katie asked, "So how are we going to find Trevor this time?"

"We? You're the one who made the promise to Lena," Dave teased his wife.

"You knew that resuming the search was inevitable." Katie gestured bewilderment with her hands. "But I have absolutely no idea even where to begin this time."

Dave emptied a satchel of papers on the bed. "Let's start by looking through this stuff."

"What is this?

"This is every single scrap of paper and picture Lena has from Trevor. She gave it all to me and prayed that we would find a clue here. I promised to return everything before she catches the train with Dingo and Beatrice for Melbourne tomorrow. The least we can do is make copies of her more recent pictures of Trevor."

The Parkers started examining each piece. In a few minutes, Katie passed the stub from the sixteen-thousand-dollar cashier's check to Dave. "Look! The check was issued in Dunedin. And the date is less than a month ago!"

"Maybe God answered Lena's prayer."

"If so, then we're on a mission. Maybe we should stop whining about going home," Katie responded.

Dave shook his head. "God doesn't mind us expressing our feelings. He knows we're trying to do the right thing."

"Then I'd better email the Fogles again. I'll let them know a little about what we're doing. This time I'll tell them that their guess is as good as ours when we'll be home."

Chapter Eighteen

"I never thought I'd see Scotland. But it couldn't be much different," Katie commented about Dunedin.

Dave held open the door to the police headquarters for his wife. "You said something a few weeks ago about Christchurch being more English than England. So I checked London off of our list. Now I'm checking off Edinburgh too."

"You can throw away the list as far as I'm concerned. The only place I want to go right now is warm Mobile."

Dave brushed the slushy snow off her back. "I'll bet Scotland in the middle of winter has weather just like this."

An hour later, Dave and Katie walked the streets of Dunedin again. A gusty wind from the Antarctic blew a mixture of sleet and snow into their faces. The police had performed a criminal record check—or as they called it, "vetting"—on Trevor. The search had revealed nothing.

Dave shouted above the howling of the wind between buildings built of natural stone. "At least we know that Trevor isn't incarcerated, in the hospital, or in the morgue."

Katie shivered in the penetrating cold. "Is that the good news or the bad news?"

They reached their rental car. Inside, Dave revved the engine slightly to speed warming while Katie turned the heater to maximum.

"Do we go back to the old drill? You'll go to the must-be-warm-inside casino? I'll be canvassing the run-down hotels and pizza places in this miserable weather?" Dave asked.

Katie warmed her hands over the heater vent and took pity on her husband. "Let's take a gamble and both go to the casino first."

"Ha, ha. Take a gamble."

Katie shook her head. "I'm not in a mood for puns either. That one was just an accident. But Trevor came up with sixteen thousand dollars in only a couple of weeks. Where else around here could he get that kind of money so quickly?"

"I'm with you, as long as it's warm inside."

"This is Denyse's room, luv. You can stay in here," Beatrice said to Lena.

"I'll go borrow a basinet from our neighbor," Dingo offered. "We can set it up by the window. Plenty of fresh air for Vlady." He departed.

Beatrice saw Lena's eyes admiring Denyse's teenager bedroom. "I've seen pictures of rooms like this," the young mother said. "Thank you much."

"You're welcome. Graham and I are very happy to have you and Vlady here."

Lena hesitated. Her voice revealed trepidation. "Mama, I need something else, please."

Beatrice sat down on the bed. "What's that, luv? Tell me about it."

"I left Ukraine to help my mother, brothers, and sisters. They have nothing. Trevor sent them money before the hospital bills for the baby. Until he comes I need to earn the money to send. Could you help me find a job?"

Beatrice suddenly realized the burden this young girl carried: a new baby, a missing husband, and a fatherless family back home depending on her. She hugged Lena like she was a child. "Yes, I can help you get a job at the hospital where I work. But it would be a nasty job cleaning up bedpans and . . ." Beatrice's voice trailed off. Her instinct told her that Lena could endure nearly anything.

"Thank you again, Mama. Would you also help me care for Vlady while I'm working?"

"Of course. Dingo will too."

Katie could hardly believe her eyes. There at a pokie

machine sat a familiar-looking young man. She took out a copy of Lena's most recent picture of her husband. The image looked like the player before her. Only unlike the happy young man in the photo, the man she watched reflected a demeanor of despair and hopelessness. She edged closer to hear his Aussie accent as he tried to entice a fellow pokie player into a face-to-face poker game. *That has to be Trevor,* she thought and hurried to find Dave. *Lord, please don't let Trevor wander away.*

⁂

"You're right! That's him." Dave started toward their long-sought quarry.

Katie pulled her husband back. "Wait! What are you doing?"

"I'm going to kick Trevor's butt all the way back to Melbourne. Then we're going to get on the first flight back to Alabama."

"Hold on, Dave. Something is wrong. Does that look like the joyful kid in the pictures with Lena? Why would he send Lena the sixteen thousand dollars and then linger down here in this wretched place? Why would any Australian stay here in the winter's wet and cold? This doesn't add up. And if you approach him abruptly, you might even spook him. Do you want to continue chasing Trevor around the South Pacific? Let's watch awhile."

Dave hung his head in resignation. Katie knew he missed summertime back home, crabbing in Mobile Bay, catching largemouth bass in the rivers, and trolling for king mackerel in the Gulf of Mexico. She missed home too, even their cat, Old Yeller. "Okay," he said. "Let's finish this well. But if Trevor takes off again, I'm done."

Katie met Dave in the casino hotel's lobby where he watched the elevators for Trevor, who had gone up an hour earlier. "Something funny is going on," he told her. "Another man was watching Trevor while he tried to recruit poker players on the gambling floor. That man looks like some sort of Pacific Islander. And get this, before Trevor went upstairs, the man slipped him a stack of bills. Maybe six or seven thousand dollars."

"What does that mean?" Katie asked.

"I don't know. But I followed Trevor to room 384. Several other men joined him one at a time. I'm guessing they're playing poker illegally inside." Dave sat quietly for a minute. "I'm really tired. Did you check us into a room?"

Katie passed him a key card. "We're in 418. Why don't you go get some rest? I'll watch the elevators to see if Trevor leaves the hotel."

At 4:00 a.m., Dave felt Katie crawling into bed with him. "Did Trevor leave?"

"No. And I couldn't keep my eyes open any longer."

At 8:00 a.m., Dave dragged himself out of bed and headed for the shower. *Wherever Trevor is, he's likely sleeping late,* he thought in the hot spray. *But we don't know that for sure*. Picking up Katie's cell phone and leaving her sleeping, he headed downstairs. At a small café in the lobby, he sat down where he could watch the elevator doors and ordered tea and toast.

Not until after 11:00 did Trevor appear. Looking like a dead-eyed zombie, Trevor walked by Dave without looking to his right or left. He entered the hotel's restaurant. Dave followed and took a table where he could watch.

A waitress brought Trevor breakfast and a pot of coffee without asking. *Trevor is a regular here,* Dave realized. Another waitress came to Dave's table. He ordered more tea and a croissant. When the waitress left with the order, he dialed their room.

Katie's sleepy voice answered, "Hello."

"I'm watching Trevor in the hotel restaurant."

"Should I come down?"

"No, I've got this right now. But I'll need a break in an hour or so. Call me using the room phone when you're ready."

"Can I order breakfast in the room?"

"Sure. I'll keep an eye on Trevor."

Dave watched as a man of European descent wearing a suit and tie sat down at Trevor's table. They talked earnestly. Trevor shook his head. The man appeared to be insisting. Finally, Trevor passed him some money under a napkin. Without another word, the man picked up the money with the napkin, stood, and walked away. Trevor sat a few minutes in resignation, counted out money on the table to pay for his food, and headed toward the gambling areas.

⁂

Dave's cell phone rang. "Where are you now?" Katie asked.

"I'm playing on a slot machine where I can watch Trevor."

Katie knew how Dave thought such gambling to be pointless and a waste of money. "You're playing a slot machine?"

Dave didn't bother to answer her question. "Trevor's trying to recruit marks for his poker game. He's not going anywhere soon. I'll meet you in the lobby."

Katie saw Dave waving from a couch when she left the elevator. She walked over to join him. "Shouldn't we be watching Trevor?"

"I can see the entrance to the casino from here. As long as he doesn't come out, he's somewhere inside. Did you enjoy breakfast?"

"I had an omelet and fruit cup. It was good. Thanks for letting me rest."

"Okay, Ms. 'Let's watch awhile.' What are we going to do next?" He told her about the encounter he had observed in the restaurant.

"Was that the same man who passed Trevor money yesterday afternoon?"

Dave shook his head. "No, this man looks like a European. The islander who gave Trevor the money walks through the casino occasionally checking on him."

"So one man gives Trevor money and another man takes money away?"

"That's what appears to be happening. And Trevor isn't very happy with either of them."

"Okay. Last night sitting in the lobby nearly all night I had a chance to think." Katie explained her plan to her husband. At first, he disagreed, then gradually consented.

How did I end up in this mess? Trevor wondered as he sat in front of a pokie machine without really seeing the electronic cards. *God, if you're listening, please take care of Lena and Vladimir. And give me a way to help them. Maybe you could send an angel or something.*

A petite older woman took a machine not far away. She had straight salt-and-pepper hair cut to end just above her shoulder. He heard her talking to the machine. Her voice revealed her to be an American, probably from the South. She wasn't wearing a wedding ring.

"Damn this machine," the woman said as she stared at the screen. "It's rigged."

Trevor spoke to her with a note of sympathy in his voice. "They're all rigged to favor the house. That's how the casino makes money."

"Ah!" she exclaimed and struck the screen lightly with her little fist. "This is so aggravating."

"Are you alone here?" Trevor asked.

The woman kept her eyes on the screen. "Yes, I took my former husband to the cleaners during our divorce. I worked to put him through medical school. Then I found out he had slept with every nurse who would let him for the next thirty years."

"Why are you in New Zealand?"

The woman still hadn't looked at him. She answered, "I'm kicking around the world trying to spend my ex's money. New Zealand looked good in the travel brochures. I guess they take those pictures on the few clear days. I'm just in here waiting for a break in the weather."

"You know that playing poker against a machine is like hitting a tennis ball against a wall. There's no way you can ever win."

For the first time, the woman looked at Trevor. He could see that she was still pretty, despite being older. "What alternative is there?" she asked.

"Some guys and I are planning a little unrigged game upstairs later. At least there'll be winners and losers without the house slowly bleeding everybody."

The woman apparently wasn't a stranger to poker. "What're your stakes?"

"Fifty-dollar ante, first three bets with a hundred-dollar limit."

"Is it real poker? I don't mean made-for-TV elimination drama where players sometimes declare, 'I'm all in,' before all the cards are dealt. That lowers poker to mere luck."

Trevor shook his head. "Oh, no. This is old-fashioned five-card stud. Sometimes we play variants like 1-3-1 with the river card down. If the players want, we can play draw poker or Texas hold 'em. But this isn't tournament elimination poker."

She turned away from the machine she had been playing on. "Where would I find this game?"

"About nine o'clock tonight, come to room 384. You leave when you want to. Bring casino chips. We don't take cash."

She smiled at him. "My name is Katie. And yours?"

"Trevor."

"See you tonight, Trevor."

Chapter Nineteen

"So, how much did you lose?" Dave asked when Katie came in about 2:00 a.m.

"Less than three hundred dollars. Could you hear me on the cell phone in my pocket?"

"Well enough to know you weren't in physical danger. But not well enough to follow what was going on."

"I'd have screamed loud enough for you to hear if I'd needed help."

"Your clothes smell like tobacco."

"A couple of them were smoking. I nearly threw up."

Dave smiled. "Well, what happened?"

"Four other men played, plus Trevor and me. Plenty of liquor was handy. I told them I was a recovering alcoholic and couldn't drink. The four all got drunk on the free liquor. Trevor acted drunk. But I think he always filled his glass with Coke or seltzer when the others didn't notice.

"Now here's the surprise. Trevor lost about six thousand dollars to one man. That man wasn't a very good poker player. Beating him was how I kept our losses low. The other three lost five to seven hundred dollars each to Trevor. I think Trevor controlled the game for this man to win and all the rest of us to lose, but not lose so much as to not come back." Katie paused to let Dave think. "Do you have any idea what Trevor is doing?"

Dave continued thinking and then spoke, "Most of the men losing, but not enough to scare them off, sounds right. But Trevor losing to an amateur seems phony. That could be about the amount I saw somebody give him. Maybe he deliberately loses that money to someone his handlers send to the game."

That didn't make sense to Katie. "Why would they do that?"

"It could be a method of payoff. A method mixed with money laundering. Because the casino chips cashed in would be legal money. Even criminals need legal money to pay credit card bills in a cashless culture." Katie waited while Dave's accountant brain sorted out the implications. He continued thinking out loud, "The marks, you and the other three, would see Trevor lose a lot to one man and likely return thinking that they might get lucky and clean him out the following night. This could be hustling and money laundering combined in a single game. If so, some really bad people could be connected to the money laundering."

Katie started to get ready for bed. "Why would Trevor get involved in this? It doesn't seem like his style."

"Maybe he doesn't have a choice."

"I did see some healing burn marks on his arms. And one under his eye."

Katie played poker for two additional nights. "The big winner is a new man each night. Then he doesn't come back," she reported to Dave. "That supports your theory about payoffs and money laundering."

Dave nodded. "Today I followed the man who gives Trevor money. Once the game started in room 384, he got into an expensive car and drove off. I don't know where he went. I also followed the man who took money from Trevor in the restaurant. He went into the casino's security offices."

"What does that mean?"

"He's probably security here, aware of Trevor's poker game in room 384, and demanding a cut."

"Wow! This is getting complicated."

"We're probably just scraping the surface. Likely the corruption goes deeper. I'd like to try following the man who gives Trevor the money. But I need to listen to you on the cell phone during that time."

"I'll be okay without you listening."

"Maybe. But I'm not taking that chance. And I've been hanging around watching so much that I'm afraid someone will start to recognize me. We'll need to get some help."

This surprised Katie. "Help? Who would we get? Until we contact him, it would have to be someone Trevor doesn't know."

"He doesn't know Jeremy," said Dave.

Katie reacted, "Jeremy? You're not involving my *only* son is this situation. You said yourself that we only know the surface of what could be going on."

"*You* got your only husband involved," Dave answered back.

"I can get another one of those if I need to."

After laughing, he reassured her, "I'm not going to expose my *only* son to any danger either. All Jeremy has to do is listen to the phone and call the police if anything goes wrong."

"Denyse won't like that."

"Trevor is *her* brother. And she's Dingo's daughter. The problem we'll have is keeping her out of it."

"Maybe Dingo too."

Denyse felt her heart jump. "Dave and Katie have found Trevor?"

"Yes. But they think he's in big trouble. He may have gotten involved in some criminal enterprise way over his head," Jeremy explained.

Denyse put down the teacher's lesson plan she had been working on. "I'll go bring Trevor home."

"No, you probably can't just bring your brother home. Mom and Dad think he's being coerced into some illegal activity. Trevor would react to you and could expose them. He might even bolt."

"Why don't they just call the police and let them sort it out?"

"I asked them that. Criminals do terrible things when

they feel threatened. Mom and Dad are great friends of the police, but they know police can't protect everyone when bad guys want retribution. You remember that the police made them leave Minnesota for their own protection last year? And in this case, they suspect the hotel police might be dirty themselves. Do you want Trevor's throat cut or Mom's and Dad's?"

Denyse sat in stunned submission. "This is serious, isn't it?"

Jeremy nodded. "That's why they asked me to come help them."

"What? You just talked about people getting their throats cut and now you want to join them?"

"Trust me. Mom and Dad won't let their son near any danger." He described their cell phone monitoring system. "My job would be to call the police if Mom and Dad needed help. And I'm the only one of you Trevor doesn't know. But I'll have to use that week of vacation we had saved for when the baby comes."

"We'll manage somehow. Mum will come up to help me with the baby when we need her."

Beatrice directed her husband and daughter-in-law to the couch. "Sit down. I need to talk to you both."

"What's this about? Hogan will be expecting me at the body shop," complained Dingo.

"Then I'll get right to the point. Denyse called. The Parkers have found Trevor. And like Lena suspected, he's in some sort of trouble. Jeremy has gone to New Zealand to help protect his parents while they try to sort out the situation and contact Trevor."

Lena crossed her arms across her chest and bowed her head. She started to pray silently in gratitude and for protection for all of them.

Dingo jumped to his feet. "Protection? I can provide protection."

"But Trevor will recognize you, luv. He might run. This all has to be done on the hush-hush until the Parkers understand what to tell the police."

"Then what can I do?"

Lena still had her eyes closed in fervent prayer. In silence, Beatrice pointed at the girl and then her tiny son. Her lips silently mouthed, "Take care of your family."

For once Dave was enjoying a pleasant dream. He and Jeremy and Denyse trolled for king mackerel off of Alabama's Gulf Coast. His rod suddenly bent under a heavy load. Jeremy stopped the boat. Slowly Dave pulled his line in against the weight. His hook had snagged something. One last pull brought it to the surface. The dream became a nightmare as Katie's lifeless body looked up with uncomprehending eyes.

The vision startled him awake. Instantly, he could feel Katie's warmth and gentle breathing beside him. He lay in the darkness awake until morning.

Dave and Katie stood facing Jeremy, whom they had made sit on the bed. Dave spoke directly. "Okay, Jeremy.

Here are the rules. You're a kid again. Eight years old. And we're the parents. You'll do exactly as we say and no more. If you can't do that, then get back on the next jet to Sydney."

Jeremy sat transfixed. Katie spoke next. "We do know that you're an adult. As an adult, your first responsibility is to Denyse and your child. This could be a bad situation. We just don't want you to endanger yourself unnecessarily. But we really do need your help."

Jeremy had mixed feelings. They had just relegated him to eight years old again. On the other hand, how many parents ever asked their eight-year-old for help in such a difficult situation? In that regard, he had never felt so grown up.

He decided he felt more respected than chagrined. "Got it. You're the bosses. What's my job?"

"Thanks, son," said Dave. "Your job tonight is to listen on your cell phone while your mother is undercover."

"Mom is going undercover with criminals?" Jeremy interrupted, the same tendency he had as a boy.

Dave paid him no attention from long practice. "If she calls for help or is discovered, you'll call the police. She'll be in room 384. Have you got that?" After his son nodded, Dave continued, "Tonight she's going to give Trevor the first hint that she's here to help. We don't know how he'll respond. You'll sit here in the lobby with the cell phone to your ear. Watch the elevators. If you see Trevor running, call the police." Dave handed Jeremy a picture of Trevor and Lena.

"What would I tell the police?"

"Say that he's a fugitive or a shoplifter. Just get him

arrested, if you can. We don't want him to disappear again. While you're watching over your mother, I'm going to try following the money man's car. If I'm not back by eleven p.m—"

"I know. Call the police."

"You're catching on."

Jeremy sat in the hotel lobby. His cell phone rang. "I'm in the hall outside room 384 now, Jeremy," his mother's voice came to him clearly. "Mute your end on the phone. And stay listening as long as I'm inside."

"Okay."

Thunk, thunk, thunk. He heard knocking on the door and the door opening.

"Come in, Katie. We nearly started without you," a male voice said.

Jeremy heard his mother's voice answer, "Maybe my luck will be better tonight."

A dull hour of mostly monosyllabic poker playing followed. Occasionally, the routine would be broken by complaints about luck or groans over losses. The Australian voice that had admitted Katie seemed to be getting drunk and mostly losing. *That must be Trevor,* Jeremy realized.

After an hour, Trevor excused himself to the room's toilet. "Would you mind if I went first?" Katie's voice asked. "I'll only be a second."

Jeremy heard the toilet door close, a flush, then the door opened again. Apparently, Trevor had waited just outside the door. His mother's voice said, "Thank you. And Trevor, some friends of mine asked me to say 'Hello' to you. Their names are Lena and Denyse."

No response came back from Trevor. "Deal me in," Jeremy heard his mother say back at the poker table.

⸻

Trevor initially thought he had heard wrong. *Lena and Denyse?* How could this American woman know the names of his wife and sister? The distraction bothered him so much that he forgot his job and played by habit. Looking down he saw three thousand dollars more than he had started with. Losing the additional three thousand dollars on top of his regular loss took all his concentration the remainder of the evening.

At midnight, Katie excused herself from the game. "I've got a headache," she explained. "And I want to quit ahead one night. I'll see you tomorrow, if you're here." She looked Trevor directly in the eye. He twitched in uneasiness. The other players didn't notice.

Chapter Twenty

"Hey, this is like the vacation we took in the Smokies," said Jeremy when the Parkers convened back in their hotel room.

"You're a little tall for the couch now, though," his mother answered.

"I'll be fine on the floor. It's not much harder than the bed Denyse and I sleep in."

Dave ate another cookie from a nearby mini-mart, or as New Zealanders called it, a "dairy." "Wasn't the Smokies trip when you got poison ivy?"

Jeremy laughed. "I think I got poison ivy on nearly every outdoor trip."

"You figure out what the leaves look like yet?"

"I always knew. I just didn't pay much attention in the woods."

"What I recall," said Katie, "is when we all got food

poisoning on the way home from New Orleans. It started when Jeremy threw up in the back seat."

"I got as sick as Jeremy," Dave remembered. "You had to drive us all home."

"I didn't eat as much of that jambalaya from the street vendor as you two."

"Do you remember the day Dad caught the sailfish while trolling for king mackerel?" asked Jeremy.

"Remember? He still carries a picture of that fish in his wallet," Katie retorted.

They all laughed.

Jeremy tried to get more serious. "Who would have expected that someday we'd all be here in New Zealand trying to save my Aussie brother-in-law?"

Banter was Katie's element. "Who would have expected that someday we'd have such colorful in-laws? And I'm pretty certain that we owe both circumstances to you."

Dave, laughing, nearly choked on his last cookie. "Denyse is a winner, though, son. You made a great choice."

"So what happens next?" Jeremy asked after they all settled down.

"Did you learn anything following that guy?" Katie asked Dave.

"He went to a house a couple of miles away. Maybe that's where he picks up and delivers money. How did Trevor react when you mentioned Lena and Denyse?"

"Well, he didn't deny knowing them. And he didn't run either. He seemed distracted the rest of the evening. I think tomorrow we could try meeting him."

"How would we arrange that?" asked Jeremy.

Katie shared some ideas, after which they all discussed them. She went to bed, leaving Dave and Jeremy talking quietly at the room's couch and coffee table.

"Thanks for letting me help, Dad. This is exciting."

"Sorry I was a bit hard on you at first, son. Your mother and I need your help. And you're doing great. But we don't want to endanger you either. Our greatest hope is that you'll be around to be a wonderful husband to Denyse and good father for your children."

"I've got a great example to go by."

"Thanks. But that wasn't always true. You probably remember I wasn't around as much when you were younger. I had become obsessed with my business. I had even convinced myself that the reason I worked so hard was for you and your mother. Your mom helped me see that my excessive work hurt our family. 'Children are in your home only for a few short years,' she told me. Although they don't always seem like short years, she was right." Dave smiled. "Your mom and I together made the decision to put our family first. We got a babysitter for you and went out to a nice dinner. She had written up a little contract that we both signed over dessert. I framed the contract and hung it in my office for the rest of my years at the firm. And that's when we bought the boat. I'm encouraging you to make that same decision now, one I wish I had made sooner. You have the opportunity to make that commitment before your child is even born."

"Okay, I'll tell Denyse that we're buying a boat."

Dave could hardly stop laughing. He choked out, "You have your mother's quick wit. But you know what I mean."

"Yes, I do. Thanks, Dad."

Jeremy stretched out a very late morning breakfast in the hotel restaurant while he waited. *That's Trevor.* He recognized his brother-in-law as he entered and took a table. As Dave had predicted, the waitress brought Trevor coffee and a plate of food without taking an order. Jeremy sipped from his own coffee cup while staring at Trevor over the rim. Although Jeremy knew him to be five years younger than himself, Trevor looked older. *Maybe haggard would be a better description*, Jeremy thought.

After eating, Trevor laid money on the table and headed for the casino. Jeremy lingered a few minutes then drifted into the casino. He picked a slot machine where he could watch Trevor and look for the money man his father had described. At first Trevor slumped despondent over his own machine. When a tourist sat down nearby, Trevor tried to initiate conversation.

Two hours of dropping coins passed slowly. Finally, Jeremy identified an islander checking up on Trevor. After satisfying himself that Trevor was at work, the man wandered off elsewhere. Once the islander had gone, Jeremy shifted machines to sit near Trevor. "Maybe I'll have better luck over here," he announced to no one in particular.

"You must be an American," Trevor spoke to him.

"How can you tell? Do Americans usually have bad luck in Dunedin?"

"Nah. It's your Texas accent, mate. And Americans have used up their bad luck by not being Aussies."

"Oh, then I suppose Australians have used up their good luck."

At this retort, Trevor smiled. For a brief instant, he looked like the happy young man in Lena's picture. Trevor changed machines to play pokie next to Jeremy. "Where in the States are you from, mate?"

Jeremy dropped another coin. "I'm from Mobile. But I'm working in Sydney. I just came over here to get away from all the Aussies. I guess my bad luck isn't all used up."

At this, Trevor actually chuckled a little. "Mobile, that's in Texas, right?"

"Not hardly. The rest of us Americans are thinking about giving Texas to Australia. That would be bad luck for both places."

"You're alright, mate." Trevor gestured at the machine in front of him. "You know that these machines are set up to slowly bleed you to death. Playing against a machine is like playing tennis against a wall. You can't win. Would you be interested in a real game, a game where you might win?"

Jeremy glanced at him. "What kind of game?"

Trevor leaned forward and spoke softly. "Me and some other players get together in the hotel for old-fashioned face-to-face poker. Somebody wins. Somebody loses. The house doesn't get anybody's money."

"When?"

"Tonight about nine o'clock."

"I've got a date tonight. I can't make it. But maybe some other time." Jeremy held out a note. "But I've got a message for you, *Trevor*."

At the sound of his own name, Trevor froze. His eyes focused on the piece of paper before him. Taking it and turning away he read, *The woman in your game in room 384 represents Lena and Denyse. Tonight she will act like she's flirting with you. You should feign a romantic interest and follow her to her room. We are here to help you.* Trevor turned back, but the American had gone.

Dave waited in the lobby. Jeremy nodded to him as he passed out of the casino. Dave's eyes scanned the crowd, looking for Trevor. If Trevor tried to run, Dave planned to tackle him and accuse him of pick-pocketing. He had his own wallet ready to insert into Trevor's pocket, if necessary. But Trevor didn't appear.

"Now you don't want to be late on your first day at work, luv," Beatrice warned Lena. "Me and Vlady will be happy here until you return."

Lena pulled on her coat. "Thank you, Mama."

"I've asked Dingo to ride with you on the bus to make sure you don't get lost. Then he'll go on to his own job. Are you sure you can get home on your own?"

"Yes, Mama."

"Well, if you get lost, phone us. Dingo or I will come get you in the car."

Dingo held the door open for her.

"Thank you, Poppa."

"My, aren't you handsome tonight," Katie said for all to hear when Trevor admitted her to room 384 just after 9:00 p.m. The other players had already started the first hand. "You let them start without me? Naughty boy." She hit

Trevor on the bottom. A couple of the men glanced at each other.

As the poker play continued, Katie laughed and reacted to anything Trevor said. The men turned their heads to watch her lithe figure as she sashayed to the toilet. They were all surprised to see her return to the table with a drink. "Didn't you say you're an alcoholic?" a man who had played there on several nights asked.

"One little old drink won't hurt me," Katie assured them. But Katie kept returning to the bar. Each time she ran her hand across Trevor's shoulders. As she apparently got drunk, Katie chatted about the doctor she had recently divorced. She confided that he had never been much good in bed anyway.

Jeremy, listening on the cell phone, had never imagined his mother could be a temptress. Even knowing her to be acting made him feel uncomfortable. He was glad when she finally said, "That's all for me tonight, boys. Y'all might take advantage of a woman who's a bit tipsy."

Katie stood and headed for the door. Trevor stood up as well. "That's all for me too. The rest of you can play awhile longer. The last man out, please lock the door." As Trevor closed the door behind him, he heard raucous laughter from the game.

Katie put her arm in Trevor's and guided him to room 418. Inside the room, she dropped her inebriated act and closed the door behind them. "Trevor, Lena and Denyse sent me to help you." His apprehensive body language warned her to act fast. She handed him a photo. "Now, look at this proof."

Trevor looked at the family picture Jeremy had suggested taking at his flat. "Lena! Along with Denyse, and Mum, and Dad. How—"

"We found your wife up in Auckland. She's in Australia now."

Trevor looked at her in amazement. "Who are you?"

"Sit down and we'll talk." Katie pointed to the couch in the hotel room. "My name is Katie Parker." She pointed out Dave and Jeremy in the photo. "This is my husband, Dave. And this is my son, Jeremy." Trevor recognized Jeremy from the casino. Katie continued, "Now don't panic, Trevor, but Dave is going to come out. Dave!"

The closet door opened and Dave emerged. Trevor looked at the photo, which showed a smiling Dave standing behind Lena and Vladimir. A rapping at the hotel room door drew all their attention. Dave opened the door to admit Jeremy. "Did anyone follow them?"

"The poker game broke up a little after Trevor left. And no one followed him," Jeremy answered. "But I did see the guy you call 'the money man' talking with someone who looked like another islander. Then the first one left the complex. It was sort of like they were changing shifts."

"Nice work, son."

Jeremy saw Trevor and extended a hand. "Jeremy Parker. I'm Denyse's husband."

Trevor shook his hand. "Uh . . . Trevor Larkin. You're Denyse's husband?" All three Parkers nodded to him. "What are you? A team of detectives?"

Dave spoke for them all, "No, we're actually accountants.

Jeremy and I, anyway. Katie is a former school teacher. You've been missing for three years. Your family asked us to try finding you. After we found Lena, she prayed for us to find you. She thinks you're in trouble. And so do we. A mysterious man was even looking for you at Denyse and Jeremy's wedding. Now we need you to tell us what sort of trouble you're in."

Trevor tried to divert Dave. "How did you find Lena?"

"That's a long story, Trevor. But she was penniless in Auckland. Some bad men were trying to take advantage of her," said Katie. "She's safe right now. But we," Katie indicated herself, Dave, and Jeremy, "have gone to a lot of trouble and spent a lot of money plus put ourselves at risk to find you. Now you need to tell us what's going on. Start with when you left Lena in Auckland."

Jeremy sat entertained as he watched his parents work together interrogating the younger man. Both of them stood while Trevor sat. *This is just how they operated on me that time in high school I got caught cutting classes,* he remembered. *They took away my car keys for two weeks.*

Trevor looked from face to face and began, "I'm working on a business plan to provide tours for tourists Down Under that could—"

"Cut the bullshit, Trevor!" Dave broke in. "We've followed your trail all over Australia and New Zealand. You've hustled people everywhere you went. You'll be straight with us now, or we'll dial the police to sort out your little operation here while we're on the first jet back to America."

Next Trevor tried defiance. "What keeps me from just walking out that door?"

"Fine. Walk right on out," said Katie. "Isn't 111 the right number to dial for police services here in New Zealand? Then we'll call Lena to suggest she look for a new husband while you're in jail."

"Wait. Give me a minute to think." The Parkers waited quietly as Trevor considered what story he could give them. He remembered the photo. Finally the thought occurred to him that maybe he could trust them.

Trust didn't come easily to Trevor. He started hesitantly, "Please don't call the police. If I don't cooperate with these men, if anything goes wrong, they'll find Lena and my family to take revenge."

Actually, this is a bigger deal than when I cut some classes, Jeremy realized.

Chapter Twenty-One

Trevor sat quietly, then sighed. "Lena is the best thing that ever happened to me. If she had needed a heart transplant, I'd have donated mine. Marrying her made me happier than I had ever been. I played poker; sold some cars. She picked up a few temporary jobs and improved her English. We worked toward starting a business that could employ some of her brothers and sisters from Ukraine. Then we found out she would have a baby. Being pregnant with my baby thrilled Lena. The baby came early and needed medical care. We had to have sixteen thousand dollars fast. I came down here to Dunedin where I wasn't known. You can get money quicker when nobody knows how you operate.

"I won some money playing poker and making bets in sports bars. I sent what I had to Lena. Then an Asian man came to a poker game I had organized. He had plenty of money to throw around. Later he approached me in the hotel restaurant bar. He bragged about how smart he was. So I brought out this little game I play with circles. I beat him for a thousand dollars. Then I offered him double or nothing. He probably thought he could win once and break even if he kept doubling. I beat him five times and had the sixteen thousand dollars for our baby. As soon as I had the money, I quit playing and went to a bank where I got a cashier's check for Lena."

When Dave cleared his throat, Trevor stopped. "I know the circle game," said Dave. "You can't lose if you know the trick with binary numbers and the other guy doesn't."

Trevor nodded and resumed, "I kept playing poker here to get money for us to start somewhere new. A couple of men surprised me at the place I stayed. They tied me up and claimed I had cheated their boss, Mr. Wong. They demanded the sixteen thousand dollars back. They tried to burn it out of me, but I didn't have the money anymore." Trevor showed the burn marks. "While one of them burned me, the other searched my things. He found a picture of Lena in Auckland. From my passport, they discovered that I was from Melbourne. A few weeks later the Asian man showed me pictures of Denyse in a wedding dress and my family in Melbourne. He said that if I didn't work for him, they would hurt Lena and Denyse. I've been stuck here ever since."

They all waited in silence. Dave spoke first, "I think you've been the one hustled this time, Trevor. The circle game might work with high school kids, but a gangster would know better than play double or nothing five times. For sixteen thousand dollars, the Asian man, Wong, bought himself a slave."

"I had to have the money," Trevor insisted.

"He probably sensed that. Men like him can," said Katie.

"Who are the two men who watch you and give you money?" asked Dave. "They look like islanders."

Trevor pointed again to his partially healed burns. "They're the ones who beat me up and burned me. I think they're both Samoans. They go by Fetu and Rangi."

"And you deliberately lose the money each night to the man they tell you."

"Right. The money I take from the other players I recruit is supposed to repay the sixteen thousand dollars plus a thousand in interest a week. But I have to pay for everything at the hotel myself. I'm barely breaking even."

Dave looked Trevor in the eye. "Even if you somehow gave them the money, they would make up some reason to keep you working for them. That's the way gangsters work. Do you realize that the money you 'lose' is probably a payoff for something and money laundering combined?"

"I suspected it was something illegal."

"And the man who takes money in the restaurant?"

"That's the casino security chief. He knows I'm recruiting players on the pokie floor. He gets two thousand dollars a week. I don't know if he keeps the money for himself or represents someone. I don't think he knows about the other part."

"You mean the money laundering."

Trevor, sounding like his father, said "Yeeah."

Jeremy spoke up, "Why can't Trevor just go to the police and tell his story?"

"Several reasons, I think," Dave answered. "One, Trevor would be confessing to cheating a man for sixteen thousand dollars and also bribing the security chief. Those are both felonies, at least in the US. Two, Trevor's been involved in bigger crimes, money laundering and accessory to whatever that's tied to. Three, Trevor doesn't have any evidence to implicate anybody but himself."

"All true," Trevor added. "But the most important reason is that they would hurt Lena if I went to the police."

"She's completely safe in Australia," Jeremy protested.

Katie shook her head. "Nobody is completely safe when criminals want to hurt them." She sat down. "This is a mess. With this many crooks involved and the laws Trevor has broken, there will be no easy way out."

Late the next afternoon, both Samoans met Trevor in a dark corner of the casino to transfer the money to be laundered. "We hear you like older women," one taunted him. "Maybe you'd like my grandma."

"What makes you think I don't already know her?"

The Samoan who had spoken planted a fist on Trevor's cheek before he could duck. "You watch your mouth. You mess with us and you'll be looking for a new set of balls." The pair frisked him roughly, checking for hidden money or wires. Satisfied that he wasn't hiding anything, they pushed him away. "Get to work, you bloody worm."

Trevor turned away rubbing his cheek and walked back to his room.

One of the poker players arriving for the nightly poker game needled Trevor. "Where's your girlfriend tonight? She finally get lucky?"

Another player added, "She thinks she hit the jackpot already." All the men laughed. "Are you leaving early again tonight?"

Trevor smirked and shrugged. "Maybe."

Denyse picked up the phone to hear her husband greet her. "Hi, sweetheart," Jeremy said. "Everything okay at home?"

"Jeremy! Tell me what you're doing."

"Me? All I do is watch, listen, and be ready to call the police. But Mom and Dad have managed to contact Trevor." Jeremy described Katie's ruse and meeting her brother in the hotel room.

Immediately Denyse pressed for details about her brother. "How is Trevor? Does he look alright?"

"To tell you the truth, he looks pretty awful." Jeremy didn't mention the burn marks. "And he's in a lot of trouble. Some criminals are forcing him to work for them. They search him to make sure he's not hiding money or wearing a recording device. Tonight I saw one of them hit him."

"Where can I call him?"

"No! Don't do that, Denyse. And don't come here. The criminals somehow have a photo of you from our wedding. You wouldn't be safe. We even know that the casino police are cooperating with the criminals at some level. They're watching your brother and could monitor his calls. Trevor wants to phone Lena, but Mom and Dad won't let him. You should tell Lena that he loves her and will join her as soon as he can."

Tension brought tears to Denyse's eyes. "What about you?"

"I'll come home in three more days. Can you pick me up at the airport?"

"Of course. What will your parents do next?"

"They're not sure what to do. Dad is calling somebody in the States to ask advice."

"Jeremy, your parents are something else. I've never had anybody do anything like this for me. I'm really glad to get to know them."

"I'm sort of getting to know them myself right now."

Richard Christensen sat at his desk preparing notes for an arraignment hearing. "You have a call from Dave Parker," his secretary reported through the intercom.

"Put him through." Richard picked up the phone. "Dave! Glad to hear from you. How are things in Mobile?"

"Fine, I hope. Katie and I are in New Zealand."

"What are you doing down there?"

"We came for our son's wedding. But we ran into some difficulty. I hate to impose on you, Richard, but I really need legal advice related to some criminal activity we've found."

Richard listened carefully as Dave described the situation. "Wow! That's serious stuff. You and Katie really know how to find trouble, don't you?"

"No, we're just caught up in circumstances for only the second time in our entire lives. I spent most of my career managing financial books and trying to minimize taxes for businessmen. All we wanted to do here is attend our son's wedding." Dave paused before continuing, "I was thinking about approaching the police to ask immunity for Trevor. What do you think?"

"No, don't go to the police yourself. You don't have privilege. The national police of New Zealand can force you to talk or hold you in contempt. Once the court forced you to talk, the local police's crown prosecutor would likely start by indicting your son's brother-in-law. As a non-citizen, he's an easy target. Juries worldwide love to convict foreigners.

"You'll need a local lawyer who can hold Trevor's comments in privilege until the police agree to immunity. Even that is fraught with risk. Locals and their own police can be pretty tight. If you get the wrong attorney . . ."

"Richard, this is a lot to ask. Could you phone the New Zealand police for us and get some sort of feel for what they might do?"

"Dave, I could. But I'm just an American small-town DA to them. Here's a better idea. I'm tight with our FBI right now because of the work you started. And our FBI guys know what you did to break open the case in Minnesota. Let me ask our federal officers to call their counterparts in New Zealand. You say some of the thugs are Samoans? They could be American citizens. That gives our guys an excuse to call the national police down there.

"Here's what you should do: Make a recording of the kid's entire story to give to the FBI. Don't let him mention any names until granted immunity. Make sure he talks about his wife and her situation. That makes the situation an international threat. You send that recording to me. I'll review it and see what the FBI might do for you. If you get a chance, record the Ukrainian girl as well."

"Thanks, Richard. Sorry I didn't ask before, but how is the investigation going in Minnesota?"

DA Christensen laughed. "Criminals are falling like dominos here. But you and Katie still need to keep out of sight. Some thugs managed to post bail. Not the McReady cousins, but some other rough characters. They could do anything."

"How's the man I shot?"

"I hear he's breathing on his own now. It's rough, Dave. But don't feel any guilt. You only did what you had to do. The other cousin is cooperating for life without parole." Richard paused. "One last thing. Please don't tell anyone in the US that I'm helping you. Our local voters would want me concentrating on our own crisis. I'll wait for that recording."

Trevor left the game that night to catcalls and hoots. Inside room 418, he found Dave and Katie waiting for him. Jeremy slipped in a few minutes later and signaled, "All clear."

"You need to retell us the story you did last night." Dave positioned Katie's camera where it could pick up Trevor's voice, but not his image. "Once I hit *record*, you tell us everything since you met Lena. Include her account of escaping the human traffickers and you paying them. Then tell about the baby, you coming to New Zealand, the circle game, and being forced to work by the thugs and Mr. Wong. I may interrupt occasionally to ask questions. Don't make any personal descriptions or mention any names or places."

"Why not give those specifics?" asked Trevor.

"We want to get immunity in exchange for your testimony first."

"Who is this recording for?"

"The American FBI."

St. Paul's Cathedral

Chapter Twenty-Two

By the time Trevor had finished retelling his story and departed, Jeremy had fallen asleep on the floor. Dave used Katie's laptop to upload the recording to Dropbox and emailed the link to Richard Christensen. He and Katie looked at each other in exhaustion. "What now?" she asked.

"Richard won't get back to us for a few days. Starting tomorrow morning, you and I could take a twenty-four hour vacation."

Katie looked incredulous. "Take a vacation? Right in the middle of what's going on?"

Dave climbed into bed. "We've been stuck at this hotel for nine grueling days. And there's nothing more we can do until Richard gets back to us about the recording. We might as well look around the area of Dunedin. We're not likely to be here again."

"I don't expect to ever come back," Katie agreed as she started getting ready for sleep. "I just hate to neglect Trevor."

"Jeremy can watch over Trevor here at the casino. Leaving him in charge will demonstrate our confidence in him too. Come on, sweetheart."

Katie climbed into bed next to Dave. "I guess hanging around this hotel tomorrow wouldn't get us home to Mobile any sooner."

"Exactly."

After some sleep and explaining their planned leave of absence to Jeremy, Dave and Katie slipped out of the casino hotel. The hillsides surrounding Dunedin appeared yellow. Katie pulled over the rental car next to a patch of the flowers. They found a coarse plant covered with yellow blooms. Dave pointed to some yellow blossoms poking through some residual snow. "Not many plants bloom in the middle of winter."

The science teacher in Katie emerged. "I think this is gorse. The plant covers the hills in Scotland. I guess the early settlers transplanted some here. They really made Dunedin into a little Scotland."

As Katie resumed driving, Dave read in their guidebook, "The name 'Dunedin' is even Gaelic for Edinburgh."

Despite the damp cold, Dunedin's stone buildings exuded charming Scottish heritage. Fortunately, the intermittent drizzle held off while the couple explored The Octagon at the center of town. "The bronze statue is of the Scottish poet Robert Burns," Katie explained from the guidebook.

The Parkers admired the vaulted nave of St. Paul's Cathedral. Otago Museum nearby contained an impressive section on the original Maori culture as well as exhibits on New Zealand's unique natural history. "I had never known that New Zealand had no indigenous mammals other than bats and seals," Dave commented. "Australia by contrast has a cornucopia of odd native animals, but much less geological interest. Both countries are strange worlds compared to South Alabama."

"New Zealand has never been linked to any other land mass," Katie explained. "Two thousand miles of ocean is a long way to swim for most animals. The bats could fly. The seals swam."

For a late lunch, Katie selected a cozy café. The only soup available was pumpkin. "They like their pumpkin soup here, don't they?" said Dave.

"It's warm and filling," Katie answered. "But I sure could use a seafood gumbo or some jambalaya."

"Maybe we'll get home in time for Mardi Gras."

"You mean next year? Seven months from now?"

Dave admitted, "I spoke sarcastically. But who knows when we'll get home with these complications."

That night Jeremy surprised Trevor by opening the door to Dave and Katie's room. "Where are your parents?" Trevor asked.

"Dad sent your recording to somebody in the States." Jeremy waved Trevor inside. "He doesn't expect a reply for a few days. Mom and Dad needed some time to unwind. They went somewhere, sightseeing and another hotel, I think."

Trevor exhaled a long breath in relief. "Good. Your parents are pretty tough."

Jeremy laughed. "I've been where you sat a lot of times. Not in as serious trouble, of course. But Mom and Dad are tough. Growing up, I knew they would do anything for me except put up with nonsense. They're trying to do the same for you. Have a seat. Let's talk a bit as brothers-in-law." Jeremy sat down on the bed.

Trevor sat on the room's couch. "What do you think will happen here?"

Jeremy gestured uncertainty with his hands. "I have no idea. This is all beyond my experience."

"How's my sister doing?"

"Denyse is pretty eager to come over here and help you. But Mom and Dad have asked her to stay away for her safety." Jeremy then told about meeting Denyse, their life in Sydney, and even the fight at the wedding.

Trevor laughed at Jeremy's description of Denyse upbraiding them all. "My sister is a corker, alright."

"She takes after Dingo."

"The good parts anyway." Trevor's comment made Jeremy laugh.

The two young men continued talking about family and life. "I always wanted a brother," Jeremy confessed.

"My sister was like a brother to me. We stuck together. I'm glad she found a good husband."

Jeremy accepted the indirect compliment and said, "I don't understand how anything works."

"How what works?"

"Getting money from people. What you do."

"You mean hustling?'

Jeremy leaned forward in interest. "Maybe that's what it's called. You're what? Five years younger than me? But I wouldn't have any idea how to live the way you do."

"What I do is get people to act on their emotions, not their heads. Sometimes I make them react in anger. Other times I tell people what they want to hear, then add just a little more to my advantage." Trevor made a sour expression. "But this situation now is more than I can or want to handle. Mine is not a good life for having a wife and a baby. I wish that I could be like you with a job and a home for my family."

"Denyse and I are expecting a baby, you know?"

Trevor smiled. "No, I didn't know. But that's great. Congratulations. My sister will make a good mother. I myself hope to be a good father someday."

After a silent moment, Jeremy commented, "You're already a father. Lena and Vlady came to our flat when Mom and Dad brought them to Sydney. Everybody loves them."

Trevor didn't understand. "Who's Vlady?"

"Oh, that's the nickname your dad gave to little Vladimir. Your mother could hardly put him down." Jeremy continued to tell Trevor all about Lena and Vlady meeting the family. When he noticed a tear running down the younger man's cheek, Jeremy reassured Trevor about everybody's commitment to Lena.

"I appreciate you and Denyse taking care of Lena and Vladimir in Sydney. I'll pay you back when I can."

"Family doesn't need to pay family back. And Lena and Vlady are in Melbourne with your parents now."

Trevor stood up in alarm. "My son is with Dingo?"

"We know that he mistreated you, Trevor. But your dad promised to reform to care for Lena and Vlady. He got a full-time job in Melbourne. And he's committed to only two beers a day. That should keep him sober."

Trevor sat back down. "You're sure?"

"Everybody in the family thought we could trust him to keep his word."

"Is Mum there, Dad?" Dingo heard Denyse ask over the phone.

"Beatrice is working her shift at the hospital. Lena and Vlady are taking a nap."

"Well, tell them both that the Parkers have talked with Trevor. Like Lena suspected, he's in big trouble. Some criminals are forcing him to work for them. It's a bad situation. He can't phone because they could be listening. But Trevor sent a message to Lena that he loves her and will come when he can."

"Kiwis are holding Trevor against his will?"

"I guess you could put it that way. There are some rather nasty thugs involved. Jeremy saw one of them hit Trevor."

"I'll get on the next plane. I'll save my son."

"No, Dad. Dave and Katie are waiting for some legal advice from the United States."

"Bloody 'ell! What do the Yanks have to do with this? We can't depend on a bunch of frigging American lawyers. We need to stick up for our own blood."

"Stay out of this, Dad! For Trevor's sake, give the Parkers time. Goodbye for now."

Dingo slammed down the phone and stood fuming. *I need a beer,* he thought. He opened the refrigerator. *Blimey, we're out.*

Beatrice was going to bring some home with her.

A few hours later, the ringing phone woke Lena. Fearful that the noise would disturb her baby, she picked up the receiver. "Hello."

"Is this the Larkin residence?" a male voice spoke.

Lena could hear glasses clinking. "Yes."

"This is Joe, down at McGinty's Pub. Dingo is down here. We had all heard about his two-beer pledge. Then he came in an hour ago in a funk. He's been drinking steady ever since. Now he's threatening Kiwis and Yanks and criminals and anybody who looks at him funny. I've seen this trajectory before. We'll have a big fight in here before the night is over unless someone comes and gets control of him. If there's a fight, the police will arrest Dingo, and he's a repeat offender."

"I'll come." Lena hung up then took Vlady in her arms and started the mile-long trudge in a cold wind to McGinty's.

All the patrons' heads turned as a petite girl carrying a baby hurried into the pub. The baby started to bawl. Dingo stood holding a tankard of beer and berating anything and anybody that came into his mind. Every ear listened as she approached him. "Poppa, what are you doing here? Are you drunk, Poppa?"

"Yeeah, who cares?"

"I care, Poppa. And hear Vladimir cry. You made a promise. Will I need to move to Sydney to live with Denyse and Jeremy? I love you and Mama. And I want Vladimir to love you too."

The pub remained totally quiet as everybody waited. Dingo himself stood like a statue. "Trevor's son. Your grandson," Lena said and placed the crying baby in his arms.

No one made any sound as a tear rolled down the tough man's face. He put down the tankard and hugged the child to himself. He choked out, "I'm sorry Lena. I'll behave from now on. Let's go home. I'll carry Vlady." A smattering of approving applause started among the patrons. Dingo walked out the door to a chorus of voices cheering, "Good on ya, mate!"

The bartender, Joe, spoke to one of the customers at the bar. "Why don't you give them a ride home, mate? I'll save your stool." The man stood and followed them out the door.

Beatrice had arrived home to an empty house. Her heart ached in fear and frustration. A car pulled up from which her husband and Lena emerged and approached the front door. She met them on the front porch. Dingo handed Beatrice the baby and said, "Vlady crying in the pub nearly broke my heart. Can you comfort him?" He then walked inside and headed to the bedroom to fall sleep.

"Why did you go to the pub with the baby?" Beatrice whispered to Lena.

Lena explained the phone call. "Poppa could have been hurt or arrested."

"Was Dingo drunk?" Beatrice asked.

Lena only shrugged.

"You can go to Sydney to stay with Denyse and Jeremy if you feel you need to, luv."

Lena sat down. "No, I stay here with you. You heard Poppa say about the baby crying. I don't think he get drunk again."

"But why was the baby crying?"

"I pinch him."

Chapter Twenty-Three

"I listened to the kid's story you sent," Richard Christensen said over the phone. "Nice way you asked questions without leading him, by the way. Obviously, the young man makes his living as some sort of con man and hustler. Dave, are you convinced that he's not trying to pull something over on you?"

Dave answered from their overnight hotel room, "You're on speaker, Richard. Katie is listening, too. To answer your question, Trevor has visible burn marks, plus the girl and baby are real. Her story collaborates with his. I think Trevor is a small-time hustler who abandoned all caution to help the girl he loves. That got him in over his head. The check stub Lena showed us supports that."

"Well, he's not a very sympathetic victim," said Richard. "His testimony alone won't be worth much in a court. On cross examination, the defense would put him on trial. They could even make it sound like he abandoned his wife and baby. And as I had said, juries are eager to convict foreigners."

Katie spoke up, "Richard, we've learned about Trevor's background. He was mistreated as a teenager and ran away from home. He's just a mixed-up young man in trouble."

"If all that was explained in court, the trial would be even more about him rather than the criminals. I'm just making the point that the New Zealand police will see things pragmatically. They're going to insist on seeing hard evidence on the worst offenders. Otherwise the kid is an easy conviction for them."

"Are you suggesting that we try to collect some evidence?" asked Dave.

Richard spoke firmly, "Absolutely not! The kid's story indicates human trafficking, coercion, money laundering—certainly linked to something more sinister, and even police corruption. How these fit together, if at all, is unclear. Are you sure you don't want to throw in some international terrorism?"

Katie spoke again, "All we want is to send Trevor back to his family and go home to Mobile ourselves."

"Okay, then. No heroics. Or you could get killed this time. I'm having Trevor's story put into a transcript. This afternoon the FBI guys are coming in here for a planning session on our local cases. I'll talk to them about your situation. They understand better than I do how the Kiwis operate on different rules than we do in the States. You just sit tight. These things take time."

"Thank you, Richard."

Two days later, Denyse hugged Jeremy at the airport upon his return to Sydney. "Hugged" is an inadequate word. She squeezed him until he could hardly breathe. "Thank God you're home safe," she said. Jeremy transitioned the hug into a passionate kiss.

On their walk to the car, Jeremy displayed a young man's excitement after an adventure. "I wish you could have been there, Denyse. That was quite an experience. Mom and Dad were terrific."

"And you saw Trevor?"

"I talked to him. I liked him. Look at this." Jeremy pulled out his cell phone and thumbed up a selfie of him and Trevor together. "I took this when he and I talked alone."

Denyse stared at the picture while Jeremy put his small suitcase in their trunk then took his place behind the steering wheel. Tears brimmed her eyes. "That's Trevor, alright. He looks a lot older, though. What did you talk about?"

Jeremy started the car and headed toward their flat. "Oh, lots of stuff. He was alarmed when I told him that Lena and Vlady are in Melbourne with your parents. I assured him that your dad has reformed and won't get drunk anymore."

"Oops."

Jeremy glanced at his wife. "What's 'oops' supposed to mean?"

"Nothing really. Dad just feels useless and frustrated not being able to help. Mum told me that Dad fell off the wagon. But Lena straightened him out."

"Lena? How'd she manage that?"

"She pinched Vlady to make him cry and make Dad feel guilty."

"Jeremy laughed. "Lena pinched her own baby to trick your dad? She'll really fit into your family."

Denyse stared at her husband. "My family? What's that supposed to mean?"

⸻

Katie opened the hotel room door to admit Trevor. She couldn't miss the young man's look of disappointment.

"Where's Jeremy?" he asked.

"Jeremy needed to go back to Sydney. He said to tell you to hang in there."

Frustration emerged from Trevor. "Hang in there, for what?"

"Smart people are working on your situation," Katie told him.

"You mean the American FBI? Why would they help me?"

Dave put his hand on the young man's shoulder. "We don't know for sure if they will help, yet. But they're the best chance we know to keep you out of prison."

Trevor shook off Dave's hand. "Why would I go to prison?"

"New Zealand authorities could see you as laundering money, abetting a criminal enterprise, and even bribing a public official. You'll need to be patient. Just keep doing whatever your handlers say. Don't do anything to arouse their suspicion."

Trevor stood in sullen silence. Katie addressed him, "We're going to disappear for a few days while our contacts in American law enforcement try to communicate with New Zealand's national police. The more Dave and I hang around here, the greater chance someone will wonder what we're doing and associate us with you. We don't even know who all might be involved here at the casino. If anybody at the poker game asks about me, you can say that I've joined a tour group to see New Zealand."

Dave interpreted Trevor's continued silence as acquiescence. "Once we learn something, Katie will reappear in the casino. We'll keep up the paramour act. If there's an emergency, you can reach us at this number." He extended a slip of paper with Katie's cell phone number. Trevor grimly took it from him.

"What did you mean about my family?" Denyse repeated to Jeremy.

"Come on, Denyse. Surely you've got to admit that the Larkins are a bit dysfunctional."

"What about me?"

"You're a Parker now."

Anger tinged Denyse's voice. "Oh, and the Parkers are so perfect, I suppose."

Jeremy parked the car in their garage. He tried to flatter his way out of the brewing situation. "Well, I think you're pretty perfect."

"No, what you think is that the perfect Parkers are riding to the rescue of the Larkins like the cavalry in your American western movies."

Jeremy felt his own ire rising. "That's what's happening, isn't it?"

"Now I understand why Dad got drunk!" Denyse slammed the passenger side car door and stomped up the steps. Once inside, Jeremy found the door to their bedroom closed.

In a local neighborhood north of Dunedin, Katie and Dave found a small shopping area. A dozen shops included three fish-and-chip places. They chose a restaurant run by an oriental family, open 365 days a year. For about four dollars a person, each of them received a large slab of fried hoki and a huge serving of hot French fries wrapped in yesterday's newspaper. "This is convenient," commented Katie. "There's plenty to eat and something to read as well."

"I saw an ocean-side campground by the road. Let's take our food there," Dave suggested.

The campground, nearly empty in winter, offered a few efficiency cabins for lodgers. Dave and Katie selected a cabin close to the ocean. Periodic rain and sleet showers tinkled on a metal roof. Waves crashing onto the shingle beach tumbled stones over each other, creating a clicking noise. The sounds of heavy surf mingled with the clicking noise sounded odd to the Alabamians. "What a wonderful place to hole up for a few days," said Katie.

Katie dialed Jeremy's number in Sydney to tell him where they would be. Dave caught a hint of sympathy in her tone as she responded to something Jeremy said. "What's wrong?" he asked after she hung up.

"Oh, Jeremy and Denyse are having a tiff. She isn't speaking to him right now."

Dave sighed. "What next?" Then he added, "What was the fight about?"

"All the Larkins are feeling left out of our efforts for Trevor. They feel the Parkers are running the family now. They're understandably frustrated."

Dave responded with some frustration of his own. "Then

let's tell them where to find Trevor and go home. In two days I can be fishing on the Gulf."

"You know that we can't do that." Katie sighed and suggested a diversion. "We haven't been on a walk in a long time."

"It's freezing out there."

"Not as cold as Minnesota, though."

"Okay, after we eat our fish and chips. Pass the vinegar. They smell great."

Trevor sat in front of a pokie machine. *Dave and Katie treat me like a child. They won't even let me call Lena. And now they've abandoned me here. They're probably telling Lena that I'm a criminal, to forget about me.*

Gamblers passed without noticing the young man simply sitting. *What happened to my life?* Trevor asked himself. He remembered trying to live with Dingo. *Now Dingo has Lena and my son. Does Lena know why I didn't come back to Auckland? Does she believe that I still love her? Will my son ever know I love him? I've got to get word to her. I can outsmart those Parkers.*

Trevor left the casino floor to return to room 384. With a hotel ballpoint pen and stationary he found in a drawer, he scratched out a note:

Dear Lena, I think of you and little Vladimir constantly. You are my reason for living. I will join you as soon as I am able. All my love forever. Trevor

Trevor next checked his financial resources. $1,163. He

folded the note around ten one-hundred-dollar bills and sealed them in an envelope furnished with the stationary. Then he addressed the envelope to Lena Larkin and used his parents' address. *Nobody can trace this to me without a return address,* he thought. In the hotel gift shop, he purchased an international stamp, affixed it, and carried it to the hotel's front desk. "Would you place this in the outgoing mail, please?"

"Certainly, sir," responded the desk manager.

Trevor returned to the casino with a lighter heart and renewed purpose. *I need to get more money to free myself and to send Lena.*

⸻

The hotel desk manager dialed an internal number. "Sir, the man you instructed me to watch just left an envelope at the front desk."

"Bring it to me, please."

Inside the Security Department, the desk manager entered the chief's office.

"Close the door behind you," the chief ordered. With the door closed, he looked at the address, ripped open the envelope, read the note, and counted the money Trevor had enclosed. Separating out five hundred dollars, he handed it to the desk manager. "Good work. Keep watching."

Chapter Twenty-Four

"Don't you feel better now?" Katie asked Dave as they walked along the rocky shore next to the turbulent ocean. A cold drizzle fell in temperatures near freezing.

"Surprisingly, I do feel better," he answered. "Even though I'm miserable in this weather. Minnesota in a blizzard didn't feel this cold."

"That's because you stayed inside in front of a warm fire."

"I wish I was there now."

"In Minnesota?"

"No, in front of a warm fire. Let's get back to the cabin."

Katie's cell phone rang as they entered the cabin. "Katie, this is Richard Christensen. I just wanted you and Dave to know that the Feds have forwarded the transcript to their counterparts in New Zealand. Remember this in case it comes up: The kid in question is now an official informant of the FBI. That gives our guys some latitude to protect their source and strike a deal."

"Thank you so much, Richard. This may be our best chance to help."

Katie told Dave what Richard had said. He had already stripped off his wet clothes and started tinkering with the cabin's propane heater. "Won't this thing burn hotter?"

"What should we do about Denyse and the Larkins?" Katie asked while changing into dry clothes.

Dave had given up on the heater. Instead he turned on the oven and left the door open. "You mean besides bailing out?"

"Precisely."

"Why don't you call Denyse with the news from Richard? Maybe that conversation will suggest something."

Denyse answered on the second ring. "This is Katie; I have some good news. The American FBI is sending Trevor's story to their counterparts in New Zealand. They're talking to the Kiwis on our behalf. We hope that leads to an offer of immunity for Trevor."

Denyse politely thanked her mother-in-law and remained otherwise silent. "I heard you and Jeremy had a disagreement," Katie prompted.

"Jeremy really hurt my feelings. But it could have been mostly what you told me before about new husbands not thinking before they speak."

"What did the stinker say?"

"He called my family dysfunctional. Even when Mum and Dad are trying so hard."

"Jeremy was insensitive. I've already told you how clueless young husbands can be." Denyse forced herself to laugh. Katie first laughed with her, then probed deeper. "Denyse, how do you feel about the situation with us and Trevor?"

Denyse spoke with emotion. "I feel useless. And I feel left out. We've hoped to find Trevor for so long. Now he's been found. You, Dave, and Jeremy—all the Parkers—have talked to him. But me, Mum, and Dad—all the Larkins—can't. Even Lena can't talk to him."

"You know that we're trying to protect your brother and your family in a dangerous situation?"

"Yes, I know." Denyse's voice softened. "I've even stopped Dad from flying to New Zealand and barging in. I just wish that I had something to do to help."

Katie had an idea. "Maybe there is something you could do."

Denyse sounded hopeful. "What's that?"

"Our American advisor thinks that the New Zealand authorities will also be interested in Lena's story involving human trafficking. You could research that angle and get her story. Your work could be part of the immunity deal for Trevor. His helping Lena the way he did might even earn him more sympathy from potential prosecutors."

"Could I get Mum and Dad involved, too?"

"Sure."

Jeremy woke up in the night on the mattress in their spare bedroom. His body ached. Previously he had thought the thin mattress on his and Denyse's bed to be hard. The floor mattress had been much worse.

The glow of a computer screen from downstairs attracted his attention. He walked down and found Denyse there staring intently at the screen. She had heard him descending the stairs and spoke without looking at him. "Did you know that human trafficking is a two-hundred-billion-dollar-a-year business? Sex trafficking affects four and a half million people, most of them young women. Debt bondage is the most widely used method to capture these girls. Human traffickers cruise areas of economic hardship and promise legitimate jobs to attractive girls. They especially look for girls who are of legal age but look younger. Proving coercion of legally aged girls is difficult. But once the girls are removed from their families and transported to another country, their identification is taken away. Then they can be locked up, beaten, forcibly addicted to drugs, and compelled to serve as prostitutes. Organized criminals can generate several thousand dollars a day from just one attractive girl."

Jeremy leaned over to look at the computer screen. "No, I didn't know that. And you mean that's true even here in Australia?"

"And in America."

Jeremy stood back erect. "Listen, Denyse, I'm sorry for what I said."

She turned from the screen to look at him for the first time. "You're sorry, alright." Her smile conveyed forgiveness.

"I won't be so stupid again."

Denyse turned back to the screen. "That's not true. But according to your mother, you will get better."

Jeremy patted her on the back in acknowledgement. "So why are you researching human trafficking?"

"Katie gave me an assignment. We're going to see what we can find out about Lena's experience. Your parents' American friends think Lena's story might help convince the New Zealand police to accept Trevor's immunity deal."

The casino security chief approached the two Samoans during their shift change. "I thought you'd want to know that we intercepted a message from the Larkin hustler in 384." He handed them the envelope and note.

The two men looked at the note then the addressee. One said, "This must be his girlfriend. The envelope gives her the same name, Larkin. Maybe they're married now. Even under persuasion he wouldn't tell us where to find her. She's gone to Melbourne. Makes sense. He's an Aussie." He recorded the address in a ledger.

The other Samoan spoke to the security chief. "Anything else come in this envelope?"

"No, that note was all."

"Alright, Mr. Wong will appreciate knowing this." He returned the note with envelope and counted out a thousand dollars for the security chief.

"Mum, this is Denyse. I'm working on a project that might help Trevor come home. Would you help?"

"Of course, luv. But what could I do?"

"I want you and Dad to talk to Lena. Find out all about her life before going to New Zealand, how she came, and about the men who deceived and wanted to use her. Record what she says and send the recording to me. I'll call her with additional questions later."

"How will this help Trevor?"

"Trust me, Mum."

After Denyse hung up, Beatrice summoned Lena and Dingo. "We need to ask you some questions, luv," she explained to Lena. "Denyse thinks you can help Trevor. I'll video you on my cell phone."

A few hours later Denyse answered a return phone call from Beatrice. Her mother could barely contain her excitement at having learned so many key details of Lena's story. "Lena's father was a farmer killed during their civil war. Because the family was ethnically Ukrainian living in an area taken over by pro-Russians, Lena, along with her mother and five younger brothers and sisters, fled to western Ukraine and became refugees. There are no jobs for unskilled farm workers in Ukraine, especially women.

"Men came to the refugee camp looking for especially pretty blond girls to take 'housekeeping' or 'nanny' jobs outside Ukraine. Because she's good with children, they promised Lena a nanny job in New Zealand. She suspected that they had more sinister motives, but she felt like she had no other choice. As the oldest child, she thought maybe she could get a foothold for her family in a country with more opportunities. So she signed a contract like an indentured servant. That's how she came to New Zealand.

"The men had paid for a Ukrainian passport, a New Zealand tourist visa, and her airline ticket. Lena was willing to work hard as a nanny. But once she left Ukraine, she overheard the men offering her for sale to work in a brothel. They then sold her contract to some pimps in Auckland. Even street prostitution is legal in New Zealand, you know. But before those men could make her do anything, she mingled in with a tour group leaving immigration at the airport. Then she ran and hid from the men who had bought her contract. But that left Lena in a strange country with poor English and no money, job skills, or work visa. She got a series of menial, revolting, and dangerous jobs and stole food to survive. Lena kept hiding and slept in parks at night until she met Trevor. He rescued her and paid eleven thousand dollars for the contract from the pimps. After Trevor disappeared, the men came back again and tried to force her to work for them as a prostitute.

"I recorded lots more, luv. Dingo asked Lena most of the questions."

"This is wonderful, Mum," Denyse responded. "Can you Dropbox the recording to me?"

"I don't know how to put this on Dropbox."

"Go to the computer, Mum. I'll walk you through it."

Four days later, Dave and Katie had turned on the speaker phone in the cabin to listen to Richard. "The Kiwi police are interested in what Trevor and his wife, Lena, have experienced. But they've gotten reports about an Australian hustler working bars and casinos from several places in New

Zealand. They think your Trevor could be the guy. So the current situation withstanding, they're pretty interested in getting their hands on your boy. If they do, there'll be plenty of eyewitnesses to identify him."

"So, there'll be no immunity deal?" said Dave.

"No, I didn't say that. Here's the deal they suggested through the FBI. Trevor must fully cooperate, and that includes some sting operations to get evidence. He has to be willing to testify, although I doubt the crown prosecutor would use him that way in a criminal trial. We also forwarded the related report about human trafficking and Lena's personal story your daughter-in-law, Denyse, compiled. The Kiwis also want cooperation and testimony from the Ukrainian girl about her experience as part of the deal. I think that report tipped the balance to make the Kiwis agree to an immunity they found distasteful and were reluctant to accept."

Dave paced back and forth while listening to Richard. "Okay, and what happens to Trevor?"

"I'm getting to that. The New Zealand police also contacted the Australian police since he's their citizen. Rugby rivalry aside, the two countries work pretty closely together. Still, the Aussies don't like the idea of one of their citizens incarcerated or detained a long time in New Zealand. They proposed that Trevor confess to a couple of charges to which he could easily be proved guilty. Then Trevor gets ten years of probation to be served in Melbourne and immunity for the other charges. If he's caught hustling in either New Zealand, Australia, or any other Commonwealth country, he goes to jail in New Zealand to serve the remainder of his time without probation."

"Wow! That's pretty tough, Richard."

"From what the FBI tells me, crown prosecutors Down Under don't give free passes as part of plea bargains. They're being lenient by their standards in cooperation with our FBI. And if Trevor is willing to be cooperative, this should keep him out of prison and get him home in one piece."

Richard's tone of voice became more persuasive. "Dave, our American legal system is more rights-based than theirs. Probable-cause limitations aren't as strict Down Under as in the States. Just knowing that your kid could be the key to a big case, they'll start seriously looking for Trevor. And the Kiwis will probably find him in a hurry. It's their island, you know."

"What should we do next?"

"You'll still need a lawyer licensed in New Zealand to make the immunity agreement with Trevor binding on the police. I made a few calls for you. Aarav Kapoor is a barrister in Dunedin and a stickler for details. The Kiwi authorities respect him. But Dave, he wants a fifty-thousand-dollar retainer in New Zealand dollars. That's about thirty thousand in US currency. From what I hear, he'll be worth it. The police detective whom Barrister Kapoor should contact is Malcolm Fraser in Dunedin. They probably already know each other. And Sergeant Fraser participated in the talks with the FBI."

Katie spoke for the first time. "God bless you, Richard. How can we ever thank you?"

"You've already done plenty for me. And I love bringing justice where it's needed. Just remember to not mention my name. My voters don't live Down Under and are focused on local affairs." After goodbyes, the Minnesota DA hung up.

Dave stopped pacing and sat down. "This is turning out to be an expensive wedding."

Katie sat next to him and put an arm around his back to squeeze him. "If Jeremy had been a daughter rather than a son, her wedding in Alabama would have cost us as much. And now we have a daughter, and soon a grandbaby too."

⸻

Trevor stared at the pokie machine, daydreaming about himself and Lena walking on a warm, sandy beach. In his thoughts, Vlady toddled behind them, stooping to pick up bits of seashell or debris tossed up by the waves. *Don't put that in your mouth*, he imagined Lena telling their son.

A hand caressing his neck made Trevor turn around. "I'm back, big boy." Katie kissed him on his cheek. "And I'm in the same room. You remember 418. See you tonight?"

"Uh, sure," he managed.

"I'll be waiting."

Chapter Twenty-Five

"Come right in, big boy." Katie spoke seductively and held the door open for Trevor. She closed it immediately after him.

A slightly built and dark-skinned Indian man waited inside. His suitcoat remained buttoned over a conservative red tie. "Are you Mr. Trevor Larkin?" Trevor nodded in response. "I'm Aarav Kapoor," the man continued. "I've been retained by Dave and Katie Parker to be your barrister. Won't you please sit down?" He waved toward the couch.

Once Trevor had seated himself, the barrister drew a chair closer. "Mr. Larkin, a lot of people have been working on your behalf. Even the American FBI has intervened for you. The New Zealand police have reviewed the transcript of the recording you made and also a summary of the experiences of a Lena Travnikov, whom I understand to be your legal wife. Local authorities have made what I believe to be a generous offer to secure your cooperation." He opened a file and outlined the conditions.

When Aarav Kapoor mentioned Lena's cooperation, Trevor balked. "No, I won't have Lena involved."

"Don't you want those who victimized her brought to justice?" the barrister appealed. "And this offer is contingent on cooperation from both of you."

"Leave Lena out of this," Trevor insisted.

The barrister looked at Katie. She had anticipated Trevor's reaction. Without comment, Katie dialed on her cell phone and handed it to Trevor. A girl's voice answered. "Trevor is that you? I love you."

"Lena! Where are you?"

"I'm here with your mama and poppa in Melbourne. They have been so good to me and Vladimir. We all know you are in trouble. I want to help you. I will happily cooperate with the police. Do what this man called Aarav Kapoor tells you to do. He can bring us all together again."

"How is Vladimir?"

Lena laughed. "He is getting fat. Your mother spoils him too much, I think. Your father is good to him too."

Katie gently took the phone from Trevor's hands. "I know this seems cruel. But we have important business to do right now."

"I love you and Vladimir," Trevor shouted before Katie said goodbye to Lena.

A tapping at the door drew their attention. After checking through the view port, the barrister opened it to admit Dave. "One of the Samoans followed Trevor here," Dave reported. "But he left when he saw Katie open the door. We need to be even more careful."

Katie dialed again and handed Trevor the phone. "Trevor, you need to follow the Parkers' advice," Denyse demanded.

"Is that you, Sis? I've missed you so much."

"I've missed you too, Trevor. And now we need to bring you home."

"But they want to involve Lena in their evidence gathering."

"She's ready. Lena would do this even if it didn't affect your immunity. Other Ukrainian girls are being victimized. Terrible things are happening. You and Lena can help to stop them. Maybe something good can come out of this."

"Alright. I'll do it. And your husband, Jeremy, is a stand-up guy, by the way."

"Thanks, and we all love Lena. She and Vlady have made a big difference in Dad."

Katie gently took the phone away again. The barrister restarted, "As I said, the offer is a generous one. If you accept, I'll need your signature on this agreement." He handed Trevor a document. "As your barrister, I'm required to warn you that once I file this with the New Zealand authorities, you can't back out. Because they have acted in good faith, the police could arrest you and charge you for various crimes should you fail to keep your bargain. But, on the other hand, if you fully cooperate, you should be home in Australia with your family in a few weeks."

Trevor signed the agreement and handed it back.

"Thank you. Now that's just the first step. Our next step will be to document everything for which you will receive immunity." Aarav Kapoor took out a recorder. "I need you to tell me everything you've done that even might be illegal since first arriving in New Zealand. Tell me every hustle, every con, every payoff, everything you can remember. If you've committed any crime and try to keep it secret, immunity won't apply to it. You could still be charged for that separately."

Trevor reached into his pocket and pulled out a stick drive. "Fortunately, I have a record of my activities. Can I use somebody's computer?"

The first light of dawn had started to break over the ocean when Trevor finished. Although Dave and Katie had dozed off, the barrister remained sharp and attentive. He summed up, "Now go back to your routine, Mr. Larkin. Don't do anything to draw attention to yourself. We'll meet again—not tonight, but probably the night after."

When Trevor returned to Katie's room the second night, he found two men waiting with her. Aarav Kapoor introduced the second man. "Mr. Larkin, this is Sergeant Fraser of the New Zealand police. He'll be supervising the investigation."

A short, rotund man in his mid-forties stepped forward to shake hands. "G'day, mate. Call me Malcolm." His jolly, round face broke into a big smile revealing uneven teeth. "Trevor, I've been reading the agreement drawn up by your lawyer. I'm afraid there's one item we just can't give you immunity on." The Kiwi police officer let his words hang in the air. "You'll still have to pay the fine for that littering ticket up in Auckland."

Trevor looked at his barrister, not knowing how to react. Even the dour barrister had smiled at the policeman's surprise jest. Aarav Kapoor regained his professional demeanor. "I've worked with Sergeant Fraser in the past. He's crazy and drives a hard bargain. But he will honor our agreement unless you fail to cooperate. And he has not only the interests of the law at heart, but genuinely wants to get you back to your wife and baby as soon as possible."

"Hey, we're all on the same side now," said Malcolm. "And young fellow, having learned about your litany of escapades, believe me when I say that I want to be on the same side as you. Just tell me one thing, though. How did you become an informant for the American FBI?"

"Don't answer that, Mr. Larkin," Barrister Kapoor interrupted. "Nice try, Sergeant. You'll get the whole story after my client is free to leave New Zealand."

Malcolm shrugged and returned such a guilty grin that all had to smile again.

Dave's entering through the door drew everyone's attention. "All clear," he announced. "What are all of you smiling about?"

Rather than explain, the barrister said, "Then I'll slip out. Mr. Parker, you still have some money in retainer. If you need me, do call. Otherwise my presence could draw unnecessary attention to the operation. No more tricks, Malcolm?"

"You have my word, Aarav."

Left alone with Trevor and the Parkers, the policeman eyed the hotel-furnished coffee pot. "I could make us some coffee," he suggested.

"Malcolm, while I appreciate your effort to not be sexist, I don't mind making the coffee," Katie offered.

"Thank you, madam," he responded with an exaggerated French accent. "Jolly good then. Let's sit down. And Dave and Katie, the FBI knows you and spoke highly of your abilities. You're welcome to participate as observers and consultants."

Dave sat with Trevor on the couch facing Malcolm in a chair. "Now as I understand it, two Pacific Islanders, perhaps Samoan, are your handlers. And they apparently report to a man they call Mr. Wong."

"That's right," answered Trevor. "They call themselves Fetu and Rangi."

"Could you identify this Mr. Wong?"

"Yeeah, I think so."

Suddenly Dave had an idea. "Katie and I might have a picture of him." While Katie served the coffee, he shuffled through their notes and produced a photo, which he handed to Malcolm hopefully. "This man was looking for Trevor in Melbourne."

The policeman looked at the photo and shook his head. "I don't recognize him." Then he spoke to Trevor, "Make sure you look closely and be certain before you speak." He handed the photo to Trevor.

"Nope, that's not Mr. Wong." Neither Trevor nor Malcolm noticed Dave's hopes deflate.

"You're certain?" Malcolm reasserted.

"That's not him."

Malcolm looked at Dave. "You say that this man was seen in Australia?" To Dave's affirming nod, he offered, "We could send this to the Aussies to run a facial recognition program on him. After the 9/11 terrorist attacks in New York, the Americans came up with some truly amazing technology. Do you have the original picture in electronic form?"

"Sure." Dave located the original photo on Katie's laptop.

Malcolm looked at the photo closely. "Wait a minute; this looks familiar. This is from that fight at the wedding where the bride tackles some old guy. The video went viral. What a hoot! Have you seen that clip, Trevor?"

"No, I don't think so."

Malcolm took the laptop and connected to the online clip. He moved to sit beside Trevor. "See the guy take a sucker punch? Then the bride tackles him."

Malcolm and Trevor sat chuckling as they watched. Suddenly Trevor said in surprise, "That bride is my sister, Denyse!" He pointed at the screen. "And there's my dad."

"Then the old guy would be . . ." Both Malcolm and Trevor looked up at Dave.

In spite of himself, Dave had to smile. "Yes, that's me."

Katie stood apart observing. *Malcolm is trying to establish a bond with Trevor. He wants a willing participant, not just reluctant cooperation.*

The two continued to tease Dave. "What were you thinking?"

"Apparently not anything," he played along.

After some more laughter, Malcolm got back to business. "Trevor, together we're going to try and take down some bad guys. Are you with me?"

"Sure."

"What we'll need to do first is track the islanders and

hope they lead us to this Mr. Wong. Then maybe we can establish his identity."

Trevor obviously relished being a confidant. "Will you have somebody tail him?"

"Nah! That's just in old movies. Nowadays we put a GPS position-locating device under their car bumper."

"What do you want me to do?" All noticed Trevor's eagerness to cooperate.

"For right now, you just keep up your routine. Don't do anything different that might make them suspicious." Malcolm noticed Trevor's disappointment, then added, "But I understand from Dave and Katie that you're a good actor. Let's talk about some ways we can leverage that to our advantage."

Chapter Twenty-Six

The casino security chief sat down at Trevor's breakfast table. "Let's have the money, Larkin."

Trevor shook his head. "It's too much. I'm not clearing enough to pay down my debt."

"I'm tired of this. I'll tell the Samoans that you're causing more trouble. Too bad. I see your burns are almost healed."

"What do you do with the money, anyway? Do you keep it all yourself?"

"None of your bloody business. Just know that I'm the one that looks the other way so that your little operation can continue. And this argument is going to cost you an extra five hundred."

"You can't do that. I'll tell Mr. Wong."

"Go ahead and tell him. You think Mr. Wong cares about your sorry ass? He could snap his fingers and somebody you know would disappear. Your sister or maybe that little blond girlfriend of yours."

"Wait, I'll give you the two thousand dollars. But could you maybe forget about the extra five hundred?"

"Not a chance. And remember that plenty of people are watching you."

Trevor hid the money under a napkin and slid it over the table. After the security chief left, Trevor paid for his breakfast and stopped by the hotel gift shop on his way to the casino. Nobody noticed him laying down the police's radio transmission device or Dave picking it up.

"You did great baiting the security chief, Trevor," said Malcolm when they met that night in Katie's room. "We've got him on tape admitting bribery, threatening you, and implicating Wong. Now we need to try to get the Samoan thugs to incriminate themselves."

"They frisk me all the time," Trevor warned.

"Then we'll need to get you the device after you're frisked."

Trevor approached the two Samoans during their shift change in the hotel lobby. "I need to talk to both of you."

"You know what to do first," Fetu, the night shift man, said. Trevor stepped into a secluded corner, held up his arms, and turned around to be frisked. "He's clean."

Trevor walked back to the more public area of the lobby followed by the Samoans. "As I was saying, I need to talk to both of you. We have a problem."

"You'll have another problem if you hassle the security chief about payment again."

"That's not what I mean. But couldn't you get him to reduce that charge a little? I'll never get my debt paid off."

"Again, your problem, not ours."

Katie passed by dressed for the hotel spa. "Hi, big boy." She approached to kiss Trevor on the cheek and rub her hand up and down his waist. "Sorry for interrupting," she said to the Samoans. "See you later, Trevor." The three men watched her walk away.

Both Samoans sneered at Trevor. "Still lusting for old women, huh?"

"Why don't you guys give me a night off? Then I could go to town and meet your younger sister."

Rangi looked around to see if any hotel patrons were watching. When none were evident, he stomped on Trevor's toes. "I warned you about that smart attitude."

Trevor lifted his foot in pain. "Take it easy, guys. I'm here to help you."

"What do you want, maggot?"

"I want five thousand dollars off my debt for saving your asses."

"How are you going to save us?"

"Last night you gave me six thousand dollars to lose to the Malaysian guy."

"So what?"

"After the game, he stayed behind and claimed he was due seven thousand dollars. He said he was going to tell Mr. Wong that you're skimming the payments. He said that the other mules are also going to complain."

Fetu looked at Rangi with suspicion. "Rangi, I swear that if you're doing something that could get me killed—"

"No. Look at the records." Rangi pulled a ledger book out of the satchel he carried. "See, the book clearly says six thousand dollars."

"But you wrote in the entry."

"Listen," Trevor interrupted, "you knock five thousand off my debt, and I'll convince Mr. Wong that I lost the entire seven thousand dollars to the guy. He'll think the drug mules are trying to pull a fast one."

"How did you know they were carrying drugs?"

"The Malaysian said the risk for carrying drugs is too high to be shorted payment by a couple of fish heads."

"He called us fish heads?"

"Yeeah. I know that you eat fish heads. But I would never call you that. Because I know that you would hurt me and my family."

"You're right about that. That's how we keep scum like you in line."

"Maybe you could threaten the Malaysian's family. Better yet, you could kill him. He's probably out spending the money on booze and hookers."

"He wouldn't be the first we killed."

"Do the records show any other discrepancies?" Trevor asked. "Could I look?" Rangi handed the ledger to Trevor, who scanned the entries and said, "Wait a minute. There could be a lot of problems here. Mr. Wong isn't going to like this. Let's go up to my room where you'll have privacy to call him and straighten things out. Better that you speak to him before the others."

"Alright."

"Don't forget. I want five thousand dollars off my debt."

"You'll settle for us letting you and your pretty girlfriend live."

A ringing phone interrupted Lee Wong during his meditation. He answered with irritation. "Who is this?"

"Mr. Wong, this is Fetu at the casino. We haven't been skimming off the money you gave us for the drug mules. If the Malaysian has already talked to you, he's lying."

"What? Nobody has talked to me about skimming."

"That's good. Because we've got the books to show. We can prove that we passed on every dollar you gave us."

"And how would you prove that?"

"We've got the Larkin hustler right here. He can back us up."

"Put Larkin on."

Fetu handed the phone to Trevor, who spoke fast with a tone of urgency. "Mr. Wong, I want you to know that if you'll let me be part of your operation, I'd never shortchange you. I could manage the books and launder the drug money. All I'm asking is that you forgive my debt. I could even supervise this pair of thugs you've got running things at the casino. I could make more money for you—"

A massive blow to the side of his head knocked Trevor down. He dropped the phone and vaguely heard "Who are you calling thugs?" shouted from one of the Samoans. Trevor curled into a fetal position as both Fetu and Rangi kicked and stomped him. The punishment stopped for a moment. He opened his eyes to see Fetu's hand reach down to pick up the phone.

Trevor heard, "Sorry, Mr. Wong. We're managing this operation just fine. You don't need to bring this worm on. He's just proved that he can never be trusted. What do you want us to do with Larkin? Should we get rid of him?" Rangi kicked Trevor again.

Some indiscernible words answered Fetu on the phone. Trevor closed his eyes again. *This is evidence for the police. Lena will be safe now,* he thought before another kick from Rangi knocked him dizzy. His mind saw Lena's face.

Lee Wong heard more yelling in the background. The meaty sound of blows came over the line.

Fetu came back on the line asking instructions. "We've made plenty of money off Larkin," Wong told Fetu. "Losers like him are only good for a few months. And he'll likely try to run now. Just terminate him."

"That'll be easy enough. We can cut his throat here in the room where he runs the poker games. The police will think one of his poker marks killed him in anger."

"You're in his room?"

"Yeah."

"Is this the hotel phone? I told you to never call me except on a burner phone. You stupid fools. The police can trace this call to me. Get out of there!"

Lee Wong immediately hung up. Then he placed a call of his own. This time to Melbourne.

From outside his house, Wong heard a shout. "Open up. This is the police."

"We've been tricked," Fetu said to his partner. "We've got to run. But we can spare a couple more seconds." He pulled out a knife and moved to where Trevor lay semi-unconscious.

The hotel room door banged open. "Freeze! This is the police!" Three plain-clothes officers rushed in with drawn handguns. Fetu dropped the knife. The Samoans backed away from Trevor and raised their hands.

Malcolm pushed through the policemen and knelt by Trevor. "Lie still, lad. We'll protect you now."

"Did you get them?" Trevor managed to whisper.

"That depends." Malcolm removed the transmission device Katie had placed in Trevor's pocket. He spoke into it, "Did you get it recorded, Bennie?"

"Every bit. And the bug on the hotel phone will pick up Wong's words too."

"We got them, mate," Malcolm told Trevor. "But you went a little off script, didn't you? We hadn't planned on contacting Wong so soon."

The policeman at the door let Katie and Dave through. The Samoans had been cuffed and placed on the floor. The Parkers helped Trevor to stand. Shaky legs forced him to sit on the edge of the bed. "Are you dizzy? Do you need a doctor?" Katie asked.

Trevor shook his head a little and looked around. "No, I've been beat up worse than this before."

Dave handed Trevor a towel to put under his bleeding nose. "Son, you're going to look worse than I did a couple of months ago."

Katie spoke to Trevor, "Come with me to our room and lie down in a quiet place. The police are going to be all over this scene. I'll get you some ice and some aspirin." Trevor got to his feet and allowed himself to be led away.

Dave leaned over and picked up the record ledger the Samoans had dropped. He showed it to Malcolm. "This could be important. Do you mind if I look at it?"

Malcolm waved over one of the plain-clothes policemen. "Document the discovery of this piece of evidence. Then watch Mr. Parker look through it. But keep it at all times in our official chain of custody."

Trevor lay on the bed in room 418. Katie brought him a towel with ice and the aspirin. Then she dialed on the hotel phone. "Trevor, if you feel like it, I've got somebody who wants to talk with you. You can talk as long as you want." She held the phone to his ear.

"Trevor, this is Lena. I love you. Are you coming home soon?"

"What are you finding?" Malcolm leaned over Dave as he perused the ledger.

Dave kept his eyes on the page in front of him. "I think these guys," he motioned toward the Samoans restrained on the floor, "are or were managing about six other operations here at the hotel and casino. One almost certainly was another money distribution and laundering operation. A couple were probably drug sales. This one here . . . I can't tell."

"Could have been extortion," Malcolm speculated. To Dave's quizzical look, he responded, "They take photos of people in questionable situations and threaten to post them online. If some old guy is partying with a hot young girl, a photo of them together and a threat can pay off big rewards.

As for the drugs, the buyers can pay in chips. The dealer simply claims to have won them. Who is to prove he didn't? The mules are paid off in chips too. Gambling winnings aren't taxable here either."

"Looks like a couple of other operations had already been terminated," Dave continued.

"That's what they were about to do with Trevor." Malcolm then attempted a poor joke. "Must be tough on criminal kingpins. They just can't get good help." When Dave didn't respond, he added, "What else have you found?"

Dave flipped to a section he had marked with a piece of hotel stationary. "This operation marked 'Aussie poker' is undoubtedly Trevor. See all the names listed under six thousand dollars? Those have been paid off for services. Each one is likely a lower-level criminal like a drug dealer or mule. If you got them, some would undoubtedly roll over on the higher ups."

Malcolm looked at Dave with amazement. "You've done this before, haven't you?"

"I've had a little experience."

"Now I know how your FBI knew you and how Mr. Larkin became an FBI informant," said Malcolm. Dave only shrugged in response.

The police sergeant then spoke to his own men. "We need to wrap up here and get this record logged into the evidence locker." He turned to Dave. "They'll make copies. How about you come to headquarters tomorrow and take a more thorough look along with our detectives?"

"I'd be happy to. Did you arrest the security chief?"

Malcolm shook his head. "He disappeared when

somebody reported our arrests of the Samoans. But New Zealand is a small island. We'll get him."

"Could I ask about what happened with Mr. Wong? Did you catch him?"

"Barely. Lucky we had a pair of patrolmen on surveillance at his house. But he destroyed some evidence before they could stop him. Our lad Trevor jumped ahead before we had everything set in place."

Dave smiled. "You're the one who turned him into an enthusiastic partner."

"True. I've got a young son myself. He might have tried the same dumb thing. Inexperienced enthusiasm can be dangerous."

Jeremy answered the ringing phone. "It's for you." He held it out for Denyse.

"Sis, this is Trevor."

"Trevor, where are you? What's happening?"

"I'm here with Katie. She says I can talk as long as I want this time."

"Don't you want to call Lena?"

"I've already talked with her. Mum and Dad too."

"What did Dad say?"

"Mostly he told me about Vlady. And he asked me to come home."

"You should come home, Trevor."

"I will as soon as they let me."

"What's happened, Trevor? Why can you talk now?"

"The police busted my handlers tonight. They were

about to kill me. The police recorded them saying so. And their boss has been arrested too. We're in the clear now, Sis."

"That's the address Lee Wong sent," one of three men said as their car passed a darkened house in an east Melbourne neighborhood later that night.

"Park someplace down the road," an Asian man ordered. "We'll approach on foot. Remember, it's the girl and baby we want. Get the baby and you'll have the mother. Just disable anybody else. And keep it quiet."

Chapter Twenty-Seven

"Wake up," Beatrice whispered as she poked her husband. "Someone is outside."

"What makes you think so?" Dingo replied groggily.

"I heard the possums run away."

"A dog probably scared them off."

"No, I saw a flash of light."

Dingo sat up in the dark. He heard the soft scrunch of human steps on dry winter leaves outside. "Lock your dogs in the bathroom. And stay quiet," he told Beatrice. He silently moved to Trevor's old room where Vlady was sleeping in the borrowed bassinet. A window remained cracked to let in fresh, cool air.

"Here," a whispered voice came through the crack. "Cut through the screen."

Dingo picked up the baby and tiptoed out as the knife made a low zipper sound cutting through the plastic mesh.

In the hallway, he found that Beatrice had already wakened Lena. He passed the baby to Lena and ordered Beatrice, "Take them to the back door. When the commotion starts, all of you slip out and hide in the dark."

Returning to Trevor's room, Dingo saw a man stand erect after having just crawled through the window. Darting forward, Dingo used his body momentum to magnify a massive fist blow to the man's face. A cracking sound indicated breaking hand bones. The man went down. Dingo straddled him while continuing to strike.

The front door crashed open from the shoulder of a huge man. Dingo left the first man lying nearly inert. For a fraction of a second, he and the big man faced each other in the hallway. Dingo screamed a battle cry and charged. Instinctively the other man accelerated as well so that the two hurtled toward each other. The bigger man knocked Dingo backwards with his greater weight and momentum. But Dingo had grabbed on to him, pulling the huge man down.

On the floor, the two men grappled, using head butting and gouging. Fingers groped for Dingo's eyes. He grabbed that hand with his teeth and bit down as hard as his jaw muscles allowed. Dingo felt a tooth crack and tasted blood. The man jerked his arm back as he screamed in pain. Dingo used that reaction to tuck his head under his opponent's arm and push backward with his neck. This gave him leverage to get behind his opponent. Dingo extended his right forearm under the man's chin and held it in place with his left hand. The big man started to choke as he thrashed around.

The choked man's exertions ceased as he blacked out. A tremendous blow to Dingo's temple suddenly dazed him. Another blow followed. Without releasing his grip, Dingo looked up. An Asian man cursed and pulled his leg back for another vicious kick. The kick landed, nearly taking Dingo's consciousness. He barely heard a dull thud. Then the Asian man fell on top of him. Dingo peered up in time to see Beatrice, with two hands on Denyse's old cricket bat, lean over to deliver a second head blow to the Asian. Dingo pushed the man off him. "Check on another intruder in Trevor's room," he told his wife. Beatrice went to Trevor's room carrying the bat. Dingo heard another dull thud as he struggled to his feet, gasping for breath.

Beatrice returned. "He was trying to stand up. I had to hit him again." She started to cry in shock and trauma as she looked around her home.

Suddenly Dingo became aware of pain in his right hand. He looked down. Bones protruded. "Where are Lena and Vlady?" he asked his wife.

"I sent them out the back door when the fight started. Then I called the police," Beatrice answered between hysterical sobs.

Other sounds came to Dingo. Yapping of Beatrice's corgis from the bathroom. The cricket bat falling to the floor. And sirens, lots of sirens in the distance. He blacked out and fell over.

Jeremy turned on the morning news while he had toast and coffee prior to leaving for work. "A frightening home invasion occurred in Melbourne last night," the morning anchor announced. "Our Stephanie Ingles is on the scene. "What have you found out, Stephanie?"

"Thomas, sometime in the early morning hours, several intruders entered the home you see behind me. Apparently, a fight ensued with the homeowner."

Jeremy stopped chewing. *That looks like the Larkin house*, he thought. "Denyse, come and look at this!"

Stephanie went on, "Four men have been taken to the hospital. Two women residents of the house have been questioned by the police. One of the women reportedly has a baby with her."

"I'm just getting into the shower," Denyse yelled back.

"Come right now!" Jeremy demanded.

Denyse came in with a towel wrapped around her. Irritation accented her voice. "What is *so* important?"

Jeremy pointed to the TV screen. "Isn't that your parents' house?"

"Mom, Dingo has been hurt in a fight. The morning news covered it," Jeremy told Katie. "He's in surgery now. Denyse is on her way to the airport to fly to Melbourne. She wanted Trevor to know that Lena and the baby are okay in case he saw the news."

Katie's first impression was, *Why would Dingo's fight be on the news?* "What caused the fight?" *Alcohol?* She silently wondered.

"Somebody invaded their house in the middle of the night. Dingo fought three men to protect Beatrice, Lena, and Vlady."

That explanation brought terrible memories to Katie of the experience she and Dave had faced in Minnesota. "How about Beatrice?"

"She's hysterical. The emergency responders gave her a sedative. She's sleeping at a neighbor's house. Lena took the baby and went to the hospital."

"Trevor is asleep, too. I gave him one of your dad's sleeping pills last night after he talked to Lena and Denyse. He won't know anything for several hours."

"Is Dad there?"

"Dave's helping out down at the police station."

"Okay, you can tell Trevor about the home invasion when he wakes up."

Dave sat in a conference room with three young Kiwi detectives looking through copies of the records captured the previous evening. As the detectives watched, he used three colors of magic marker. "First, I think these nine records represent the operators being managed by the Samoans. I don't know whether they're willing operatives or coerced like Trevor." He marked them in blue. "Notice that no entries have been made for several months on these three. They're probably inactive." He added an asterisk by each.

"They might be inactive in more than one sense," a detective quipped.

"Could be," Dave agreed. "Second, I'm marking in pink the ones who are probably collaborators such as hotel and casino employees who report things or look the other way. See the security chief here? The records show periodic smaller disbursements, usually less than a thousand dollars, without any revenue.

"Finally, these are what I'll call contractors, maybe drug mules. The records show irregular payments of a larger amount, usually six thousand dollars. I'll mark them in light green."

"Because some of those names are documented, we can notify immigration," another detective suggested. "The name can be confirmed by dates coordinated with immigration records. We should be able to pick them up trying to enter the country again."

"Unfortunately, a lot of nicknames are used and occasionally just a nationality," Dave replied. "You guys have a lot of work ahead."

"These are solid leads, though," another voice said. Dave and the three looked up to see Malcolm had slipped in while they were concentrating. The sergeant indicated the three detectives. "These blokes will be like three beagles discovering a field full of rabbits." They all laughed. The detectives, eager to get started, took Dave's marked copies and hurried out.

Malcolm's voice became serious. "Dave, the Aussies have reported a home invasion in Melbourne. The reason they informed us is that one of the assailants matches the photo you gave me of an Asian man. We checked the phone records, and Lee Wong phoned Melbourne just before our officers arrested him. We're working on the theory that the two Asians are linked and that the attack was intended as retribution against Trevor, because his family was their target."

Dave sat stunned. "What happened? Was anybody killed?"

"The Aussie police are having trouble figuring out what happened. Apparently, your in-laws sent Trevor's young wife out the back door with the baby. Then they fought the attackers. The woman," Malcolm checked his notes, "Beatrice Larkin, became hysterical and had to be sedated. Her husband, Dingo Larkin, has a severe concussion and is unconscious. The doctors are operating to relieve pressure on his brain. What the police do know is that they found three dazed assailants, one of them the man in your photo, inside the Larkin home. They found their car parked down the street."

"Trevor told us they had threatened Lena," Dave mumbled to himself, but out loud.

Malcolm thought the statement had been directed at him. "Yes, he did. And I am truly sorry. Trevor caught us by surprise when he phoned Lee Wong. We weren't ready for that."

Dave uncharacteristically bit his lip. "What happens next?"

"We thought you and Katie would be the best ones to tell Trevor."

Trevor woke from a long sleep to find both Dave and Katie waiting. Katie had brewed coffee and brought him a cup.

Dave started, "Son, we have some bad news for you." Trevor's head jerked up from sipping the coffee. "First, know that Lena and Vlady are fine. Denyse is on her way to be with them. But your dad is hurt bad physically and your mother is experiencing severe emotional trauma."

"What happened?"

Dave and Katie each told him what they knew about the home invasion and ensuing fight.

Trevor absorbed what they said and then reacted. "These bloody cops. I told them Lena had been threatened. This is their fault. Your fault too."

"I understand why you're upset, Trevor," Dave responded. "But please be reasonable. Your meeting with the Samoans was just intended to tempt them to threaten you while being recorded. Malcolm didn't expect you to involve Lee Wong at that point. The police weren't ready."

"They should have thought of that. I'll not cooperate any more. Neither will Lena. I'll go to prison first."

"That won't help anyone—"

Trevor cut Dave off. "The cops certainly aren't helping. Neither are you and that bloody Indian lawyer. You're all just using me. And I'm the only one Lena has got to look out for her."

Dave sat quietly, allowing Trevor to vent.

Katie had watched the exchange between Dave and Trevor and thought, *I wonder how the criminals knew Lena was in Melbourne.*

Chapter Twenty-Eight

Since Denyse had grown up without a car in the Melbourne area, she knew the quickest way to get where she needed using public transport. She took busses from the airport directly to the hospital. There she found Lena asleep in a chair next to a bed where Dingo lay inert, connected to various monitors. His head had been heavily bandaged. A glove-like cast encased his right hand. Vlady lay fussing on a blanket spread in the corner.

"Lena, Lena," Denyse spoke softly.

The girl stirred and opened her eyes to see her sister-in-law. "Denyse! How did you know to come? Did Mama phone you?"

"Jeremy and I saw the story about the home invasion on the morning news."

Tears rolled down Lena's cheeks. She stood to hug Denyse. "Bad men came. Poppa is hurt."

"Can you tell me what happened, Lena?"

The girl noticed her baby fussing and went to pick him up. "Mama woke me in the night. She sent me with Vlady out the back door and told me to hide. She stayed in the house. I heard screaming and fighting. Then quiet. I came out when the police and ambulances came. A policeman drove me to the hospital to follow Poppa."

"Do you know where my mum is?"

"A man gave her a pill. I think she sleeps at her neighbor's house." The baby quieted when his mother started to nurse him.

"Lena, I talked to Katie in New Zealand. The police there think the men came to hurt you and Vlady."

"Why would they do that?"

"Trevor has been helping the police, and the criminals found out."

"Then Mama and Poppa saved us." Lena started to cry in earnest.

Denyse nodded and then asked, "Have you been here all day?"

"Yes."

"Have you had anything to eat?"

"No."

"You wait here. Let me talk to the doctors and nurses. I'll be back in a few minutes."

A nurse directed Denyse to a small room where several physicians had desks. She approached the one who matched the description the nurse had given her. "I'm Denyse Larkin. Can you tell me about my father?"

"Mr. Larkin is suffering a subdural hematoma. We've relieved some of the pressure from the brain swelling," the attending physician explained. "We'll keep him sedated for at least several days. I told the girl with the baby, Mr. Larkin's daughter-in-law, I think. She's been here all day praying. We let her into Mr. Larkin's room."

Denyse thanked the doctor and returned to her dad's room. "You need some rest," she told Lena. "The hospital will call me if there's a change in Dad's condition. Let's you and I go. We'll hire a taxi."

Malcolm stared at Trevor's barrister. "What does he mean, 'The deal is off'?"

Aarav Kapoor maintained his professional demeanor. "Mr. Larkin contends that police actions resulted in bodily harm to his father and an attempt on the lives of his wife and son."

"We'll need Trevor's testimony here, at least in preliminary hearings. And we need his wife's cooperation to uncover the human trafficking operation. That's unrelated to what happened here in Dunedin," the policeman explained. "Don't you want to see abuse of girls stopped?"

"I'm just relaying my client's decision."

"We have a signed agreement. The government could withdraw his immunity."

"My client's position is that the danger to his family supersedes the agreement. And he could have a good case. Let me remind you that judges have total discretion in such matters in New Zealand. But, if the court rules otherwise, my client is willing to go to prison to protect his family."

Malcolm's shoulders slumped in exasperation. "That makes us, the police, sound like the threat to his family." He sat thinking while the attorney waited. "We'll tell the court that the kid failed to follow instructions by contacting Lee Wong prematurely. Had he not done that, no call would have been made to Melbourne. Trevor's actions caused the assault."

"That could be true. But do the police have the instructions given to Trevor documented?"

"I verbally told him to try provoking the Samoans into an incriminating statement. Why would we need to document that?"

Without answering the question, the barrister claimed, "Then you can't prove what the police told Mr. Larkin or what latitude was implied, much less what he understood. My client can contend that he acted based on directions given by the police."

"Lord help us. I know you have a daughter yourself, Aarav. Isn't there something we can do?"

The attorney dropped his professional role for a few seconds. "Of course, I want to see you arrest and convict criminals, especially those who take advantage of women, Malcolm. But I have a legal obligation to represent my client's interests regardless of my feelings."

Malcolm nodded in recognition of the barrister's responsibility. Then he turned to Dave, who had watched the police sergeant and attorney sparring. "Dave, can you appeal to the kid? A court action would likely alert the criminals to our plans. And I don't want to send Trevor to prison either."

Dave spoke to both the policeman and attorney. "I've already tried. Trevor has been under intense pressure for months. He's obsessed with protecting his wife and son and not thinking rationally."

"After all that's happened, I can't fault him for that." Malcolm sat back, thinking. "How did they know his wife and son were in Melbourne? Did Trevor tell them? All of us have seen the torture marks."

"Those marks happened before Katie and I found Lena in Auckland. We took her to Australia."

"Gentlemen, could I make a personal suggestion that doesn't directly conflict with my client's interest?" Aarav Kapoor spoke up.

"By all means, please do," Malcolm responded.

"This young man has been through a lot. Let's give Trevor a couple of days to settle down. Our fighting in court right now won't help anybody."

Denyse found her childhood home surrounded by bright yellow crime-scene tape. A middle-aged policeman in uniform sat on the front porch to guard the crime scene. "Can she sit with you a few minutes?" she called to the man and waved toward Lena.

The policeman saw a tired girl carrying a baby and waved her up. "Thanks," said Denyse. "Do you know where my mother, Beatrice Larkin, is?" The policeman pointed toward a neighboring house.

There Denyse found her mother having tea with Mrs. Farmer, an elderly widow. Beatrice's corgis lounged nearby. "The police came here and asked questions. Your mother doesn't remember anything," the woman whispered as she showed Denyse to her parlor.

"How are you, Mum?" Denyse said and kneeled in front of her mother.

"You know how I mope when your father is at the sheep station, luv. I hope he comes home soon. Is Lena with you?" When Denyse nodded, Beatrice went on, "I do love her and little Vlady."

Denyse looked at the widow who returned an *I told you so* expression. "I hope Dad comes home soon too, Mum. Why don't you stay with Mrs. Farmer for a few days? I'll take care of Lena and see if we can get Dad home."

"Thank you, luv."

Back in front of her parents' house, Denyse asked the policeman, "Can I take my mum's car? We don't have a ride." She indicated herself and Lena with the baby.

"It's not inside the crime tape. I can't stop you."

"What about the car keys?" The policeman grimaced and looked up and down the street as though somebody might be watching. He waved Denyse inside the tape and followed while she located the keys. Inside, Denyse saw her former home in disarray. Blood splatters marked the floor and walls. Her old cricket bat lay bloodied with an evidence label attached. "Thank you," she told the officer.

"Lena, let's get some supper and then get some rest at a motel."

"Here's what we can do for you, mate." An Australian police interrogator and prosecutor sat in front of a huge man restrained with shackles. A severe bite mark with stitches showed on one of the big man's hands. His court-appointed attorney sat beside him. "We found you inside a private home in the early morning hours. The homeowner, a Mr. Graham Larkin, is near death at the hospital. If that phone rings telling us that Mr. Larkin has died, then we'll have you cold on first-degree murder. Or we can offer you ten years for assault of Mr. Larkin right now. All you have to do is tell us everything about your accomplices and what they intended. If you don't want to talk, one of your partners will take the deal and leave you with the murder."

"Could we eat there?" Lena pointed at a McDonald's.

Although not a frequent patron of fast foods, the convenience appealed to Denyse. "A great idea." She pulled Beatrice's car into the parking lot.

Denyse wouldn't have thought such a small woman could eat so much. Lena sat devouring a loaded hamburger, chicken nuggets, the largest order of French fries, and a large chocolate milkshake. Vlady slept beside her. "You are hungry," Denyse commented as she ate a grilled chicken sandwich.

"Yes. But also, McDonald's is my favorite place to eat. Inviting me there is how Trevor made me a friend." She told Katie about their first date at McDonald's after his hesitant approach to her at the library. "Trevor is wonderful," said Lena. She thought to herself for a few seconds, then confided, "All my life, I do my best for others. This is the Christian way, I think. I take care of brothers and sisters while Mama and Poppa work on the farm. I help Mama when we became refugees from the war. I come to New Zealand to make a new home for our family. I care for Vlady. I work to send money home. But Trevor takes care of me. He makes me happy."

"How did your father get killed in the civil war? Was he a soldier?"

"Some Russian men came to our farm. They want Poppa to take a gun and go with them to fight. But Poppa point to wife and children and say, 'No.' Three men tied him with a rope then took him away in a truck. Three days later, Ukrainians found his body with several other men from our village. They had all been shot in the head. Then Russian police come and say that our farm now belongs to others. They forced us to leave."

Denyse sat aghast at Lena's story. "Are you saying that police came and took your farm?"

Lena nodded. "Police in our country, not always so good."

Denyse could still hardly absorb Lena's story. "You lost your father, your home, and had to leave your mother and family?"

"Then I thought I had lost Trevor, until Dave and Katie find us both. There are many other girls like me. They must do bad things to live. Sometimes their own families are so desperate that they sell them. Then the girls have no choice or chance of escape."

"Do you believe that the police in New Zealand want to stop these men? They need your help."

"Yes, this is part of what they call an 'immunity agreement' for Trevor. I don't trust the police. In New Zealand, I was afraid they would put me in jail and take my baby. But I will do anything to help Trevor. And I do want to stop the men who sell girls like they tried to do me."

Lena had finished her supper but showed no inclination to leave the reassuring atmosphere of McDonald's. "Let's you and I make a partnership," proposed Denyse. Lena paid close attention. "Together we can work to do something about men who abuse and sell women."

"That would be very good." The two young women shook hands to seal their partnership.

The phone rang in room 418 where Dave and Katie were resting while watching sports on TV. Dave was attempting to explain the nuances of rugby to his wife. Happy for any distraction, she answered the phone. "Hello."

"Mrs. Parker, this is Detective Barry. I'm downstairs going through the office of the former security chief of the hotel and casino. I've found something that Sergeant Fraser would like Mr. Parker and yourself to see. Could you both come downstairs, please?"

Chapter Twenty-Nine

Malcolm handed Dave the note written to Lena by Trevor. "Detective Barry found this in the former security chief's desk. This is how Lee Wong knew where to find Trevor's wife and baby in Melbourne. Hell, the envelope even has the address to find her. And it's handwritten on hotel stationary."

Dave examined the note and stationary. "Some hotel staff Wong had corrupted must have intercepted this when Trevor attempted to mail it. They turned it over to the security chief for a reward, I imagine."

The police sergeant spoke with confidence, "This should take away any legal grounds for abdicating the immunity for cooperation agreement we made."

"Yes, it should. But I don't think that guarantees Trevor's cooperation."

"Why not?"

"Malcolm, the kid doesn't trust authorities. Beating them

has always been a game to him. And he's genuinely fearful for his wife and child. Right now, he's more likely to trust his instincts and run."

"Without his wife and baby?"

"My daughter-in-law told Katie that Trevor's wife, Lena, has an inherent distrust of police as well. Apparently in Ukraine police aren't very . . . honorable. She would probably also disappear and meet him someplace with their child."

"We have an officer monitoring Trevor at the hotel."

"You've seen how clever and resourceful the kid is. If he wants to get away, he'll figure out a way."

"Maybe I'll just arrest him and keep him in jail."

"You think Aarav Kapoor would allow that? Even if you've got the legal high ground now, Trevor would be gone before the legalities could be sorted out."

Irritation sounded in the policeman's voice. "Alright then, you talk some sense into him."

"I'm afraid Katie and I are authority figures to him too. He doesn't trust us much either."

"Dave, you're angling toward something. So just get to it."

"I think Trevor trusts my son, Jeremy, as much as he trusts anybody."

"What about Trevor's wife, the Ukrainian girl?"

"She trusts my daughter-in-law."

"Can you bring your son over here to talk to Trevor and get your daughter-in-law to get the girl's cooperation?"

"I'll sure try."

"Thanks! By the way, you'll be glad to know that our Aussie police brethren got one of the Larkin assailants to implicate his partners. They gave him ten years for assault for a written statement. Otherwise he could have gotten life for murder should Mr. Larkin die. Too bad for him his lawyer forgot to include the charge for attempted kidnapping of the girl in the deal. Or maybe his lawyer just didn't care to remember. The thug is scum. Have you gotten any recent word on Mr. Larkin's condition in the hospital?"

"Stable. He's still sedated."

The hotel restaurant's toilets are just past the staff entrance to the kitchen, thought Trevor. *All I've got to do is take the wrong door, pretend I'm drunk, and slip out the delivery door. Then I'll call Lena . . .*

A knock on the hotel door interrupted his planning. Opening the door, he found Jeremy accompanied by Aarav Kapoor and Detective Barry. The three being together seemed odd. "Jeremy, why do you need a lawyer? And what does this cop want?"

"I'm here as your legal representative, Mr. Larkin," the barrister answered for Jeremy. "And Detective Barry is required to maintain chain of custody of the evidence. Mr. Jeremy Parker is here in an unofficial capacity as your advisor. As your barrister, I recommend that you listen to him."

"What evidence?" Trevor wanted to know.

"We'll get to that in a minute," Jeremy spoke. "Can we come in?"

Trevor held the door open. Inside, the barrister and policeman hung back while Trevor and Jeremy sat down facing each other. "Any more news from Melbourne?" Trevor asked.

"Denyse got there day before yesterday. She and Lena are staying at a motel together with Vlady. Lena wants to eat every meal at McDonald's." Trevor smiled at the mention of McDonald's. "Denyse says the doctors are keeping Dingo sedated."

"What about my mum?"

"She's staying with a neighbor. A Mrs. Farmer, I think. Denyse tried to talk with your mother. She's uninjured, but can't remember anything that happened. Sometimes your mind just blocks terrible memories. Your mother thinks Dingo is out at a sheep station. But she remembers Lena and Vlady."

Trevor answered bitterly, "Things would be better if Dingo had just stayed out at the station."

"Not this time, Trevor." Jeremy looked at him directly. "Your dad fought to protect Lena and the baby. He saved them."

Trevor wouldn't give up assigning blame and shook his head. "That wouldn't have been necessary if the cops hadn't screwed up." He gave a nasty look to Detective Barry, who returned a blank face.

Jeremy spoke gently, "Trevor, once I thought I was in love with a girl I met at the beach over the summer. She was different from anybody I knew. A free spirit. She asked me to drop out of school to kick around the country with her in a van. It seemed like such a good idea compared to studying accounting. Then my father said," Jeremy mimicked Dave's deeper voice, " 'Son, each moment divides our lives into before and after. Be careful when the moment will divide your life into never before and always after.' There's no way to know what would have happened if I had gone with that girl. But later I learned that she had become addicted to heroin. And eventually I met and married your sister."

Trevor nodded appreciatively. "You got the best with Denyse. But what's that story got to do with me?"

"You're at a 'never before and always after' moment, mate. You signed an agreement with the police. Whatever you do next will affect your life and Lena's and Vlady's always after."

Trevor glanced at his barrister. "Because of what happened in Melbourne, that agreement might not be enforceable."

Jeremy extended his arm to Detective Barry, who handed him some papers protected in a plastic sleeve. He took a deep breath and passed the sleeve to Trevor. "Did you write this note?"

Trevor sat in disbelief looking at the note, then demanded, "How did you get this?"

"Detective Barry found this note in the hotel security chief's desk. Someone must have intercepted it when you tried to mail it to Lena. Notice that the address directs the criminals to your parents' home."

Aarav Kapoor spoke up, "Mr. Larkin, as your legal representative, I must tell you that this evidence severely undermines any potential we had to overturn the cooperation and immunity agreement. Furthermore, my services require a retainer. To pursue that elective legal course, I would need a hundred thousand dollars deposit."

Trevor stood and faced the others. "Is everybody against me?"

Jeremy picked up the sleeve where it had fallen and returned it to Detective Barry. He spoke forcibly to Trevor. "*No one is against you.* Everyone here wants to keep you out of prison and get you back to Lena. My father even fronted fifty thousand dollars for your legal bills. But everyone also wants to stop these criminals. The police need your testimony as leverage to get more information and then get convictions here in Dunedin. They need Lena to set up the pimps in Auckland."

"No. Lena can't be involved. All I have to go on is my own judgment," Trevor shouted.

Jeremy answered deliberately, "Listen to me, Trevor. You know that I'm on your side. By sending this note, you directed the criminals to Lena. Your acting without police guidance allowed Lee Wong to issue the hit. That poor judgement is why Dingo is near death in the hospital. These poor choices need to stop here. You need to trust the people trying to help you. What will it be, Trevor? What kind of ever after do you want?"

Trevor stood stunned at the revelations. *What have I done?* he thought. He looked at Jeremy, detected sincerity, and took a deep breath. "I'll trust you, mate. Tell me what you think is the best thing to do."

Denyse stared out the airplane window as the jet approached the Auckland airport. "I've never been to New

Zealand," she told Lena. "You'll need to show me around."

Lena leaned over Denyse, also trying to catch a glimpse of the city. "I know the best places to sleep hidden in the park and where to get warm on cold days," she teased.

Denyse laughed. "You did a good job explaining to Trevor on the phone how you want to help stop human traffickers."

"I still don't think he would have agreed without Jeremy's encouragement and unless he knew you would come with me."

"I was surprised when Trevor asked Dave and Katie to meet us in Auckland."

"Jeremy advised him to do that."

Two familiar faces waited for Denyse and Lena outside of customs at the Auckland airport. The sisters-in-law gladly exchanged hugs with Dave and Katie. "We'll take you to the hotel in our rental car," Dave offered. "The police will meet us at their offices tomorrow morning."

Katie surprised both women by getting behind the steering wheel. "Beatrice taught me how to drive in the city on the left-hand side. Then I taught Dave. He still feels more comfortable driving on the left out in the rural areas," she explained.

"Trevor wanted to come himself," said Dave. "But the Dunedin police are somewhat reluctant to let him out of their jurisdiction while they're hot on the trail of Lee Wong's henchmen and collaborators. They need Trevor's testimony at nearly every arraignment hearing."

"I'm glad Jeremy's company allowed him extra time off," said Denyse.

"Sergeant Fraser calling the CEO in Sydney to explain certainly helped," Dave responded. "Is there any news about Dingo?"

"They did another smaller surgery yesterday," Denyse said. "The hospital anticipates keeping him sedated for several more days. They won't revive him until his brain swelling subsides. The Melbourne news media has picked up the story. They're making Dad a hero for protecting his family against three men."

"How about Beatrice?" asked Katie.

"The doctors say that she may regain part or possibly all of her memory. The police are eager to hear what she saw and did, especially if Dad doesn't survive. The forensic people claim that only Mum's fingerprints are on the cricket bat along with mine," explained Denyse.

"What does that mean?"

"Nobody knows for sure. Even the one thug the police got to talk to about a plea deal didn't see what happened after Dingo choked him unconscious. Apparently, Mum joined Dad in the fight."

"And you trusted Beatrice with the baby even in her condition?" Dave asked.

Lena spoke up. "Yes, of course. She has Mrs. Farmer to help her. The only danger is that they might love Vlady to death."

"Here's the hotel," Katie announced. "Shall we check in, then meet for dinner in about an hour? We made reservations for one room for you two. Is that okay?"

"Thank you," both young women answered.

Chapter Thirty

The next morning, Katie drove them all to the police headquarters in Auckland. "This is Sergeant Crowley of the Auckland police," Dave introduced.

Denyse and Lena saw a tall and lean man. His tanned and wrinkled face showed many hours of racing sailboats in the waters of New Zealand. His crisp, professional demeanor contrasted the folksy approach of Sergeant Malcolm Fraser in Dunedin. "Ms. Larkin, we appreciate your cooperation." He pointed to a map of Auckland. "This park is where about a month ago the men attempted to coerce you into working for them as a prostitute, correct?"

Lena had not previously seen the map. "I think so. The bench I used is across from a café. Mr. and Mrs. Parker found me in that park." Dave nodded to the policeman to confirm the park's location on the map.

"And the men approached you on foot?"

"Yes. They were walking."

"And these two men are the same ones who had purchased your contract from the Ukrainians who brought you to New Zealand on false pretenses?"

"Yes. I had to run away and hide from them then. Later they found me with Trevor. He paid them the money they claimed I owed. Once Trevor was gone, they came back to get me again."

"Alright, what we'll do is make up a bundle to look like your baby. Inside the bundle we'll put a sensitive radio to transmit all that is said. Three undercover policemen will be in or around the park. We'll also watch you carefully from across the street. A camera mounted in a room above the café will record everything that happens. Hopefully the same men will see you again, approach, and say something incriminating. Then we'll arrest them."

"Will we wait in a police van with the listening equipment?" Denyse asked.

The dour sergeant smiled. "You've been watching a lot of TV, ma'am. With today's technology, you can use a password I give you to log into the police operational website. You can listen to the radio and watch the camera's feed from anyplace you want."

"I think Trevor would want us close by," Denyse insisted.

"We can't have you attracting attention and risking the operation," the policeman asserted. "And frankly, all three of you would stand out. Them," he indicated Dave and Katie, "because they're Americans. Their dress and mannerisms give them away. You . . ." he indicated Denyse and searched for the proper words, " . . . well, most men would notice you."

"I've got an idea," Katie interjected. "Why don't the three of us park the rental car on the street about a block away. We'll be able to actually see Lena. We can also watch and listen by logging in on Denyse's phone."

"That could work," agreed Sergeant Crowley.

"I never realized stakeouts could be so tedious," Dave complained. "We sat here all afternoon yesterday for nothing. And nearly all afternoon today."

"Think about Lena," Katie returned. "At least you're dry and out of the wind. She's been outside the entire time. She didn't even go in when the rain showers passed over. By contrast we've been taking turns getting snacks and drinks and using the toilet."

"I've been trying to spot the undercover policemen," Denyse volunteered from the back seat. "One is that workman by the water fountain. That or he's taken two days to change a washer. The second is that woman pushing the baby stroller. She must have been around the block a hundred times. That man washing windows across the street is one, too. I'll bet those store owners are happy for free window washing."

"What about Sergeant Crowley?" Dave asked.

"He comes out from the café occasionally to give each of the others a break. I'll bet he's upstairs with the camera most of the time."

"The sun is going down. We won't be able to see anything directly much longer," Dave observed. "Sergeant Crowley had said something about cockroaches coming out after dark. I guess he plans to stay later tonight."

"We can still hear, though. And I can still see Lena on the cell phone through the camera feed. It's a good thing that street light is nearby," said Denyse.

"I'm thinking of an object," Katie began for the umpteenth time.

"Is it bigger than a breadbox?" her husband responded without any enthusiasm. "And run the engine some more. Our being cold doesn't make Lena any warmer."

I wonder what is Trevor doing? Lena asked herself. She felt a little guilty about personal thoughts diverting her from praying for Dingo. She fussed with the blanket a bit to act like she held a real infant. For Beatrice, she wasn't certain how to pray. *Maybe she is better not remembering*, Lena considered. *Lord, you know what Beatrice needs most. Please take care of her.*

A man stopped in front of her. Lena looked up. He was one of the two men who had threatened her earlier. "Well, girlie, we haven't seen you here for a while. Since you've run away, your debt has gotten a lot bigger," the man sneered. "Are you ready to come work for us now? Or should we call immigration to put you in jail and take away your baby?"

Lena shook her head without speaking. The man continued, "Well, we know how to take care of runaways. A few drugs in your system will make you a lot more cooperative. And to make sure you don't disappear again, we'll just take your baby."

A white van pulled up next to the curb beside them. The man reached for the bundle in her arms. When Lena resisted, he slapped her and pulled away the bundle. The blanket fell open to reveal an electronic device. The man didn't recognize it as a transmitting microphone. "What's this? You're listening to a radio while you're panhandling?"

"Just bring the girl," his partner ordered from the driver's seat of the van. The man grabbed Lena by the wrist and roughly jerked her to the van. He opened the sliding door and manhandled her inside. Eleven seconds after stopping, the van started away.

In the distance, a voice shouted, "Stop! Police!"

"Is the object a rabbit?" Dave attempted.

"Wait! Something's happening!" Denyse proclaimed from the back seat. "There's a man . . . a white van . . . they've got Lena . . . they're coming this way!"

Katie saw a white van approaching on her right. She put the rental car into drive and pressed down the accelerator. The van's driver didn't have time to react as she steered into the other lane and hit the van corner-to-corner on the driver's side of each. The impact shattered glass and spun both vehicles around. Denyse's body hit the back of Katie's seat, pushing Katie's face into the air bag at the moment it inflated.

Katie heard the passenger side open and her husband get out. Although dazed, she watched through the broken windshield as Dave approached the van, opened the sliding door, and reached inside. With his left hand he grabbed a man, pulled him toward him, and used his right fist to smash the man in the face. Blood gushed from the man's nose. Suddenly, police swarmed over the scene with drawn weapons. They forced the two men from the van to the ground. Denyse had untangled herself from the car and rushed to assist Lena. Dave stepped back shaking his right hand in apparent pain.

Katie felt something dripping from her chin. She looked down. Blood from her nose dropped onto her lap. "Are you hurt, ma'am?" The policewoman Denyse had spotted pushing the baby stroller stood at her window. The policewoman tried to open the door, which had been jammed by the collision.

Dave returned to the passenger side door to check on Katie. "Great work, sweetheart. Can you try to come out this side? Let me help you." Katie nodded and scrambled across the seat. Dave took her arm and helped her to stand up. He took off his shirt. "Here, use this to wipe your face."

Katie took the shirt and held it under her nose. She saw Dave shaking his hand. "How's your hand?"

"Still hurts a little." He showed the redness on his knuckles. "But it's not broken. That auto-body shop owner, Hogan, had good advice about aiming for the nose."

Dave pulled his jacket from the wrecked car and put it on in place of his shirt. Nearby, Denyse consoled and congratulated Lena. Dave and Katie consoled and congratulated each other with a prolonged hug.

The Parkers heard Sergeant Crowley talking to one of the other officers. "This couldn't have worked out better.

We've got the scumbags threatening the girl on audio and a kidnaping attempt on video." He turned to see Dave and Katie watching him. "What are you two smiling about?"

"We'll get to go home to Alabama now."

The next morning, Sergeant Crowley led raids of the addresses found on the arrested men. They freed several other girls of various nationalities. Lena and Denyse then began searching the streets of Auckland for other girls lured into or held in bondage as prostitutes. Several New Zealand organizations that were dedicated to helping such girls rendered assistance. The sisters-in-law found many of the girls difficult to dissuade. Some had become addicted to drugs. Others had lost all sense of self-worth. Few could envision any other alternative.

Fortunately, nearly all the women agreed to supply the names of those who had ensnared them. "All we need to do now is wait for them to attempt reentering New Zealand," Sergeant Crowley promised. "Immigration's computers will identify them. They'll be detained at the airport. I suspect we'll find a lot of witnesses willing to accuse them."

Auckland's most popular TV station did a report on Lena and Denyse's search. Lena told about her situation in Ukraine, coming to New Zealand to work as a nanny, running away from forced prostitution, meeting Trevor, and being rescued from kidnapping by Dave and Katie. The outpouring of public support created a demand that government authorities crack down on human trafficking all over New Zealand.

⸻

"Dave Parker?" a male voice on the hotel phone questioned.

Dave recognized the voice of George Ferguson.

"How are things on the farm, George?"

"As busy as ever. And that was wonderful, what you did for Holly."

"You're welcome. She's a nice girl. It was our pleasure."

"Dave, we saw the report on the telly. Wasn't Trevor Larkin the Aussie you and Katie were looking for?" After Dave confirmed that, George continued, "His young wife, Lena, doesn't look much older than Holly. We felt . . . well, we wanted to do something for her Ukrainian family. I'm just saying that, if someone brought her family here, Nikki and I could take care of them on the farm until they wanted to go elsewhere."

"Lena's family are refugee farmers, you know."

"The news covered their story in an interview with Lena. They could stay in the cottage. Lena's brothers and sisters could go to Holly's school. I think the whole community would welcome them. I'd pay them some whenever they could help me on the farm."

"Judging by Lena, they're good Christians and hard workers," said Dave.

"Send them to us."

⸻

"Trevor! Trevor! Trevor!" Lena screamed. Her husband pushed through the crowd at the Dunedin airport. Wordlessly, the young husband and wife embraced and held on to each other.

After two full minutes they separated to look at each other. "What's this?" Trevor touched the bruise on Lena's cheek from the slap she had received.

Lena in turn saw the marks remaining from Fetu and Rangi's beatings. "Oh, Trevor. Look at you." Lena started to cry with both joy and sorrow.

Trevor then noticed Denyse standing quietly nearby with tears on her own cheeks. "Sis!" He hugged his sister. "I thought I'd never see you again."

"We never gave up on you, little brother. Now you, me, Mum, and Dad can make a fresh start."

"How is Dad?"

"The doctors say the pressure on his brain is decreasing. They hope to revive him in a few days." Denyse pointed to Lena. "And you've added to the family."

"You too. Jeremy is great."

"Where is Jeremy?" Denyse wanted to know. "I expected him to be here."

"I had trouble finding a place to park," Jeremy spoke from behind her. "Trevor couldn't wait to come inside to see you." He hugged his wife and sister-in-law. "But where are my parents?"

"They sent us ahead while they waited for all of our luggage. Here they come," Denyse answered.

Dave and Katie soon emerged from baggage claim each carrying two bags. Two black eyes marked Katie's face.

"Mom! What happened to you?" Jeremy exclaimed.

Denyse answered for her, "There's a dramatic story to tell. Your mum is a hero. And the Auckland police even gave us a video clip. Let's all go somewhere we can rest and catch up."

"There's a nice ocean-side campground north of Dunedin. They aren't busy this time of year. I'll rent three cabins for us all to rest. We can tell our stories there," Dave offered.

Chapter Thirty-One

Dingo felt somebody touching his cheeks. He forced open his eyes. A blurry white-coated figure standing before him leaned over to shine a light in one eye, then the other. The figure shouted, "Mr. Larkin, can you hear me?"

Dingo attempted to nod. Pain in his head stopped him. "Ehhh," he managed to grunt.

The white-coated figure stepped back. "He's still heavily medicated. But you can talk to him. He should understand you."

"Dad, it's me, Denyse. You had a head injury and concussion. You've been unconscious for three weeks. We love you and have prayed for you. You're on the way to recovery now."

Blinking cleared Dingo's vision a little. He barely discerned Denyse leaning over him. She squeezed his left hand. "Ehhh," he managed again.

"I brought someone with me, Dad. Do you recognize Trevor?" Denyse reached back and pulled her brother closer. "Trevor has come home."

"Trevor?" Dingo fought to focus his eyes.

"Yeeah, it's me, Dad. I'm here. And I'm staying." He squeezed the hand Denyse had relinquished. "We want to get you better and back home."

A tear ran down the stricken man's cheek. He squeezed back at Trevor's touch. "Beatrice?"

"Mum is fine, Dad. She's waiting for you at home. The doctors wanted to have you get a little better before she sees you. Lena and little Vlady are safe with her. Do you remember them? She always called you Poppa."

Unlike Beatrice, Dingo remembered everything. "Yeeah. My grandson."

Trevor cried, "You saved them both, Dad. My wife and son. Good on ya, mate."

Dingo's eyes focused on Trevor. "My son."

"You're a hero, Dad," Trevor went on. "Everybody in Australia knows about what you did. And Mum too. I'm going to write a book about you."

The white-coated figure stepped in again. "Let's give Mr. Larkin time to get some natural sleep now. He should feel better tomorrow."

"Are you ready for guests, Mr. Larkin?" the attending nurse asked the next day. To Dingo's nod, she spoke to someone in the hallway. "You can come in now."

Denyse and Trevor entered the hospital room followed by Lena. But Dingo looked past them to the fourth figure entering. "Beatrice?" he mumbled.

"Oh Dingo! They told me you were hurt." The three young adults held back as Beatrice came to her husband's bedside. "I missed you so much. I can't remember all that happened. But I know that you're a hero. I'm so proud of you."

Dingo spoke more clearly, "I can remember everything. You're the hero. You saved all of us."

The others crowded around the bed talking. Dingo acknowledged each with eye contact and a nod. But his eyes returned and rested on his wife. "Where's Vlady?"

"The hospital wouldn't allow him inside, Poppa," Lena replied. "But he's fine. You won't believe how he has gained weight."

Dingo looked at the smiling faces surrounding the bed before his eyes returned to Beatrice. "And what about the Americans? The Parkers?"

Beatrice answered gently, "Jeremy went back to work in Sydney, luv. Dave and Katie headed home to America after your doctors told us you would be alright. Dave asked us to tell you that you had taken care of your family well. He said, 'Tell Graham, Good on ya, mate!' "

"So, what all has happened?" Dingo wanted to know.

Everybody started talking at once until Dingo waved for quiet. He pointed at Trevor. "You first, son."

Each of the family members told their stories, assisted by the others, of course. The stories culminated with Denyse showing everyone the dramatic video of Katie and Dave stopping Lena's would-be kidnappers in Auckland. Dingo chuckled after seeing Dave punch one of the abductors. "Those Yanks are alright."

Dave grumbled as he and Katie drove toward home from the Mobile airport. "Three months of airport parking fees. Jeremy's wedding was supposed to be a two-week trip. After we settle with the car agency for the wrecked rental, we may have spent two hundred thousand *American* dollars on that trip."

Long years living with Dave had accustomed Katie to him grousing over expenses. She knew reason always soothed him. "Didn't we have car insurance?"

"That doesn't cover deliberate acts like your kamikaze attack in Auckland."

"You know that was necessary." After Dave responded with a grudging nod, she consoled him. "Even so, the amount we spent was a drop in the bucket compared to what we accomplished. I think God helped us to save a family, maybe several families. We've got the daughter we always wanted, and our grandbaby will be well cared for. Now stop complaining. You know that we have the money from the settlement you got from the firm."

"No, we *had* that money."

"Well, what's Jeremy and Denyse's happiness, not to

mention our grandchild's security, worth to you in dollars?"

"A lot. And God probably did help us to do something important," Dave admitted. Then he looked at Katie and smiled. "Remember how concerned you were about Denyse and the marriage?"

His wife laughed. "Yes, I do. Compared to my fears then, everything turned out wonderfully."

"Do you feel more than ordinary again?"

"I found out that more than ordinary often isn't a picnic."

"We had some fun Down Under too," Dave reminded himself as much as Katie.

"Yes, we did." Katie then reviewed some of the interesting and entertaining experiences of their trip.

Dave glanced at her. "What are you going to tell people about your two black eyes?"

Katie shook her head before breaking into her mischievous grin. "I'm going to mount pictures of both of us with black eyes on the wall and challenge people to guess what happened."

"Down Under was quite an adventure," said Dave as he chuckled at the mental image of his and Katie's pictures on the wall. "But I'm ready for some ordinary peace and quiet for a while. Fishing sounds like adventure enough for a long time."

Dave pulled the car into their driveway. Katie unlocked the front door while Dave removed their two bags from the trunk. Other than a light coating of dust, everything inside their home appeared just as they had left it. A mountain of unpaid bills and other mail waited on the dining room table. A noise greeted them, *rrrow*. An orange cat trotted out from a bedroom to welcome the couple. "Are you glad to see us, Old Yeller?" Katie picked him up for a squeeze. *Rrrow*, he answered.

Back on the floor, the cat rubbed against Dave's legs. Dave put down the bags and scratched under the feline's chin. "I thought the Fogles had him."

"I emailed them that we would be home this afternoon. They must have brought him over. He certainly seems happy to see us."

"What do you want to do first?"

"That was a long flight. How about a nice nap?"

"My thinking exactly," Dave responded.

Katie kicked her shoes off and undressed for a long sleep. "You should call Richard Christensen to thank him and explain what happened."

Dave shed his own travel clothes. "That's a good idea. I will."

Dave and Katie fell asleep with Old Yeller content between them.

Chapter Thirty-two

Eight Months Later

Emerging from Sydney customs, Dave and Katie saw Jeremy and Denyse waiting at the same spot as they had nearly a year earlier. Katie felt a little ashamed at her attitude about Denyse on their first meeting. At this moment, she felt equally overjoyed to see Denyse as she did her son.

Jeremy smiled and waved. Denyse radiated happiness but kept her arms wrapped around a pink bundle. Katie moved directly to Denyse and gently folded back the blanket to reveal a tiny face. "She's beautiful, Denyse," Katie whispered.

Denyse handed her child to Katie. "Katelyn Beatrice Parker, your granddaughter." She curtseyed as she had seen Lena do upon presenting Vlady to Beatrice. " 'Kate' for you and 'lyn' for my mum's maiden name, Lindsey."

Katie felt as though her heart could burst with love toward Katelyn and toward Denyse. "I'm sorry we weren't here for her birth, Denyse."

Denyse picked up Katie's bag to carry to the car while Katie carried her granddaughter. "No worries. You couldn't help having the flu. And we know that Dave had to testify in court as part of his first consulting job. He couldn't control the court dates. We had plenty of help here."

After hugging his father, Jeremy picked up Dave's bag and indicated the way to the car. The women walked in front. "I'll bet Beatrice *has* been a lot of help," Dave speculated.

"Not that much, really," Jeremy replied. "Beatrice came here for a few days. Then she rejoined Dingo traveling."

"Dingo and Beatrice are traveling?"

"Not for entertainment, although they enjoy it," Jeremy explained. "They've become celebrities in Australia. They've had a lot of speaking engagements all over the country. Dingo has plenty of colorful bloke stories and self-deprecating humor. He tells the same tales he used all his adult life to entertain pub mates. He's also brutally honest about mistakes he's made. Dingo uses his platform to exhort the men about the importance of taking care of family and avoiding the abuse of alcohol."

Denyse partially turned to add, "Mum isn't bad at speaking either. She talks to the women about sticking by your man. Audiences just love them together."

Katie still cuddled her granddaughter. "Then who helped you with the baby?"

"Lena came to Sydney with Vlady for more than a month," Denyse answered. "That girl knows all about caring for babies.

Some of my teenage students have come by to help too."

"How is Trevor doing?"

Jeremy unlocked the car. "His probation keeps him in Melbourne. He served as a ghostwriter for Dingo's book, *The Right Fight*. It's just been published and is already a best seller Down Under. They included a lot of pictures, even the fight at our wedding. Dingo split the two-hundred-thousand-dollar advance and the royalties with Trevor. Dingo is bursting with pride. You can't stop him bragging about Trevor."

Denyse pulled out a car seat for Katie to place the baby in. She eagerly elaborated while Katie situated Katelyn. "Now Trevor is taking creative writing classes at uni and has nearly finished his first novel. The story is set in the world of con men and hustling. His insights into the human psyche are amazing. He doesn't have an advance for the novel yet. But several publishers have already asked to review the draft copy."

Dave laughed. "Well, Trevor's research has been thorough."

Jeremy strapped in the car seat with Katelyn and loaded their bags. "He says that writing isn't that much different than hustling." Jeremy quoted Trevor, "You tell people what they want to hear, then add just a little more. Except that the more should make readers think rather than taking advantage of them."

Denyse held the car's back door open for Katie then sat beside her and the baby. "You haven't heard the best part yet," she shared with excitement. "Mum and Dad are getting a lot of healthy honorariums for speaking. They used some of the first money to pay for Lena's family to immigrate Down Under from Ukraine. Right now they're staying on the farm in New Zealand you told us about."

Dave took the front seat alongside Jeremy. "Wow! Things have turned out well. How is Dingo handling the notoriety?"

"Dad complains that every bloke in Australia wants to buy him a drink now. But he's limited to two beers a day," answered Denyse. They all laughed. "But Dad has become amazingly humble and caring," she continued. "I guess that sharing his screw ups with the world is a constant reminder to him. He's still a bloke's bloke, though." Everybody laughed again.

"So how are things in Mobile?" Jeremy asked.

"Relaxing," answered Dave. "And I haven't had a nightmare in months. Maybe rescuing Trevor convinced me that your mother and I together could face any danger. Or maybe hitting that kidnapper without going berserk convinced my psyche that I don't have a demon inside."

"Mobile seems a bit boring now," Katie amended. "As you know, your dad did pass the forensic accounting exam. More clients than he can handle are coming to him already. All of them are out of state. So we'll be doing some traveling ourselves as soon as we get back."

"When *do* you plan to go back?" Jeremy asked.

"That depends. Do you have anyone else we need to track down?" teased Katie.

Denyse laughed. "Not this time. We could advertise your services, though."

"That's okay. Two weeks sounds about right for this trip. After that, we'd like for y'all to visit us in Mobile," invited Katie.

Authors' Note

All the characters in this novel are purely fictional and created in the imaginations of the authors. However, all the locations and the descriptions of Australia and New Zealand are as detailed and accurate as space and our readers' attention would allow.

Truly both Australia and New Zealand represent enchanting worlds, very different from what most Americans experience. Each is worth a visit, perhaps an extended stay. We have traveled in many countries and cultures. Frequently by race or ethnicity, we usually stand out among the local residents. However, whenever possible we like to blend in and observe the culture unnoticed. Being unnoticed is different from being ignored or tolerated as many cultures do Americans, especially in areas frequented by tourists. For this reason, we favor local markets and parks over tourist sites.

New Zealand and Australia offer perhaps the best worldwide opportunity to travel among a different people incognito. They have infrastructure in English and a safe environment that can assist you to travel outside tourist areas. Speaking softly and wearing drab clothes are two tips than can help you avoid drawing attention to yourself. And when you do reveal yourselves, likely by speaking with an American voice, the Kiwis and Aussies will welcome you. Both are friendly peoples and pleased to share their countries with you.

More from the Challenge Series

Challenge for Two
Challenge Series Book One

A series of difficult circumstances have forced Dave and Katie Parker into early retirement. Searching for new life and purpose, the Parkers take a wintertime job house sitting an old Victorian mansion. The picturesque river town in southeastern Minnesota is far from the climate and culture of their home near the Alabama Gulf Coast.

But dark secrets sleep in the mansion. A criminal network has ruthlessly intimidated the community since the timber baron era of the 19th century. Residents have been conditioned to look the other way.

The Parkers' questions about local history and clues they discover in the mansion bring an evil past to light and create division in the small community. While some fear the consequences of digging up the truth, others want freedom from crime and justice for victims. Faced with personal threats, the Parkers must decide how to respond for themselves and for the good of the community.

Challenge in Mobile
Challenge Series Book Three

Dave and Katie Parker regret that their only child Jeremy, his wife Denyse, and their infant daughter live on the opposite side of the world. Unexpectedly, Jeremy calls to ask his father's help finding an accounting job in the US. Katie urges Dave to do whatever is necessary to find a job for Jeremy near Mobile. Dave's former accounting firm has floundered since his departure. The Parkers risk their financial security by purchasing full ownership of the struggling firm to make a place for Jeremy.

Denyse finds South Alabama fascinating compared to her native Australia. She quickly resumes her passion for teaching inner-city teenagers. Invited by Katie, other colorful guests arrive from Australia and Minnesota to experience Gulf Coast culture. Aided by their guests, Dave and Katie examine their faith after Katie receives discouraging news from her doctors.

Political, financial, and racial tensions have been building in Mobile. Bewildering financial expenditures of a client create suspicions of criminal activity. Denyse hears disturbing rumors from her students. A hurricane from the Gulf of Mexico exacerbates the community's tensions. Dave and Katie are pulled into a crisis that requires them to rise to a new level of more than ordinary.

More from Kit and Drew Coons

The Ambassadors

Two genetically engineered beings unexpectedly arrive on Earth. Unlike most extraterrestrials depicted in science fiction, the pair is attractive, personable, and telegenic–the perfect talk show guests. They have come to Earth as ambassadors bringing an offer of partnership in a confederation of civilizations. Technological advances are offered as part of the partnership. But humans must learn to cooperate among themselves to join.

Molly, a young reporter, and Paul, a NASA scientist, have each suffered personal tragedy and carry emotional baggage. They are asked to tutor the ambassadors in human ways and to guide them on a worldwide goodwill tour. Molly and Paul observe as the extraterrestrials commit faux pas while experiencing human culture. They struggle trying to define a romance and partnership while dealing with burdens of the past.

However, mankind finds implementing actual change difficult. Clashing value systems and conflicts among subgroups of humanity erupt. Inevitably, rather than face difficult choices, fearmongers in the media start to blame the messengers. Then an uncontrolled biological weapon previously created by a rogue country tips the world into chaos. Molly, Paul, and the others must face complex moral decisions about what being human means and the future of mankind.

More Than Ordinary Challenges— Dealing with the Unexpected

Many heartwarming stories share about difficult situations that worked out miraculously or through iron-willed determination. The stories are useful in that they inspire hope. But sometimes life just doesn't work out the way we expected. Many people's lives will never be what they had hoped. What does a person do then? This mini book uses our personal struggle with infertility as an example.

More Than Ordinary Marriage— A Higher Level

Some might suggest that any marriage surviving in these times is more than ordinary. Unfortunately, many marriages don't last a lifetime. But by more than ordinary, we mean a marriage that goes beyond basic survival and is more than successful. This type of relationship can cause others to ask, "What makes their marriage so special?" Such marriages glorify God and represent Christ and the church well.

More Than Ordinary Faith— Why Does God Allow Suffering?

Why does God allow suffering? This is a universal question in every heart. The question is both reasonable and valid. Lack of a meaningful answer is a faith barrier for many. Shallow answers can undermine faith. Fortunately, the Bible gives clear reasons that God allows suffering. But the best time to learn about God's purposes and strengthen our faith is *before* a crisis.

More Than Ordinary Wisdom—Stories of Faith and Folly

Jesus told story after story to communicate God's truth. Personal stories create hope and change lives by speaking to the heart. The following collection of Drew's stories is offered for your amusement and so that you can learn from his experiences. We hope these stories will motivate you to consider your own life experiences. What was God teaching you? "Let the redeemed of the Lord tell their story." (Psalm 107:2)

More Than Ordinary Abundance—From Kit's Heart

Abundance means, "richly or plentifully supplied; ample." Kit's personal devotions in this mini book record her experiences of God's abundant goodness and offer insights into godly living. Her hope is that you will rejoice with her and marvel at God's provision in your own life. "They celebrate your abundant goodness and joyfully sing of your righteousness." (Psalm 145:7)

More Than Ordinary Choices—Making Good Decisions

Every moment separates our lives into before and after. Some moments divide our lives into never before and always after. Many of those life-changing moments are based on the choices we make. God allows us to make choices through free will. Making good choices at those moments is for our good and ultimately reflects on God as we represent Him in this world.

Visit **https://morethanordinarylives.com/**
for more information.

www.ingramcontent.com/pod-product-compliance
Lightning Source LLC
Chambersburg PA
CBHW030518310726
48979CB00010B/1711/J

* 9 7 8 1 7 3 2 5 7 8 3 7 1 *